THE Capital OF Kansas City

Also by Gary Gildner

Fiction

Somewhere Geese are Flying: New & Selected Stories
The Second Bridge
A Week in South Dakota
The Crush

Poetry

Cleaning a Rainbow
The Bunker in the Parsley Fields
Clackamas
Blue Like the Heavens: New & Selected Poems
The Runner
Nails
Digging for Indians
First Practice

Limited Editions

The Birthday Party
The Swing
Pavol Hudák, The Poet, Is Talking
Jabón
Letters from Vicksburg
Eight Poems

Memoir

My Grandfather's Book: Generations of an American Family
The Warsaw Sparks

Anthology

Out of this World: Poems from the Hawkeye State

THE Capital OF Kansas City

GARY GILDNER
STORIES

BkMk Press
University of Missouri–Kansas City

BkMk Press
University of Missouri-Kansas City
5101 Rockhill Road
Kansas City, Missouri 64110
www.umkc.edu/bkmk

Financial assistance for this project has been provided by the Missouri Arts Council, a state agency.

Executive Editor: Robert Stewart
Managing Editor: Ben Furnish
Assistant Managing Editor & cover/book design: Cynthia Beard
Cover art: Zoë Polando
Editorial consultant: Karen I. Johnson
Author photo: Michele Gildner

BkMk Press wishes to thank Zoë Polando, Anders Carlson, Brittany Green, Cameron Morse. Special thanks to Marie Mayhugh.

Library of Congress Cataloging-in-Publication Data

Names: Gildner, Gary, author.
Title: The capital of Kansas City : stories / by Gary Gildner.
Description: First edition. | Kansas City, MO : BkMk Press, University of Missouri-Kansas City, [2015]
Identifiers: LCCN 2015047023 | ISBN 9781943491025 (alk. paper)
Classification: LCC PS3557.I343 A6 2015 | DDC 813/.54--dc23 LC record available at http://lccn.loc.gov/2015047023

ISBN 978-1-943491-02-5

For Michele

Acknowledgments

I am grateful to the editors of the following magazines in whose pages these stories, as noted, first appeared: *The Antioch Review* ("Beáta" and "The Bach Suites"); *Confrontation* ("If I Could Be With You" and "Pro Bono"); *The Georgia Review* ("Three Short Tales"); *The Great River Review* ("Lark"); *New Letters* ("Celebrations," "The Capital of Kansas City," "One in a Million" and "The New People"); *The North American Review* ("Tiger Lilies" and "Stories Under the Stars"); *Shenandoah* ("My Mother's Story" and "South of Wenatchee"); and *The Southern Review* ("Timmy Sheean Is a Prime Example")

Contents

Timmy Sheean Is a Prime Example

Weekends, W.D. Deschuttes tends bar at The Triangle. On Sundays she chases bass in Gravel Pit Pond if the weather is fine or nearly; if it's asking-for-nasty she will bake a pie. Monday through Thursday she meets her students at Mesquite Community College during the day and at night grades the papers they write trying to say what they mean. A god-awful hard thing to do, she tells them, but if they can achieve clarity they might be angels. Behind the bar she wears a flannel shirt, jeans, and a fleece vest against the freezing AC demanded by the roughnecks and roustabouts who come in still sweating from the hot fields. At the college she wears heels long and sharp enough to pierce a rattler and a skirt with bounce; she can't see hiding her shapely legs in natural light. W.D. has three cats at the moment but is not a cat rancher. Two of those varmints are walk-ons she intends to place in good homes.

WD is for Wanda Delight, age thirty-eight, unattached. On the first date with a possible candidate for her heart, the candidate will almost right away ask how did she come by that pretty name? She will say she must confess to a direct descent from The Reverend Delight Deschuttes, who found that humongous gold nugget in California and started the First Church of the Vegetarian. Oh yes, great-*great*-grandpa DD. Lost nearly all his teeth, before he could vote, in a mishap—with a mule—but held on to his money until he passed peacefully at ninety-six in the rosy arms of a generous member of his little congregation. To which body he bequeathed a decent bundle to divvy up. Said his secret for a long life was of course no red flesh, which he couldn't chew anyway, no cold baths, a warm beer at breakfast, and a warm woman at night. Plus enough smarts to treat that gal to silk accessories whenever she sighed for them. Oh, and no blockages in the bowels. Wrote a whole book on health in his own curlicued hand, but declined to publish it for the public at large. Why he sat on such knowledge, except for snippets in his sermons, nobody knew.

Wanda Delight will offer this brief history in a friendly, near-breathless colloquial drawl—could be the legal truth or a made-up entertainment, your choice—then lean back, allowing that she and her progenitor had more in common than met the eye, and wait for a response. If she has brought the candidate to a point of high excitement and an inability on the spot to gather his thoughts in a consequential way—which is not difficult to observe and may even be sweet—she will then dial her tone down to its softest level, as if sharing a pillow, and say that Mark Twain is her favorite writer of all time, followed close by Emily Dickinson and F. Scott Fitzgerald—*Who are* your *personal favorites*? This is not a hard question. If his answer reveals that he is not nor ever will be a serious reader, well then, she loses all trace of tingly interest required for meaningful romance. You can teach a man to fish, even to bake a pie, but if after wrapping yourself around him trading physical pleasure he is not constructed to lie quietly and get wound fresh all over by a good book, you have made a mistake. This is not being uppity, hard to please, spoiled, cynical, or anything else anybody might want to call her—it is simply a no-frills summary of her standards, gained by hard experience.

Once in a great while, a complicated failure will revisit Wanda Delight in the form of a fire-hot dream and cause her to work extra hard for cheerfulness the entire next day, if not longer. Timmy Sheean is a prime example. Two years ago he came to town hauling a load of some kind of parts for Amos Oil Field Supply and stopped in The Triangle for a cold one. When Wanda Delight asked where he hung that Royals baseball hat on his head and he replied Peculiar, Missouri, she casually wondered, semi-flirty, what he thought of a fellow Show-Me Stater by the name of Mr. Samuel Langhorne Clemens. Both eyes weepy from driving all afternoon into the Western sun, he said, "Pretty lady, *Adventures of Huckleberry Finn* is either the greatest American novel, or it's one of a towering threesome, alongside *Moby-Dick* and *The Great Gatsby*!"

Whoa, here was a blue-collar man of scrupulous taste and tender eyes with whom Wanda Delight could nestle. And so she did, that very night, even though he carried dangerous weight—which he courteously did not press upon her. Still, a man maneuvering almost three hundred pounds around, no matter how respectably packaged, is asking for ankle, knee, and, above all, heart trouble down the road. She told him so. Holding her by the hips to help keep her fixed to the purpose of William Butler, as he privately called his member when matters were in a lyrical state, and admiring the firmness of her perky breasts, he said his basic size was a natural genetic happening—on the Sheean side especially all the men were tall, big-boned, poetry-spouting rowdies—and there wasn't a thing he could do about *that*, but what he could do was stop taking in so much sugar and salty grease while toting up the miles.

"Might chew carrot sticks," she managed, for they were rhythmically in sync to a near-combustible degree.

"Could do that," he said.

"Could practice self-denial like the—like the—"

"Like the?"

"—Dalai—Dalai—"

"Lama?"

"Oh—you—oh—you—"

"Spit it out!"

"—animal!"

When both had reached full satisfaction, Wanda Delight fell backward against Timmy Sheean's legs, which he had thoughtfully brought up to act as a chairback for her. In a moment their breathing returned to normal. Timmy Sheean said if he had a pad and pencil right then, or better yet a keyboard, he'd be keen to compose a song about what he had just experienced, it was so fine. Where did she learn to all-of-a-sudden dove coo deep in her throat like that? Wanda Delight blushed. Yes, here was a man worth nurturing: he had a good ear, a handsome head, and naturally curly black hair. But oh, he was large.

"So you write songs?"

He confessed to being a Sunday poet when he was back home in Peculiar. Which was not often enough because he could not resist buying certain first editions; also he was helping his sister support their old mother in the nursing home and financing his ex-fiancée through law school. Therefore he had to keep moving the goods down the road.

"The pay for that, though it takes a toll on my back and especially on my kidneys, is pretty good," he said.

"Your *ex*-fiancée?" Wanda Delight could not stop herself.

"Yes, that's odd, I admit. But—" He was interrupted. An orange cat of some nerve had appeared at his side and placed two paws on his chest, establishing eye contact.

"This is Emmeline," Wanda Delight said. "Emmeline Grangerford. She'd like to meet you up close."

"I don't mind cats," Timmy Sheean said. "Unless they jump unannounced out of nowhere into my crotch while I am relaxing, causing my heart to clench. Or leap up and parade across the table where I am about to sample my stack of pancakes, throwing dander my way."

"What about sharing your bed?"

"I don't know."

"Well, know this: I will never become a cat rancher."

"A cat rancher?"

"A woman who gives up on men and collects cats for comfort. Emmeline Grangerford is my limit, period."

Wanda Delight tossed her long auburn curls to one side and tilted her head that way, as if posing for a fashion photo. Gazing at the pressed-tin ceiling, she said, "Your ex-fiancée's drain on your finances is none of my business."

"Chanterelle is a good student getting a late start. Her ambition in life, she says, is to avoid the temptations of corporate money and work for the nearly voiceless. The lame, the ignorant. I know she will pay me back if she can."

"Chanterelle? That's a mushroom."

"She comes from a mean environment. Ozark trailer trash. They named her Hickey, honest to God. So when she began her pursuit of respectability, she changed it to Chanterelle, for the music in that word."

"Her contribution to your possible future need for a dialysis regimen is not my business," Wanda Delight said.

She slid off his robust body and, slipping into a cream-colored shift, left the room. Emmeline Grangerford left with her, tail high. Wanda Delight returned with a tall shaker of made-from-scratch carrot juice and an anthology of poems.

"Let's trade saying a few of our favorites from this book," she said, plumping two fat goose-down pillows to put her head and shoulders on, and snuggled beside this tender fellow whose long sensitive fingers were those of her first girlhood crush, Harvey Van Cliburn, and whose profile called up the actor Robert Mitchum. But before trading poems, for fun she wanted to tell about her great-great-grandpa Delight—*okay?*—because she had skipped that part in introducing herself over the angel-hair pasta with clam sauce she had invited him home for, and from the table to her bed. This was almost unprecedented, this fevered leap, but when he said a first edition of *The Adventures of Tom Sawyer,* in mint condition, lay in a secret hollow of his rig, she could not hold back. And the produce of that leap was extraordinary: she was quickened by three explosions. That the fevered leap was almost unprecedented went, of course, unmentioned, and those three explosions spoke for themselves. Later, she would not be able to recall giving him, if only in a pithy phrase, her professional opinion of *Tom Sawyer,* nor recall telling him, also succinctly, that such a book tucked in a secret hollow of his rig spurred her fevered leap along faster. The point and glory of their coming together, indeed of their entire splendid evening—Chanterelle notwithstanding—was that Wanda Delight was beside herself with the tingle of meaningful romance.

"I was a vegetarian once," Timmy Sheean said, after she finished telling about the Reverend Deschuttes. "Made me feel lean, that I was burning pure sunshine."

"Pure, uncluttered sunshine?"

"Pure, uncluttered, liberal sunshine, you bet."

"Why on *earth* did you stop?"

"Met Chanterelle and meat is all she will eat, practically—or is willing to cook. Fearful of becoming fat. So—"

"No call to elaborate."

"Anyway," he said, "I like your story about the reverend."

"You think it's a made-up story?"

"Well, sure. And it's a good one. I especially like your voice."

She blushed.

"I like this old house too."

"Built in eighteen eighty-nine," Wanda Delight said. "By a cattle baron who was killed in a gunfight over some water rights. Or got partially built—the fancy dance floor and solarium and porte cochere never got put up after they buried him, and poof, there went his plan to marry a refined Eastern lady. That's why the place looks like half a wedding cake sliced down the middle and how I got it cheap. One day, I'm hoping to be on the National Register of Historic Places, *la-di-da*."

"I'm not kidding, I like how you talk. Sometimes you sound like a character in a goofy stage play. It's catchy."

"Several characters, I've heard."

"You have a reputation?"

"And you have lipstick on your mouth."

"Listen," Timmy Sheean said. "I mean, full disclosure: Chanterelle and I still see each other when it's convenient."

"For you or for her?"

"Law school is real demanding."

"Okay, I can see I would have to compete."

"Says she'd feel bad, though, if she couldn't treat me once in a while—like to a Jayhawks basketball game."

"I don't share. And you'd have to shed some weight. I can't have a boyfriend drop dead on me."

"Should I sleep in my rig tonight?"

"What if I told you my story about Delight Deschuttes is true?"

"You could do that, but it wouldn't make me like it any better."

"And *who* are the Jayhawks?"

"Rock Chalk, Jayhawk—K-U! The University of Kansas."

"Maybe you'd prefer sleeping with a cheerleader?"

"I'd prefer what delighted the Reverend Delight at night."

"I meant to ask at dinner: Do you enjoy pie?"

"I am very fond of pie."

"I make devil-mean pies," Wanda Delight said, tilting her head to the side, as if posing again.

"Cherry?"

"Oh man!"

Timmy Sheean returned to Missouri. Right away, the people he worked for sent him on deliveries to Florida. "Time is, was, and always will be money," said Guido, who represented these people and told Timmy to think of him "as your personal agent." When he finally got home to Peculiar and could hang up his cap, he was road-fuzzy but wanted to declare in a letter that he missed Wanda Delight and her goofy voice and her red curls more than he realized was possible in this distraction-packed, noisy, cliché-driven republic. Driving the lonely miles away from her, chewing the carrot sticks she'd sent him off with, he kept smelling her scent on the desert air, among the juniper trees when he pulled over to stretch his back muscles, and on his left-hand fingers—which she would know referred to the sweet sting of that single drop of her perfume she deposited on William Butler before he departed her bed that last morning. He wrote that he could no longer accept Chanterelle's invitations to Jayhawks games because Miss Deschuttes was so fixed in his thoughts and he stopped eating meat. He had a plan, he said, to get down to his best open-field weight of 205. He would wear a rubber suit over his sweats and speed walk ten miles after putting his rig up every night. His letter continued:

> *Full disclosure: I was a wild black Irishman in college. I read, yes, which I loved, but usually books that no sensible beer-drinking football player would want to bother with. I was into breathing hard, foaming, breaking through to daylight, and telling coeds, "What blurt is this about virtue and about vice? Evil propels me and reform of evil propels me, I stand indifferent"—borrowing heavily from Walt Whitman to wash my spirit and get laid. So then I'm drafted by the pros. I say okay, easy money, why not? My*

> *first week in practice I crack a fairly important structure and take pills to dull the pain. I continue to bump heads, seeing more and more of these marvelous stars—totally the wrong kind—and hearing bells I can't shake. The pros don't like watching me wobble so much and tell me to go away, I embarrass them. I go home to Peculiar. By and by a man comes around, Guido, he calls himself, whose pointy shoes are always shined and whose favorite personal motto is: "Let's make a connection." I dither, but finally, because I am near-broke and feeling sorry for myself, I let Guido help me buy a certain kind of truck. I drive from Kansas City to Miami a lot to deliver beef I know is stolen and return with goods that Guido tells me are mysteries I don't want to understand. Guido's people put their own locks on my trailer. That run I made to Amos was a departure—and wonderful in that I met you and could breathe so freely. I'm skipping over a great deal because I'm fading—not much sleep lately—but I want to get this much, at least, in the mail. Chanterelle won't hear anything smelling of criminal behavior—she has her career to think of—but agrees with me that I should seek other work. I have told her about you, by the way. She says* Fine, whatever. *I say* Real fine. *I hope when we meet again you will recognize me, I will be so lean and burning. Meantime I'm sending something I think you will enjoy. Sweet dreams.*

The something was a first edition of Fitzgerald's second novel, *The Beautiful and Damned*. Holding it, Wanda shed tears—for the book, for Timmy Sheean's letter, and because life was so damn complicated sometimes that not even inventing pretty good stories and talking funny on purpose seemed to help much.

That weekend a cowboy she knew took her out for scrambled eggs after she finished up at The Triangle. He was a nice-looking man named Slim Pickens, no relation to the actor of that name. Nor a reader, never would be; his gifts were working well with horses and cattle and being good, in his way, with women. On two occasions in the past Wanda Delight had invited him to her bed, both times when she was as lonely as she could be and had not yet polished the standards she felt were needed in order to stop having her affections curtailed and her mornings gloomy. Unlike those two mornings with Timmy Sheean, which had seemed so full of promise and light that she wondered if the copper in the roof of her half-a-cake house might conduct her body and soul into the sun and melt everything grandly together. Tonight all she wanted was for Slim to tell her what delivering stolen beef might mean, even though she could guess. He said, "Big trouble." She told him she was suddenly all wrung out, but gave him a kiss on his ruddy jaw that lingered a mite too long. She said she was sorry.

That same night Wanda Delight wrote Timmy Sheean a letter on the bond paper she used only for special occasions, which you can believe were few and far between. First she told him she cried holding his gift, and if it sounded corny to hear that she had never received such a rich present, well, she had to raise her right hand and shout out *Guilty, your honor!* As for *feeling* guilty, she could eat soap for coming down so hard on his weight, but she did so only because she had already formed powerful feelings for him and could not begin to wrap her thoughts around such a handsome virile man in his prime keeling over slam-bang with one of those heart attacks against the young you read about. "Mainly, Timmy, this Guido character scares me. And these deliveries you make. Yes, yes, yes, you must quit all of that! Honey, you must fetch your pen ASAP and tell me in writing that you are completely shut of such doings!" Then she made a cup of Sleepytime tea to calm herself. She finished her letter sitting up in bed and describing their all-too-brief time together, remembering the intimate details of which brought color and heat to her cheeks. She told him about that too.

When two weeks passed without a word from Timmy Sheean, Wanda Delight tried to find a phone number for him in Peculiar and found nothing. Nor could she find him listed in Kansas City, neither him personally nor a trucking company in his name. She clearly remembered seeing SHEEAN TRUCKING on the side of his rig as he drove away from her. Another week went by without a word. She called Amos Oil Field Supply. The girl who answered the phone—who said her name was Tendril—sounded so squeaky-young that Wanda Delight couldn't form her question right away. Also impeding her speech was a sudden, fleeting image, in stark black and white, of Timmy Sheean holding her steady. Finally, she told Tendril she wanted a phone number in Missouri for the trucker who had delivered some goods to Amos almost six weeks ago. There was a long pause during which she could hear a cluster of muffled mumbles.

"Are you still there, Tendril?"

"Yes I am."

"Well?"

"I don't think we can do that."

"Do you have a boss?" *You slow-witted kitty!* she almost shouted.

"He is home sick, I guess, with something I can't pronounce good."

Wanda Delight called the local sheriff's office. A recorded voice said to leave pertinent information. Wanda Delight left her name and number. She paced for ten minutes, then got out paper and pen.

> *Dear Timmy,*
>
> *I need to hear your voice and can find no phone no. for you anywhere. Please, PLEASE call me as soon as you receive this note. I am writing fast with a nervous heart. Tell me tell me tell me you are okay, OK?*
>
> *Love,*
> *Wanda Delight*

Then she thought to call the Law School at the University of Kansas and ask for Chanterelle. But Chanterelle who? Well, how many law school students *were* there in Kansas with the name of a mushroom! Wanda Delight felt sick with something she could not pronounce good either. The sheriff's office called and, after hearing what she wanted, told her—a sarcastic woman was speaking—that the sheriff was running for reelection and had more on his mind than wondering if he should compete with the phone companies. Wanda Delight called Edna Dahl, who owned The Triangle, and said she was flat on her back and could not come to work.

"Are you sick?"

"I don't know what I am."

"You never get sick, Wanda."

"I can't move off my sofa."

"I will be right over."

Edna Dahl had a painful-to-hear voice, rough from smoking too many unfiltered Camels over the years, and cheeks sun- and wind-burned to a glossy dark orange. She stood five feet two in her snakeskin Tony Lamas. She divorced three men after being widowed. That second husband, Rail, gave her The Triangle in a trade for her barn and horses, not including her old Packy, a cutting horse of honorable lineage close to his final reward but still up for Edna to ride him around Gravel Pit Pond whenever she threw a saddle on his back. Rail lived out in the barn, in a tack room good enough for sleeping and such, while Edna lived in the double-wide with her next two husbands, neither of whom lasted any longer than Rail in the barn, though she never had a bad word to say about any of them. She liked men and they liked her, she just had trouble being married after a rodeo bronc named Muttonchops bucked Big Mack off and broke his neck. She buried him on Valentine's Day not by design but because that was the day the undertaker picked. Her heart felt so heavy she wondered what the sun was up to, up there so bright. But scratching for some dirt to throw down on the plain, pine box he requested, she remembered the day only too well and fainted.

One night after they closed The Triangle and were having a nightcap and a heart-to-heart, Edna told Wanda Delight that Big Mack broke her cherry on Valentine's Day when she was sixteen and wore a ponytail, and she could never forget the tenderness that came over her. Wanda Delight thought back to the boy who had broken hers in high school and could not imagine having an interesting cup of coffee with him now. Or even a week after the breakage, it was so sharply painful and quick. More than a decade ago, that heart-to-heart was, shortly after Wanda Delight showed up needing a job. She had just quit two back-to-back, in retail sales, and before that she quit graduate school because her dissertation adviser, who was almost old enough to be her grandfather, could not drop the subject of those underpants she stopped wearing in high school; he was bringing it up, it seemed, every time she smiled. She had made the innocent dumb blunder one hot spring day in his office of saying she wouldn't mind jumping in the university's outdoor pool later but didn't have a bathing suit or any underwear on to fake for one. Then blushed in embarrassment. Then laughed, thinking, Oh well, a professor who admired Mark Twain would laugh too. He did. But try telling him that not wearing underwear since tenth grade had nothing to do with flirting with a *grad school* professor.

Edna took one look at Wanda Delight on her sofa, and said, "Honey, tell me this ain't the lovesickness."

"Won't tell you that."

"Hell is he?"

"Trucker from almost two months ago."

"Least you're not all wore out being PO'd at our sweet, stingy governor again."

Wanda Delight closed her eyes. Edna put on coffee, then called Blue, her last husband and now one of her bartenders. She told him to double up and take Wanda's shift. "If that's okay, Blue." He said he'd get it done.

Edna sat across from Wanda Delight and drank coffee and smoked and finally broke their silence. "I know love is real. I also know it's got a greasy twin that's good for the experience, maybe. In the short run." She sighed. She had just put Packy down, she said. Did it herself. "Just before you called me." Edna then pulled off the black wig she was wearing and gave her surprisingly white scalp a fierce rubbing. "I got to get back and take a shower. You want me to send for a pizza?"

Wanda Delight shook her head. "I am so sorry about Packy."

"Stay home long as you need to, Wanda."

"Thank you."

"I wish I could be in love."

Wanda Delight smiled, but there was no joy in it.

"We are doomed," Edna said. "I guess it's normal."

Two years passed. For a while Wanda Delight Deschuttes thought she just might go to Peculiar and find him and say—if he was okay and all—*What is wrong with you? You broke my heart.* But she couldn't do that, couldn't take the chance. He might be dead. From an accident. From doing business with bad people. From a heart attack. Who would tell her? Chanterelle? His old mother? Nobody would tell her. And so she gradually stopped thinking she might go to Peculiar and instead went fishing in Gravel Pit Pond for those bass she loved to see jump, although their jumps seemed way less vigorous and fewer these days, and then she went to her classes and to The Triangle as usual. The second time New Year's Eve came around she kissed Slim Pickens hard on the mouth and took him home and in the morning felt gloomy because, as with the other two times, he did not stay long enough afterward to catch his breath hardly. That spring she had a twenty-five-year-old freshman flirt with her, a vet with a red goatee and a manufactured leg, and she sort of flirted back a little but would go no further until the course was over, if then. She was two years shy of forty and one dissertation shy of her PhD and teaching four composition courses as an adjunct instructor, which meant she was earning maybe one-third of what a tenure-track instructor was making for the same load; plus she was feeding three cats now and disposing of the dead mice the two newcomers, looking for love, were leaving beside her slippers in the bathroom where she would be sure to see them; and her house needed work just about everywhere. Near the end of the course in which the vet sat and winked at her whenever she looked at him, a large-breasted, tall girl named Timothy Lafayette came to her office to discuss her grade, which was a D minus at the moment. She couldn't afford to fail, she said, because she was pregnant. She would have no extra time and maybe no money to repeat the course—and the other courses she wasn't doing so hot in either—if she decided to keep it. "My own fault," the girl admitted. She'd been spending far too much time fooling around with Heath, not being careful.

"Heath?"

"You know, the vet?"

"*Our* Heath?"

"Yeah, with the leg? I think I love him."

"Love him?"

"But he acts kinda weird sometimes."

They were quiet. Wanda Delight looked at her nails, at the ceiling. She thought of inviting Heath the vet to stand in front of her aging Camry and running him over. She thought briefly of Timmy Sheean driving away from her. She thought about hugging this girl and weeping and then slapping her silly.

"How old are you, Timothy?"

"Old enough to know better, if that's what you mean."

"Where do you live?"

"At home."

"Does your family know?"

The girl shook her head.

"Is there anything I can do to help you?"

"Like how?"

"I don't know. Maybe provide a place to hide once in a while?"

"Hide?" Timothy Lafayette started to giggle. She got the hiccups.

Wanda Delight listened to this giggling, hiccuping girl until she couldn't take anymore. She hadn't meant *hide* hide. She said, "Timothy. Listen to me. Who are you? Your essays are about impossible dreams. Living in a big beach house in California. Being a famous popular singer, hanging out with rappers, driving some kind of ritzy, powerful sports car. We all dream, Timothy, but your dreams—"

The girl began to cry. Wanda Delight looked out the window at a sky, whose oily-gray color seemed to sum up the girl's future and her own, and she remembered Edna saying they were all doomed. Wanda Delight shivered.

"Does Heath hurt you?"

The girl struggled to control herself. Finally she spat out, "He can't hurt me enough!" She got up as if to run from the room but only stood there, her shoulders slumped in utter defeat. Wanda Delight went to her. She pulled the girl close and listened to her cry. When the girl was calm, Wanda Delight said that over the years she had had a lot of unusual names for girls on her class lists, but never one so pretty as Timothy.

"My daddy wanted a boy. He wanted a descendant to inherit his old pipe business."

"Well, when I hear your name I think of a big, wide field of tall, waving grass at sunset."

"Yeah, well, I'm all they got. All six feet. I'm it."

"I'm it too," Wanda Delight sighed, not sure what she meant exactly, besides feeling near-to-useless.

After that meeting, Timmy Sheean would make sudden appearances in her head like a guest on Letterman. Quick and smiling and gone. He would pop into her head when nothing was taking her line in Gravel Pit Pond, when she was rolling out pie dough, making her bed, cleaning the litter box, or throwing dead mice into the field next door where the raccoons rose up like dwarf bandits and flashed their eyes in her lights. Smiling and gone.

In Peculiar, Missouri, spring has come, and Timmy Sheean is thinking, as he has been for a while now, about the letter he needs to write or the phone call he needs to make. He has been away for twenty months, two weeks, and five days and during that time was too ashamed to contact her because his address then was Leavenworth where he was paying his debt for what he had already told her about. *Leavenworth Prison?* he could imagine her saying, and he would say yes. Right after he got her letter asking him to quit what he was doing he decided he *would* quit, but before he actually could—surprise—he was arrested by the FBI. They had been watching this really dumb, naughty boy for a long time. He could—and would—tell her more, tell her everything, but what he needed, what he really hoped he could do, was tell her in person—if that was possible anymore. If she could stand to see him after he ignored her second letter, one that only a cold man could ignore. Well, maybe *tune out* or *pack in a box and try not think about*, is better than *ignore*. And remember: "You don't know about me," he says aloud, "without you have read a book by Mr. Mark Twain." Would that make her laugh or at least smile? Would she be saying *Yes, yes, yes!* Or: *I have had enough of men like you to last me forever.* He would plead, *Not even one more chance?* But he can't imagine what she'd say back.

He puts on his sweats and the rubber suit and goes outside. It's a pretty day for Missouri this time of year. He sucks in a big mouthful of it. Later he will go sit with his mother, even though she no longer knows who he is. Maybe Wanda Delight would not recognize him either. The white petals of the hawthorn are exploding all over his house and somewhere close by an oriole is giving out its flute-like whistle, happy to be alive. Timmy Sheean goes down the road, getting smaller and smaller. Soon he is no bigger than a duck on Gravel Pit Pond, no bigger than a pinecone that Wanda Delight picked up beside a mountain road on a long-ago vacation, no bigger than a comma in a comma-splice error. So let him go.

Yes, let him go. He is still talking only to himself, asking why is it so hard to do this thing? The question has become part of his rhythm, and although his stride has smoothed out, his brain, or that corner of it where the question has taken root, feels like a field of thistles and rocks and he is barefoot in it. He has never—never—had a woman problem he couldn't just walk away from. Never had a problem of any kind that hung on. Not even working for Guido and his people, when he saw they were crooks, bothered him. He shrugged his shoulders and said to the face he shaved, *Hey, I'm nothing but the stooge driver.* Even refusing to finger Guido for a lighter sentence did not bother him. Of course, he might have gotten his legs broken if he *had* fingered Guido. No, no—not might have, he'd be a cripple now. Anyway, *anyway*, one night he meets Wanda. Wanda Delight. Gets into her bed bingo-bango, no big surprise, but then he gets into her story. A whole different thing. Gets into it, but not to the end. Now what? He'd like to—to what? He'd like to pull off his rubber top. He'd like to stop and crack a cold beer. He'd also like his first edition of *Tom Sawyer* back. Not the truck, the truck is theirs, he's glad to be rid of it. Glad to be free to find a new line of endeavor. Maybe play the piano in some upscale K.C. bar. Good stuff. Standards. Cole Porter. Johnny Mercer. "I Get a Kick out of You," "Night and Day," "Fools Rush In," "One for My Baby." Or maybe just work for his brother-in-law. How hard is it to sell life insurance? Accident insurance? People crash their cars all the time. *Hey, watch out! Here comes another crazy driver!* In any event—in any case—let Timmy Sheean go; forget about him; and don't worry, this is not his story anyway, as much as he'd like it to be.

If I Could Be with You

That pearly evening when Sergeant Major George Prolly, ret., did not show up for dinner, down the hall in her office Mrs. Loretta Strictor, the director of Piney Woods Rest, leaned back on the edge of her desk just so, her blouse uncurtained, to receive the flushed face of the Reverend Jarrod Lutish; he murmured something she could not make out. Seated at the table where Sergeant Prolly should have been winking at her from his wheelchair, Miss Ginger Flambeau reached one hand to her tear-stained cheek while forking creamed chicken to and fro on her plate with the other. "What did you say, Jarrod?" Mrs. Strictor whispered, caressing the neat part in his lacquered hair.

Miss Flambeau had an idea, but she didn't have it clear enough to cry aloud. It seemed when she had journeyed down the hall to dinner that the DANGER door up ahead had suddenly slammed shut. Then she thought she heard George—outside?—shout, "Olee Spit!" Who was Olee Spit? Furthermore, that door was supposed to be locked, always, because, Mrs. Strictor warned, it protected folks from something terrible enough to suck their precious breath right out. "Jarrod?" she whispered again. "You were saying?" His response was a gush. "Cheeky, dreamy, evil, grand, oh Jesus, Loretta!"

Sergeant George Prolly, riding downhill, had actually shouted, "Holy Shit!" And seconds later, leveling out, crossing Highway 7 in high thrall, he added, "Men, we are in a scoot, attacking like hell!" His words felt rich and courageous, even profound, and for an instant or two he reckoned that the swordlike length of sunlight squeezed in the stunning weave of gray clouds on the horizon was his final destination, and he welcomed this as fitting. The ugly slamming sound of the DANGER door echoed in Miss Flambeau's head, along with George Prolly shouting again, and tears refilled her eyes, her fork abandoned in a mound of creamed chicken. Beyond the DANGER door, she remembered Mrs. Strictor saying, was a very steep slope going down, down to a highway that zoomed north to the cold heartless neighborhoods and byways of the nation. Where folks, most of them, did not know how to fall on their knees. Nobody wanted to go there, did they? No, no, that's right, Mrs. Strictor did not wish for any of her residents to exit that door and go tumbling down the hillside, attractive as it might be, thanks to their wonderful handyman Pinky Fleeter's fine mowing. "Madness and glory!" the Reverend Jarrod Lutish cried into Mrs. Strictor's cleavage.

So Miss Ginger Flambeau had stayed to her purpose right past the DANGER door and into the dining room, where gentle Mr. Sun was gracing their table, warming it, and waited for Mr. Prolly. Maybe tonight she would marry the sergeant. This idea made her neck and shoulders want to stretch, her teary eyes feel tender. She began to hum a song from long ago that had lovebirds and a nice brushy drumbeat and *two* horns in it. Listen to them! "Jarrod, we mustn't do this," Mrs. Strictor whispered, twirling a strand of his hair around her index finger, "if it's madness."

After George Prolly and his wheelchair crossed Highway 7, they were still traveling fast and bumpy enough for him to lose his false teeth and for the chair to achieve the woods next to Mrs. Marble's apple orchard and to keep going for almost fifty yards. It is remarkable that George and his chair did not crash into a tree or get snagged by a picker bush or just roll over like a doughnut, but they did not. And where-oh-where was Mr. Prolly? His absence caused Wilma the nurse's aid, counting heads in the dining room, to start wringing her hands, a habit that she knew drove Mrs. Strictor crazy but could not stop. She also felt a chill and hoped that their creamed chicken tonight had not been infected by any Asian birds powerful enough to invade their shores.

One extra cold winter night in Detroit, at The Flame on Woodward Avenue, Miss Flambeau recalled, a man with a large gap between his two front teeth sat in the front row holding an armful of red roses that were intended for *her*. She just knew it! Naturally she winked at this generous smiler when she uncrossed her feathers and peeked out. Yes, of course she loved to dance, you silly man. And what do *you* like to do? "Jarrod, did you hear me?" He moaned. Mrs. Strictor felt his tears on her skin. Across the room she could see their reflections in the framed aerial view of The Church of the Piney Woods Saints next door, the slant of the day's last light striking the photo in such a way as to cancel the intended image and mirror their actions perfectly. She rather liked it, and tingled. George Prolly felt something like a tingle, coming to rest, finally, in a pile of old leaves pushed together over the years into a nicely shaped bed that smelled to him like something from his youth on the farm. At first he did not make this connection, he was too stimulated and surprised by his ride—in fact, his heart seemed to be knocking, as if wanting free of his chest to continue the campaign alone—but by and by the tingle-like pricks on his neck and the knocking of his heart eased off, and everything in his personal machinery fell back more or less into line, and he took a long moment to gaze at and smell his new terrain. "Jarrod, isn't what we do just a little bit naughty?"

Miss Flambeau, looking off dreamily, whispered, "Ladies and gentlemen, today is Sergeant George Prolly's birthday. Let's give him a really big, generous hand for coming home to us safely." She whispered this so sweetly that the words seemed part of her favorite song. Not the one with the lovebirds in it—that other one. Oh, what *was* it? She began to hum, and then softly sing, "If I could be with you . . . one hour tonight . . . if I were free to do the things I might . . ." Smack dab in a woods turning to dusk, that's where he was, and by God it was damn fine, the berries deluxe. Now he recalled his descent beginning just beyond the door he was not supposed to use but did because it was open and because he hated creamed chicken as much as he hated Piney Woods Rest and his niece June Prolly Gladdy for putting him there. He could still see her patting his arm and saying, "Buck up, soldier!" Then turning and walking off, shaking her fat hinder. But he had escaped! He was AWOL! No goop tonight! Yes sir, he was smelling ripe apples in a musky woods in early fall and remembering how good fresh apple pie tasted. He could eat one right now, the whole thing, and wash it down his gullet with a glass of cold sweet milk. Damn that place! Gumming and belching and gas-passing in almost all sectors, and Mrs. Strictor raising her voice for the hard of hearing: "Ladies and gentlemen, the Reverend Lutish will now deliver a few words of encouragement."

George Prolly made a fist and shook it. Encouragement? Was she crazy? The man wore perfume! And dyed his hair! And moved among their tables smiling like an actor on TV showing how bright his teeth looked after brushing with a curl of toothpaste that reminded George of chicken crap. Tonguing his bare gums, he shook his fist again. He would miss all that tonight unless they came in suitable numbers and secured him with rope. But they'd better move quick; though he'd lost his choppers, he still had ordnance and knew how to use it. "Naughty, naughty Jarrod, and naughty, naughty, *naughty* Loretta," the minister crooned.

"Thank you, thank you, oh my yes, thank you," Miss Flambeau nodded her head. "Yes, I have always enjoyed playing Detroit, because he is always here, in the front row, the big galoot. Those roses? For me? You are too, too kind, sir. Oh, well, yes, at one time he *was* a major attraction. People said he could hit that ball right out of the park! He even showed me his bat. Oh, please, you will have to excuse me now. I can't take it. My precious boy, my tall, tall tree. Cut down too soon from glory . . . years and years gone . . ." She quickly pressed her napkin to her cheek, glancing this way and that, fearful the other diners might see her tears and laugh. Wilma wrung her hands. She needed to send Pinky to find Mr. Prolly. They were both crazy, in George Prolly's opinion. He could see her pressing Lutish's hand between her long red-tipped fingers. They were in it together, like two dried dingle berries clinging to a sheep's stink hole. He had seen them emerge from her office touching each other the way people do when they do more out of sight. Did they think they could fool everybody? He would not hesitate to pump a slug in the polished toe of that phony bastard's black Italian shoe, if the bastard led the charge to recapture him.

"And where is the Reverend Lutish?" Miss Ginger Flambeau asked very quietly, trying to change the subject. Quieter still, she added, "My George does not like him, no, no, no," which caused her to blush, "although he does like how I sing and dance." Her breathing becoming more rapid, Mrs. Strictor said, "Oh Jarrod, where are we going? Where are *you* going? Tell me . . . tell me." "I am going down on my knees now, Loretta." "For the pain, Jarrod?" He rolled his face against her like a dog rubbing its cheeks in something rich. George Prolly hawked up a gob and let it fly. They'd wheeled him into the church, promising he'd enjoy the singing of Miss Flambeau and the Calm Waters Choir. He went for her sake. She looked real nice in that white robe, with her golden hair flowing over her shoulders, but he was disappointed they didn't let her sing; she just swayed and hummed behind Lutish while he went on and on about Heaven, what it looked like in sickening detail, until George couldn't stop himself from hacking up and expectorating on the carpet. That nurse's aid with the bad BO came and wheeled him away.

Miss Flambeau took out a hanky scented with Evening in Paris and dabbed her neck. Surely she was in love. Just listen to her heartbeat! Is it Valentine's Day yet? Really it should be Valentine's Day more often. But where is her sweet George Prolly? Pinned down in a foxhole once, he had to piss like a racehorse. Couldn't raise up on his knees, couldn't do anything except roll over and let go on his good buddy Al from Hopatcong, New Jersey, who'd been dead all morning, picked off by a sniper. "When I was a girl, Jarrod, I would cut a lock of my hair and skip around it three times. Wishing real hard for my prince. For my handsome rich prince who could take me anywhere! Take me anywhere, Jarrod, take me." Miss Flambeau closed her eyes and made a promise: "Oh George Prolly, since you are so nice to me—and he *is,* Daddy—I will marry you *if* you want me with your heart and soul." George hated that greasy hairball, but he didn't hate Mrs. Strictor because sometimes, when he lay in bed, he could smell her, up real close, as if he had his nose in her neck, and he'd feel a flippy sensation down there where he'd almost forgot he had anything left to cause such a thing. You can't hate an inspiration like that.

The Reverend Lutish issued a long, low rumbling growl-like noise from the back of his throat; he was still on his knees, latched to Mrs. Strictor's left nipple, the vein across his forehead clearly in full and splendid pulse. Loretta Strictor was reminded of the nightcrawlers her father prized from the earth behind the pig lot when he prepared to chase catfish. Jarrod's vein also filled and shone that same bright purple on Sunday, having got all worked up describing Heaven's golden arches and lush greens, its white mink-covered recliners and perfect hair. When that vein filled and pulsed, and when he cried looking at her breasts, her body simply could not hold back. George Prolly did favor how women smelled when they smelled pretty like an orchard in spring, walking into a room all flushed from the hot sun, or bending over to ask could he manage another piece of fresh pie, apple or peach, his choice. Now there was a dandy deluxe situation—fresh peach or apple and a woman's front dusted up just a little bit with flour. Until Truman dropped the big one, that's the kind of dilemma he thought about real hard when he had the opportunity. Women and pie. And don't leave out church widows. You introduce him to a good sweet-smelling church widow who's still interested in bunky and he'll show you what he's made of. Miss Flambeau wet her lips, sucked her tongue. She could taste chocolate and champagne and something else she couldn't name right then.

"Jarrod, Jarrod," Mrs. Strictor whispered, "you look to burst." "I am so full, Loretta. You have no idea." "Does it hurt yet? I want to hear, Jarrod. I want to feel closer and closer." Mrs. Strictor never bent over to ask George Prolly could he eat another piece of her pie, but sometimes on those nights he was referring to, on the real down feather pillow he paid extra for, she would leave a smell behind that made him think—no, believe—that she had just been there to give him ideas. But all she wanted was what she wanted from Mrs. Marble: additions to their contracts. Her apple orchard, his big house in Atlanta. Hah! No one lived there anymore, not even that chinless June Prolly Gladdy, his only blood kin, but it was worth a bundle because it sat on land the developers were willing to yank out their front teeth for, or so it seemed from the way they pulled at their faces when they came around to beg. *Here, take these, throw in these with the offer! For they are worthless to me without that precious deed.* "I said does it hurt yet, Jarrod?" "The pain is always with me." "I know, I know. But I mean that especially good hurt that you say is like two giant rocks you must embrace and carry forever." "Loretta"—he looked up at her from his kneeling position—"I am *touched*. Through and through. And now I must—" "Jarrod, do we have the time? You are expected in the dining room." The Reverend Lutish whimpered. He pawed the floor. How could she hold him back? Developers! By Jesus, nobody was going to develop a thing on George Prolly's land because he was giving it to the Animal Rescue League. The League didn't know this yet. Nor that they would have to use it for League work, nothing else. Let Mrs. Loretta Strictor sneak into his room under cover of darkness and leave her smell on his pillow all she wanted, his land was just waiting for dogs and cats to put *their* smells on! Which reminded him, he had to pee. All that excitement charging down here had put some pressure on his bladder.

Miss Flambeau took out her compact and quickly powdered her cheeks. Then she regarded her eyes. Were they sad? Were they bad? Were they her Daddy's or Mr. Baseball Man's? No. They belonged to Sergeant Major George Prolly, her sweet intended, so please do not confuse her. "Jarrod, hold up, I need to get more comfortable."

Unzipped, adjusted, and now aiming at that sea of rusty leaves gave George Prolly a kind of happiness: he couldn't stand up and piss across the road anymore, but by God he could make a respectable arc. Truth was, he *could* stand up, with effort, though tell him the point when he didn't have any place of interest to walk to? No—he didn't mean that, exactly. He meant something else hard to explain. Put it this way: he couldn't just stomp his heel and bow and lead his lady around the dance floor anymore. His days of holding a fair hand, his arm around a sweet waist, smelling her excitement mixing with his were done for. Bend his ear anyway you want about the pleasures and rewards of old age—wisdom, reflection, not running the rat's miserable race, busting ass for another buck, any of that—and he'll say go straight to hell. Fact is, he can't remember right now what the thrill was to make another buck anyway. But to take a lady's hand and bow and lead her onto the floor with music all around like rain after a hot, dusty march was an entirely grand thing, nothing you could ever pay a dirty dollar for. And George Prolly—God damn you—began to cry.

Loretta Strictor got more comfortable by scootching back on her back and planting her bare feet on the desk. Jarrod had flicked out his tongue to show her what he must do; her breath had caught; now, comfortable, she waited for him to flick closer. If she could afford to, Wilma would retire. Her joints hurt, her back would never be right again after lifting dead Mrs. Marble off the bathroom floor. Why wouldn't Pinky answer! She knew he was in there, comfortable on the john with his magazine and his Dr. Pepper. She raised her fist and struck the door again. Suddenly she wondered—worried—did she lock the DANGER door after slipping outside to enjoy her Mint Patty in private?

George Prolly cried for everything he missed and would never see again or smell again or do again. And he cried for the crying son of a bitch he had turned into. And for the snot on his face he could not rub off. He tried to get at the .45 in the side pocket of his chair, but his shaking hand was useless. He pulled at his nose until it felt numb, like rubber. Finally he sat still. After a while he cleared his nostrils with a farmer's blow. Then straightened his shoulders. He wished he were sitting across from Ginger Flambeau in the dining room causing her to blush a little. The old girl was dying. He could see it. The more she tried to paint herself up, the worse she looked. He was a bum, a rat, for just hightailing it like he did, leaving her to eat alone.

"What am I, Loretta?" "You are a dog, Jarrod." "Am I a good dog or a bad dog?" "Bad, Jarrod. Clearly bad, bad, oh so—oh so—bad." She gripped his ears. Privately, she thought his tongue-flicking licking in the snake category. But never mind fine distinctions, she enjoyed Jarrod's, let us say, unorthodoxies no matter what he wanted to be. She also enjoyed their reflections in the picture across the room, and the room itself, the desk, their spontaneous, perhaps even reckless, timing. Why not? She was officially free now, a widow at last, her ancient distinguished husband, Senator Hector Strictor, finally achieving his cast bronze commemorative in the statehouse rotunda—and Jarrod was free too—so she *could* love him. Couldn't she? In fact, she wanted to tell him that—and maybe they could make their relationship more, you know . . . because getting together like this made her feel so . . . so . . . but not now, not right now . . . because oh my bad, bad doggie . . .

Oddly enough, Miss Flambeau was blushing right then and could not understand why. She looked so pale lately. She closed her compact, closed her eyes tight, counted to nine. Then she reopened her compact and looked at her face again. Why did she always count to nine? Nine, nine, nine. "Bang, bang, bang!" Pinky Fleeter yelled from his stall in the john, a copy of *Travel + Leisure* open across his legs. "Okay, okay, I'm coming, damn it, never mind *my* bowels!"

Exhausted by his tears, George Prolly fell into a brief doze that felt very, very long. When he awoke, provokingly rich pieces of his dream still spun slowly round in his head; he rubbed his eyes, then stared into the moon-dusk. He had died and gone to heaven. What a surprise! Heaven started out to be the stage in his old high school gym, that dinky, paint-splattered floor that May-Star Bondurant fell on, hard, crashing off a plank and breaking her arm playing Juliet. The plank was hidden by a fake wall that George had built; in the wall he'd cut a window so she could lean out of it and talk to Romeo of their love. George had fixed that damn plank to rest on two sawhorses and when May-Star disappeared from the window and cried out he rushed to her side and held her and stroked her long blond curls and promised to love her forever.

Nine, nine, nine. It rhymed with *mine*. It rhymed with *fine* and *line*. Yes, of course! She danced in a chorus line. "Nine fine ladies, all in a line!" the MC sang, and out they came in their feathers. She must show George her feathers. For his birthday! "George, honey. May we please get married on your birthday? Please?" But May-Star Bondurant sweetly blinked her eyes and said, "Forever is too long, Mr. Prolly, I am very sorry indeed. You see, I have promised my dear mother I will take care of her when she can no longer walk in the cemetery to dispense fresh flowers on the dead." Mrs. Strictor whispered fiercely, "Faster, Jarrod, faster, faster!"

May-Star took her broken arm and her long blond curls and rode away, leaving him to study the smears of paint on the floor of that empty stage. He blinked at the moon and shivered. He *had* gone to school with May-Star Bondurant and she *had* broken her arm, but not playing Juliet. She'd fallen from her pony, whose name was Prince. In the dream, though, when she rode away, she called her pony Old Moses. "Let's go home, Old Moses." Why would a dream change a sweet young pony's name to *Old Moses*! And have her break her arm in a play she wasn't even in! Only he was in the play; well, not really *in* it—he was the props guy. Some props.

"Please, let me explain," Miss Flambeau said to the other diners, unable to raise her voice much above a whisper. "Oh, please, listen to me! We were nine fine ladies, all in a line." But nobody would look at her. Because she was an embarrassment? Crying and wiping her eyes and crying some more? Was that it? Well, too bad for everybody. "So," she took a deep breath, "so I will just have to show my pretty feathers to Sergeant Major George Prolly of the United States Army. On his very special birthday."

"We mustn't do this, Jarrod, we mustn't, mustn't—" and Mrs. Strictor was on the brink of a beautiful, beautiful climax, almost, almost, almost *there*, when a knocking at the door stopped everything cold. Shivering, George went home too. His father sat him down and explained how to treat these old bones they'd collected. "Break 'em with a sledge hammer, boy. Crush 'em. Mix 'em in manure with sawdust, muck, loam, wood ashes, and anything else that'll work. Then cover everything with more muck and more manure, real wet. In time she'll ferment up nice as pie. Then spread her out in the field. Anybody wants to know what heaven's like, boy, you tell 'em mucky bone pie." Jarrod Lutish appeared lost, confused, struggling vaguely to his feet. Mrs. Strictor wanted to know who was at the door. "It's me, Wilma. Something is awful wrong with Miss Flambeau, I can't get her off the table. But I finally located Pinky to go find Mr. Prolly. Today is his birthday." Miss Flambeau's on a table and that contrary old coot's having a birthday—or is Pinky the one having a birthday? This is why you interrupted me, you hand-wringing, overweight illiterate dropout! Lutish felt a sharp piercing pain in his lower back and fell to his knees again. Buttoning her blouse, searching for her shoes, the director snapped, "Well, go attend Miss Flambeau! I'll be—I'll be—just a minute!" She could see Wilma thumping off to the dining room, nervously squeezing her hands, sweating. She'd fire the woman if she could find a good cheap Hispanic. "Jarrod, what are you *doing* down there!"

Miss Flambeau looked slowly around the dining room, her eyes flashing. She was ready. She had her silver dancing shoes on, her feathers in hand, all she needed was Mr. Prolly. Wilma was ready too—to grab the old lady's ankles if necessary. Some of the other diners were watching them, some were still feeding themselves, some were just sitting at their places, waiting for who knew what. Wilma's heart was racing. What was taking Mrs. Strictor so long? Where was Reverend Lutish? And Pinky? And Mr. Prolly?

A long string of saliva was just about to fall off Sergeant Prolly's chin. He didn't feel it. Didn't feel the night's chill either—he was too heated, damn it, over that dream mixing everything up: the play, the pony's name, the bones, and May-Star going away to nurse her mother instead of saying *yes* to him, *yes, I will marry you, George Prolly.* Under a by God full pearly moon just like this one, exactly like it, don't tell him no—and do not come any closer, whoever you are, because he is not going back to Piney Woods Rest. June Prolly Gladdy can have her fit, can shape her mouth into a round, teethy hole like a sea lamprey, he is staying right here.

Put reasonably back together, Loretta Strictor leaned over Jarrod Lutish. "Tell me you are *not* having a heart attack." He shook his head. "Amah—amah—a muscle spasm." She patted his hair. The word *spasm* leaped in her head like a fish suddenly free, mocking her, as she turned to go see about Miss Flambeau, that old stripper, getting up on a table. God, she was so *close.* Wilma could not understand why Pinky Fleeter hadn't come back yet. She had especially wanted him to check the basement: basements were threatening dangerous places, not just damp and hard on your joints. Why an old man on his ninetieth birthday, in a wheelchair, would want to go down to the basement, even if he could manage it, made no sense to Pinky. He was still smarting from having his john time disturbed; he'd been deeply into musing upon an advertisement for Jamaica. "Once you go, you know," the *Travel + Leisure* ad said, and he wanted to know; he wanted to wear tasseled loafers and sip from a tall frosty glass harboring pieces of speared fruit, the almond-eyed tanned woman sharing his table clearly admiring him.

Did May-Star ever miss him? Did she ever cry herself to sleep at night after tending to the old woman? Did she ever wake up to a clear sunny morning, hearing birds sing, and declare she had had enough misery and loneliness, by God, she was writing George Prolly a letter to come fetch her! And he had been waiting for that letter! Day after day. For years. Until his legs gave out, May-Star. But he is still waiting if you can open your heart in any way. You don't even have to speak loud—a whisper will do it, his hearing is pretty good. You could maybe also lift your hand and wave. He remembers your waving hand, May-Star, was like a daisy in the wind. Then he dozed off again.

Mrs. Strictor told Wilma to take her hands off Miss Flambeau's ankles, and she told Pinky Fleeter he had tobacco juice on his chin and looked disgusting. Then she said to Miss Flambeau, "Ginger, honey, we've got the stage all set up for you now. The musicians are here, the beautiful colored lights, and the audience is waiting." Miss Flambeau, whose chin rested on her entwined fingers, smiled down at the director, "My feathers?" she asked. "Goodness, yes, your feathers are here, too," Loretta Strictor said. "I don't believe these people realize"—Miss Flambeau fluttered a hand to indicate the other diners—"that I am named after Ginger Rogers, the fabulous Ginger. So they can't possibly care to see me dance." Mrs. Strictor shook her head. "No, no, Ginger, they know, we all know, and we would love to see you perform, honey, but the theatre is full, there's not one more empty seat. I myself will have to stand. Which I will not mind a bit." She offered her hand to Miss Flambeau. "Let me help you down. Mr. Fleeter, please hold this chair steady so our star dancer won't fall. That's it, honey, easy does it." Pinky Fleeter marveled that Miss Flambeau's bare feet were not the ugly, scaling, horny, scabby red things old people usually have; in fact, they were kind of pretty.

So were her calves. She held out her hand to him in such a graceful way he felt his face get warm taking it.

George Prolly woke up feeling cold. He wished he had brought along his Western jacket with the fringe in front that Miss Flambeau so admired. He'd let her finger those strips of leather every time he wore the jacket to dinner. The last time he wore it, she said, "Oh, how I wish you were my houseboy, Mr. Prolly." She couldn't help it if she sometimes didn't close her mouth all the way and drooled. It was the damned medication they fed her. He let her stroke the leather strips because it made her happy. Nor did he mind her following him around like she did; there are some things that give some folks a little joy and don't cost you anything. Go to hell if you don't agree with him.

"Do you think you can escort our star to her room now?" the director said to Wilma. "My room?" Miss Flambeau said. "Yes, honey, to put on your makeup, to get ready," Loretta Strictor said and smiled. "And also," she turned back to the nurse's aid, still smiling, "can you please, please stop wringing your hands?" As she said this her eyelids, dusted a light lavender color, came tremulously down. She kept her eyes closed while Wilma took the old dancer away. She had a blockbuster of a headache coming at her. She wanted a hot bath, a neck rub, her soft, forgiving bed, Pickles purring on the pillow beside her. But she had to say something to Pinky Fleeter, smelling of tobacco gruel and oily hair. Keeping her eyes closed, she said, "Now, what about George Prolly?" Pinky cleared his throat. "Appears he is not on the premises." "Not on the premises?" "No, ma'am. I searched inside and out and even in the basement." "Why would an old man in a wheelchair want to visit our basement?" "What I said to Wilma."

The moon had gone behind the clouds some time ago, but Sergeant Prolly took note of it only just now, raising his head and glaring around to defy anyone to sneak up and surprise him. He was normally not a man to make a fuss in public. But when Mrs. Strictor and his Judas niece and even that house pet Lutish sandbagged him, saying if he wanted to leave Piney Woods Rest they could call in the lawyers to read out, real slow so he could follow, the contract he had signed, he was outraged beyond anything he had ever experienced. Their smiles sticking on him like ticks. Not even the sniper who had shot his buddy Al from Hopatcong, New Jersey, and laughed as he pissed on the poor guy's body got to him—got under his skin—so mean. Of course when they realized that his Atlanta property had not been included in the contract and they came to him with sweet talk, he was ready.

"Daddy? Daddy?" Miss Flambeau lay in her bed, drifting off to sleep. Standing beside the bed, looking down on her, Wilma decided she would quit Piney Woods Rest and go back to the Bide-A-Wee Motel and Casino if they would let her be in charge of the laundry room again and pay her medical insurance. Mrs. Strictor was too hard to work for any more. Plus, what she was putting Reverend Lutish through was a crime. Why wouldn't she marry him? *She* would. Wilma moved to the chair in front of Miss Flambeau's vanity; she had to sit down, her joints were on fire. "Daddy? George and I are getting married . . . just as soon as he comes . . . comes home from the war . . ."

"The police? Jarrod, do you think I want it broadcast that I am not trustwor—no, I want to find him!" pacing, walking her headache away. Trying to. Pinky Fleeter led the Piney Woods Rest kitchen staff around the grounds; they aimed their flashlights at bushes and trees, they banged their pots with wooden spoons. Wilma sat at Miss Flambeau's vanity, stroking her hair with a silver brush; if they found her, she would look them straight in the eye like Katharine Hepburn, and say, *You can't fire me, I quit!* Her knees hurt too much to go searching for Mr. Prolly, who wouldn't talk to her anyway. Wouldn't talk to anybody except Miss Flambeau. And today was his birthday. They had that cake ready to bring out and everything.

Something burst in Sergeant Prolly's head like fireworks almost, a fierce brilliant series of lights and explosions of such surprise that they left him unable to speak, though he wanted to—wanted to take one more step and fall in those leaves and cover up. A big truck's air brakes blasted through the trees and picker bushes, clearing his head a moment. Then he heard an owl hoot. Another one. Talking to each other like sweethearts. *Who-whoo . . . who-whoo,* they said, and down he went. Ah yes, he was tired. Keeping quiet under these leaves . . . good idea. Exactly what he'll do. Go away now.

"Wait, wait. Perhaps we do want to notify that nice Sheriff Duane. Because, Jarrod, Mr. Prolly *was* receiving callers about that Atlanta property, was he not? You don't suppose one of them has, let us say, seduced that old man into leaving us?" Miss Flambeau was almost asleep, the sedative doing its work. Wilma thought she would try just a little touch of her lipstick before leaving. And she *was* leaving. Because she did not forget to lock the DANGER door, and was exhausted worrying about it, and was not going to hang around for more abuse from that mean woman. Jarrod Lutish, bent forward and supporting himself with a hand on the edge of Mrs. Strictor's desk, said, "When things are back to normal, Loretta, including my lumbar region, I wish to get down on one knee, and take your hand in mine, and ask you a very important question." She stopped pacing and looked at him. He appeared unfinished, not completely grown up. But maybe that's what appealed to her—besides having him in the business. She resumed pacing—she had other important matters on her mind. Anyway, why would she want to marry a minister fifteen years her junior who just might not be all there? Her pacing became slower. She was tired. And she felt . . . bone-lonely. There went those owls again, seeming to coax the moon out from behind the clouds big and round and lighting up Sergeant Prolly's smile. "Good night, my prince," Ginger Flambeau whispered. "Good night, good night."

The Capital of Kansas City

When Mary Beth was nine years old and her sister Alice five, they had to sit up straight at the dinner table one evening and pay attention to their father's lecture on the subject of cash flow. He was twenty-eight, so was their mother, who also had to pay attention. Nixon had just been elected, and Mary Beth's father said, "Now we can get down to business." She remembers clearly how he paused to take a sip of ice tea and tuck in his tie before beginning. Yes, it was the cash flow lecture (following many others) that confirmed she could not only appear to be listening but actually was—enough, anyway—while at the same time go happily roaming around in her own personal thoughts, whatever they might be. Really it was a gift.

Years later when her poetry professor, in a casual aside, suggested to the class that genius was likely the ability to hold in the mind two opposing ideas simultaneously, she fancied she might well be a genius. She would rather have had longer legs, given the choice. In any case, on her long meandering early morning walks that semester, she felt a rich glow about her cheeks and neck, sometimes a tingle, when she thought about changing her major from business to English. Would her father have a goat? Yes, maybe even two. The truth was, she had a crush on her poetry professor and spent much of the class imagining him naked. Sometimes he was naked in her bed, narrow and messy as it was, but usually he was naked with her on a beach somewhere quite private. Perhaps the Oregon coast, which she had only seen pictures of.

On one of these dreamy occasions, she jerked completely awake upon hearing herself say, "Some day I will marry thee." This shocked her, this Quaker-sounding announcement, for two reasons: one, she was an Episcopalian in good standing and, two, what might her classmates or *he* think? Looking shyly left and right from her back row seat, and then toward the front, she was calmed: no one apparently had heard her.

Then, which was not her manner at all, she stared hotly at the man for at least a minute, hoping he would feel her passion and return this fierce, thrilling gaze. She was twenty years old.

What happened next was due in part to the social climate of that time, in part to her loneliness, and part was pure luck. Or so she later assessed the situation. In brief, she managed to find four quiet, nice-looking boys on campus and favored them with her fevered cries. She hadn't set out to achieve that interesting number (the four corners of the earth, the four winds, the four known directions, the Four Horsemen of the Apocalypse), it just happened. None of them knew of the others, and all were grateful, as was she. Truth to tell, she enjoyed the heat and slippery touch of a boy very much, and disappearing in that touch, and arriving at release. She would never, then, have used the earthy verb *to come*, or use earthy language of any kind during that intimate act. Now, of course, she was older and, though still shy in many ways, not afraid of frank speech or *that* afraid of sounding or looking foolish. Weren't we all of us foolish about something now and again?

But that wasn't what she wanted to muse upon these days. These days, specifically the last two, she was nervously luxuriating in an astonishing development: she was not only back in touch with her poetry professor but scheduled to have a rendezvous. The penultimate thing she remembered saying to him as a student—she was handing in her final bluebook exam—was, "Maybe one of these days I will see you in Yugoslavia!" Then she turned, embarrassed, and fled the room. Her face felt on fire.

When her grades arrived in the mail, she saw that he had given her an A.

Where on earth did her remark come from? Mary Beth had no clue. Yugoslavia? Why not Warsaw? Waikiki? Delaware Water Gap? Why not Slippery Rock?

Now here he was—here they both were—in Kansas City.

He had called her firm to complain about the trees they were preparing to cut down to enlarge the parking lot that lay behind his house, and Mr. Woodward's secretary called her to ask if she might see what she could do to calm their neighbor.

"He's a poet, we're told. Maybe even famous in his circle. And since you have an interest in poetry, Mary Beth, Mr. Woodward naturally thought . . ."

Mary Beth had written the firm's Christmas poem for the last, well, several years now. It was always a big hit, how she managed to get everyone's name in—all the partners, secretaries, the other attorneys, the receptionists, Woodward, of course—everybody!—and how cleverly she rhymed. *Litigious/religious/good for business.* God, if he ever found out. About her so-called poems, that is. He would, however, learn that she had become a lawyer. *If* he recognized her, remembered her. It had been twenty years. More important, why had he moved to Kansas City? And when? Did he take a new teaching job? Retire early? On the phone, when they talked, she could not very well probe his personal life too deeply. Their subject was the trees/parking lot below the hill where he lived.

"Such glorious oaks," he said.

"I understand completely," she said. "I adore trees."

"And those outrageous splotches of orange paint on their trunks—have you seen them?"

"I—no. But I will! You can count on it!"

"Kisses of death."

"Yes."

"Every morning we have breakfast together," he said.

Breakfast with kisses of death? No, no, he meant the trees. "Only breakfast?" she said.

"What's that?"

"You and the trees only have breakfast together?" Yikes, what a question.

"Of course not."

"Of course not."

She suggested lunch—lunch, please, to the rescue!—to discuss the matter further. "Public relations and all that"—could he tell she was smiling?—"after all, we *are* neighbors." He hesitated, then agreed. She had to say her name again, and spell the last part. "It is a tongue-twister," she laughed. She fought the urge to add, "But it's not mine, not the one you know! It came from the man—the fumble, the stumble, the utterly wrong number—I was married to!"

Was he free for lunch on Sunday, she asked. He was. Excellent. And since it was in the neighborhood, what did he think of the Nelson—that is, had he tried their new buffet yet? "I mean," she clarified quickly, "the *caterer* is new."

No, he'd never eaten at the museum, he said, but he'd been meaning to. "Excellent!" she sang out, at least an octave too high. Dropping her voice lower, "And maybe we can have a look afterward at the new exhibit?"

"What is it?"

God, she didn't know, hadn't a clue; that wasn't the point. The point was to simply be together.

"I'll find out and call you right back."

"Oh, don't worry," he said, that reassuring tone from all those years ago coming through so naturally, "we'll find out on Sunday. Surprise can be, you know, nice."

Immediately after hanging up—that was Friday—she felt exhilarated, exhausted, useless. Yes, surprise *can* be. She left the office early and spent an hour in the hands of Viva, her personal trainer, getting stretched, bent, and straightened out. If she slept that night, she did not remember it. The movies she put on and the articles in the copy of *Foreign Affairs* she held in her lap were more like minnows darting in and out of sight than plotted dramas and enlightenments.

On Saturday she grocery-shopped, dropped off suits and sweaters at the cleaners, on impulse drove through a car wash, feeling soapy/dopey, and tried on maybe two dozen pairs of shoes, rejecting them all. Then she climbed on the treadmill at Viva's and in less than a minute jumped off: she needed fresh air, space, birdsong! She drove to the park near her apartment and walked a necessary and vigorous 5K, swinging half-pound weights in time to Ry Cooder and the Buena Vista Social Club, spontaneously flapping her arms like a goose warming up for a spin to Cuba. Why not!

That night she tried but, trying too hard, failed miserably at disappearing into sleep's curative nostrums. *O sleep! O gentle sleep! Nature's soft nurse, how have I frighted thee . . . ?*

Finally she sat up in bed—Shakespeare, as usual, asked a knotty question—and waited for the sun. It was just after four o'clock. She wanted to call Alice in Cincinnati and say, "Guess what, counselor?" But her sister, she knew, slept in on weekends after paying a lot of all-night- single-mom dues getting her twin daughters out of colicky babyhood and into robust adolescence—plus, now, having good Bart to spoon with. Maybe she should tidy up her bookshelves, wax the kitchen floor, polish the candlesticks, the hall mirror, clear off the dining room table. What would Angel, who came in on Mondays with her rubber gloves, her Benson & Hedges, and her eyebrows plucked in great arches of wonder, think? Well, first she would pour herself a cup of coffee, then she would join Mary Beth at the (now gleaming) dining room table and look slowly and silently around, not even lighting up. Finally she would turn her big round brown eyes on her employer and hold them there until Mary Beth had to say something. But what could she say? "I've decided to keep a kempt apartment, and therefore, Angel, you are redundant"?

Redundant/resplendent/expectant.

She focused across the room on the fireplace, resplendent with fresh irises. Perhaps her favorite flower. Iris. The Greek goddess of the rainbow. She took this apartment because of that handsome brick-and-stone fireplace—a fireplace in her bedroom, what, please tell her, could be more romantic? But how many fires have been laid there? How many times has she been laid on its hearth is more to the point? Twice, your honor. And both times bad. Not poor, not mediocre. Bad. Don't we need that occasional rainbow?

For lunch she will wear her black French bra—she just decided. He won't know, but she will.

The last time she'd seen him, she stood on his front steps after knocking on his door. A heavy green door with a brass knocker in the form of a ring in a bull's nose. Where had the courage to do this come from? The nerve? She was a senior now, a full year older than when she sat dreaming in his poetry class. In a week she would graduate. Then what? She felt like turning around and racing down his walkway, down the street! Maybe she would join the Peace Corps. Maybe she would return to Pine Ridge and do that again, try to help the little ones catch up. It wasn't Head Start, exactly, officially, but in practice that's what she and her fellow Episcopalian Youth aimed at providing that summer on the reservation. Summer? They were always so cold! Mornings, washing up at their outdoor pump, God Almighty! Even Steve, the young seminarian, their leader, splashing water under his arms, crooned, *O fuck me fuck me*. Well, he wasn't ordained yet.

When the green door opened and her poetry professor stood there, she blurted out, "Hi! I was in the neighborhood and thought you might like to cook pasta with me tomorrow night? I'm graduating? Celebrating?"

He looked at her a long while without saying anything—or it seemed a long while. Of course he recognized her at once. She knew by that slim smile. He rubbed his chin. He was wearing jeans and a T-shirt, a white T-shirt, and holding a book, his finger marking his place. Finally he said, "I would love to, Mary Beth, but I've already promised someone . . ." He really looked flattered *and* disappointed that he couldn't accept her invitation.

She returned to her apartment confident that that was so. Because here's why: he stepped outside and looked at the sky, the grand toss of stars, then he sighed and said, "Shall we sit a moment? If you have time?"

They sat side by side on his front steps and were quiet. He wore brown loafers, no socks. She had on running shoes, black tights, a man's white dress shirt hanging out—her father's castoff.

"Well," he said, "'As I sd to my / friend, because I am / always talking—'"

And she, picking up on the Creeley poem, even visualizing the "sd"s and line breaks, responded, "'John, I / sd, which was not his / name—'"

"'—the darkness sur- / rounds us—'"

"'—what / can we do against / it—'"

But he didn't take his turn, and the poem stopped there. He looked at her, smiling, for the longest time—like he did in class when the discussion became so close, so intimate, all you had to do was open your mouth and begin, something worth thinking about would come out. You felt you could even sing—anything!—which someone in class actually said one time, though no one ever did. Sing, that is. She was so happy being looked at like that that she could easily have jumped up and dashed into the yard and done a cartwheel, finishing off with the splits, her arms raised in a Vee.

How the evening ended, exactly, was a blur. But a blur with feeling. *Long/longing/song.*

In the shower, she imagined their Sunday lunch such a success that they fell into the kind of easy riffing he'd promoted in class:

"What's the capital of Kansas City?"

"Count Basie!"

Squeezing a creamy worm of French shampoo into her palm, she altered the lyrics of the song her mother used to sing in the shower, but only by one important word: "I'm gonna wash that man right *into* my hair . . ." Her hair was still naturally, fully, red and her body, thanks to Viva—"Must always poosh, poosh, harder and harder, Missy Attorney Person!"—firm. Or firm enough. God knew she was faithful to her workout regimen. Well, why not? It beat dating Mr. Narcissus, Mr. Trophy Hunter, or Mr. Rich-Itch, the famous interchangeable ad nauseam triplets. And *please* do not mention looking for that "certain someone" on the Net. If she wanted to become truly pathetic, she could stay later and later at the office, then pick up her dinner in a carton at the deli and eat it in front of her computer at home, getting dry-eyed, stiff-necked, and numb-bummed.

"What's the capital of Count Basie?"

"'One O'Clock Jump!'"

She chose a skirt that would show her slim calves to good advantage and was capable, besides, of a nice playful swirl. Over the black French bra—no, she had not forgotten—her pale yellow silk blouse, the top buttons of which you could leave undone and allow just enough cleavage to present solid evidence without seeming pushy. For shoes she would wear these medium heels in case they went for a stroll on the front lawn among the Henry Moore sculptures. Through her bedroom window the day was blossoming beautifully and laying a speckled sunny light across the pillows, like a slowly undulating trout. Now for a slight dab of this—*whoa*—very subtle pomegranate scent on the insides of her elbows and behind her knees. She changed her mind about the medium heels and went a little higher: she could still handle an outdoor stroll, and in style.

Driving to the Nelson, Mary Beth practiced saying "Gerald," for he would surely say to her, after realizing who she was, "Please, no more of that Professor stuff." And then like *that* their words, their timing, their jokes—everything!—would fall into place. She could feel it, yes, this meshing, this blending. After parking and checking her hair in the rearview mirror, she laughed at herself—and in honor of fate—and just because she couldn't help it. Almost singing, she said, "Here we go, Missy Lawyer Person, ready or not!"

She was a few minutes early, but it was such a gorgeous day she was happy to stand outside near the main entrance—their agreed-upon meeting place—and take the sun. She briefly called up the trout image on her pillows and smiled what was no doubt a wicked little smile. "I will be the not terribly tall woman with red hair," she'd told him on the phone. "And you?" she'd asked playfully. That just slipped out: already she had started flirting! He said he would be wearing a yellow hanky in the breast pocket of his brown tweed sport coat. And wasn't he flirting back? Just a little?

Now he was fifteen minutes late. Lots of couples coming to the museum today, and many of them, she observed, composed of an older man and a younger woman. Well, maybe not *many*, but enough to notice. Wouldn't it be—what's a good word for this?—wouldn't it be *glorious* if they clicked? Is that too—oh, too, you know—wishful?

She hoped nothing had happened, because thirty minutes, now, *was* a bit late. Thirty-three, actually. Would he have changed his mind? No—he was not a man to stand somebody up. If he *had* changed his mind, he would have let her know. She suddenly blushed: what if all this time he were waiting *inside*?

Mary Beth entered the museum and looked quickly around the reception area. She saw no one who even remotely resembled him. At the desk she asked if any messages had been left for Mary Beth Urquhart. No.

Could he have had an accident? On a pretty day like this? Of course he could. She was feeling faint and found a bench. One of the women from the reception desk came over and asked if she would like some water.

"Yes, thank you."

Breathing slowly, she began to feel less weak, though still not so hot. She returned outside and looked around. He was well over an hour late now.

Had there been a time change?

No.

Was her watch going berserk? Her eyes failing?

No, no.

This was—well, she didn't know what it was. Yes, of course she knew what it was: a panic attack. She got out her cell phone—God, she hated doing this—and dialed his number, prepared to apologize all over the place for getting the time of their date wrong (though deep down she was positive she hadn't). More important, she didn't want to embarrass him, make him feel forgetful, old.

It rang and rang, then one of those anonymous answering-machine voices came on—the voice of a woman who clearly did not inhabit the world of the fallible, the world of hope and joy and hand-holding and spontaneous kisses and, yes, of failure and decay. She said: *We are not available, please leave a message*. The poor man, to have to put up with *that* for a message-bearer.

Mary Beth could walk to his house. It wasn't that far, really, and if he was walking (a perfectly reasonable explanation for his lateness:

he simply misjudged the distance) she would run into him, and what a good laugh they could have!

"Isn't this silly, Gerald? I mean, aren't I silly getting all—"

"No, you are not silly. In fact"—and his eyes would restore and enrich her—"you are quite, *quite* pretty when you blush."

She found a nice rhythm. And the heels felt fine. A lot of people were out walking: in satiny track outfits, plugged into their audio, pushing baby strollers, pulling back on dog leashes. "Brutus, quit showing off!"

His house was one of those handsome old Tudors that sat on a ridge, the front yard a generous, grassy slope harboring a dozen ancient oaks. His back yard, of course, sloped down to where her firm would be making extra parking. Not a big parking addition but, she had to admit, noticeable. And the more she thought about it, the more she was on his side.

Three young girls were standing with their bikes at the bottom of his driveway as she approached. They were about ten or eleven years old, thin, freckled, and giving her a good looking over. Mary Beth smiled and said hello.

"Hi," they smiled back, all of them wearing braces on their teeth.

"Pretty day for a bike ride," she said and started up the steps beside his driveway.

"Are you looking for the poet?"

She turned. "Why, yes, I am."

"He isn't home," said the tallest girl.

"An ambulance took him away," said another.

Mary Beth's hand covered her mouth. Time jerked to a stop—or did it?—or what? What!

A year later, almost to the day, she was interviewing a witness in an armed robbery case when that scene came back to her, along with the question of time, its elusiveness, as in how much of it had passed while she stood there on his steps, staring at those girls—seconds? hours?—and what precious little of it they had had. The witness for her pro bono client was insisting, "Look, I was in bed with the man, you know?—at exactly the time he was suppose to be doin' what the cops accuse him of doin'—but no way, lady, no way, he was doin' *me* then. An he was in no hurry to get up and go do something mean, cause he was takin' his sweet time."

The three girls regarded her, she remembered, with a kind of admiration—or even awe—as if she were a celebrity, a star, a woman in glamorous high heels who had traveled in the same orbit as the poet. And then when Mary Beth's hand flew to her mouth, they looked down at the ground. It was clearly as much as they could muster right then in the way of sympathy and sadness, being so young.

The Bach Suites

All through my major ambivalent period—fifteen to nineteen—I was the bishop's yard boy. I trimmed his lawn and walked his Irish wolfhound and when snow fell I fired up his blower and cleared the driveway he shared with his renters next door. During the latter part of the aforementioned period, his renters were the Indian professor and his American wife, Isabel, who was, astonishingly, almost my exact age. Our births, we calculated, had occurred only eighteen hours and six minutes apart. She arrived first. He, Raj, was forty-one, more than twice her age. She told me this with a shrug. "It's all part of the cosmic cycle of becoming and perishing." They were Hindu, though before she met Raj, she said, she was practically a Buddhist. She had the curliest dark red hair I had ever seen on a girl and played the cello, *I* thought, as well as Yo-Yo Ma. An opinion that got me in a lot of trouble.

They came to our little South Dakota town (home of the Honkers, rah rah) because Raj had been hired to teach at the college. They came from Kansas, where he acquired his PhD *and* pretty permanent residence status by marrying Isabel. She mentioned this last detail as if it were only a little finishing touch, like getting the loose hairs whisked off your neck after a haircut, but I knew it was more significant than that for old Raj. I knew how these residence things worked from my government class. Which, ironically, met that fall in Wesley Hall on the same floor and at the same time as Professor Singh's Intro to Econ. Once he knew who I was—the bishop's yard boy—I always tried to avoid running into him on campus. He emitted this little sniff when he saw me. I didn't think a whole lot of him, either.

For my services as his yard boy, the bishop, who was also my great-uncle, paid me a weekly salary, in cash, which was neither a mean nor a generous sum; but he threw in, once I started college, the apartment above the garage, including heat. This was a nice deal, the carriage house, because it meant I didn't have to pay for a dorm room or live at home with my mother, and the bishop basically left me alone. Which I appreciated. I actually liked the old guy, though some people in town, including my mother, had mixed feelings about him: they admired his annual free Christmas turkey to any family that was strapped (all you had to do was stop by Schmidt's Market and say you were coming for the bishop's bird), but they faulted him for being standoffish and, until I came along, letting his dog run wild. He was a Tuohy, same as my dad and Grandpa Roger.

The bishop, as it happened, retired soon after my dad fell off his ship and drowned during a training mission. We were not at war, nobody was drunk, the waters were calm, and there wasn't a cloud in the sunny sky, my mother was told. The bishop retired because he had arthritis and difficulty hearing and seeing and, bottom line, was tired. He was also overweight and short, which gave him a nearly round and sometimes comical look: shoulder to shoulder beside Hanrahan, the Irish wolfhound, for example, the two stood almost even-Steven if the dog didn't slouch.

When I first became his yard boy, in ninth grade, the bishop irritated me some by always calling me Tim. "Tim, lad," he'd say, "are the duties onerous?" Or, "Tim, you'll let us know if the hound is too vigorous for a lad slight as yourself to manage." My name *used* to be Tim. Frankly, I didn't care for the name even before I knew about sickly Tiny Tim in *A Christmas Carol.* So in tenth grade, finally, I changed it, to Samson, which he knew, it wasn't a secret. Whenever the subject came up in my mother's presence, he'd ask her, "Was the lad getting enough to eat, to make such a decision?" Anyway, I got my growth spurt and worked up to forty chins on a low branch in his front yard and he stopped calling me Tim. I held no grudges.

Full disclosure. I started the Samson thing as an ironic *joke,* which apparently not many people got. I soon came to like the name. Samson Tuohy, what's it to ye? So I kept it. My mother said, "It's your name. Wear it in good health."

This is interesting. Not long after I met Isabel, she told me she was changing her first name to Guari, to please Raj. You could have knocked me over twice with one of those pheasant feathers that Max, the bishop's handyman, was always leaving scattered around after cleaning his recent kills. I *liked* the name Isabel, it was a refreshing change from all the Brandys and Lilys and Tiffanys and Sarahs. To give you an idea of how disrupted I was, I almost stopped to ask the bishop what *he* thought. He'd come out on his front porch to smell the day, which he liked to do before his first toddy. I was going back and forth with the mower chopping up all the maple leaves on the ground, trying as I pushed the machine along to digest Isabel's latest news. But I didn't stop to ask his opinion because I *was* aware of the irony in my objection to something I myself had done. In the end I chalked up her name-change to yet another thing we had in common, besides our age. I continued, however, to call her Isabel, if we were alone, and she always forgave me, so that was nice.

The land the bishop lived on was settled by his parents, Aiden and Ada Tuohy, who fled Ireland because they were hungry and fed up with hearing the two sets of parents casting constant blame on each other. But for what, exactly, Grandpa Roger never learned. "Maybe for everything," he said. "That makes blaming easier." Aiden and Ada produced seven children over here, milking cows, and might have produced more but Ada died giving birth to twin girls, the only females the Tuohy clan in America ever brought forth, as far as we know. Grace and Maude. Both became country school teachers and lived on in the original house caring for their father until he and then they went to meet their maker. "The last words of all three," Grandpa said. "'Going to meet my maker.' Like a tic." The twins never married. Neither of course did the future bishop, who lived with them until he went away to seminary. He came home every chance he got, my mother said, because he was kind of a baby. "Well, look at him," she said.

One day—this was a lot later—fire took out the barn and most of the house, both of which were empty and falling down anyway, and all the cows long gone. My great-uncle, who had been a bishop for a while, put together the money to build the brick house now standing there. It's that pinkish brick you see in buildings from the Civil War era. I rather like it. He also had the garage and carriage house built, the latter, apparently, for guests, my mother said. "What guests?" she always added.

When the bishop hung up his miter for good, he of course refused the home for old clergy that the diocese supported down in Sioux Falls. He wasn't about to be watched over constantly by those hawks, the caretakers. He didn't even like the word; it sounded to him like "undertakers." He'd seen them—that was grim enough. He wanted his own bed in his own house; he hired Mrs. Gustafson to cook the meals he favored and her husband, Max, to put fresh pheasant and venison on the table and to fix whatever wore out and broke. On Wednesdays, his day off, Dr. Cronin came by to sip a drop of the bishop's good Irish whiskey and, I gathered, to visually check him out. Grandpa Roger, his oldest brother, came by on Sundays now and then to needle him and, since he was already there, take a drop or two; he'd bring along my mother because at some point he'd need her arm. Grandpa's views on religion and his salty tongue did not seem to bother the bishop a bit. Which was another reason I liked him. Receiving the news one day that Roger went to bed after a good dinner and did not wake up, the bishop said to my mother, who delivered this news, "By God, Maeve, by God. He's been given the best sleep there is, and it's rare, indeed." She said that was the second time she really welcomed the bishop's whiskey and company; the first time was after my dad died.

Let's see, after Grandpa Roger, who was the oldest, as I said, the rest of Aiden and Ada's children, besides the twins, were Frank, Patrick, James, and of course the bishop. Patrick and James ran off to join the Navy after Pearl Harbor, lying about James' age because he was too young. But they were so sick of milking cows morning and night and needed, Grandpa said, the adventure. They perished on the same ship as the famous five Sullivan brothers from Iowa. Years later I saw the movie and even though it was pretty sentimental about the

Sullivan boys and didn't bother to mention my great-uncles, I still bawled like a baby. But not so much for any of those sailors, exactly.

It was Frank, my mother said, who put up the money, or most of it, so the bishop could rebuild the family home. She guessed the carriage house was where Frank would stay if he came back to visit, which he never did. He had gone off to Michigan as soon as he could, to work in Ford's factory, and somehow ended up owning lots of houses in Detroit. We were going to go visit him when my dad came home from training, my mother said. I don't remember any of that; I was a baby. "A big surprise," she said. We were going to go see if Frank had something we could do there in Michigan. Then my dad drowned and Grandpa Roger, who was living with us, turned permanently shaky. Frank was generous about the money that allowed us to stay put.

I myself left after graduating from college. "Go while you can," my mother said.

She wasn't going anywhere. What would Schmidt's Market do without her? "Oh, I could go to Las Vegas, I suppose, and deal blackjack."

"What do you know about dealing cards?" I said.

"Well, I'm too skinny to be a stripper—I need to know *something* if I go to Las Vegas. Besides . . ."

She didn't finish her thought, if she had one. "Besides," followed by a toss of her hand, was how she usually ended this kind of conversation.

I used to wish my mother had come from a large noisy family full of singers and tellers of tall tales, since on the Tuohy side the bishop and even Grandpa spent so much of their time inside themselves, thinking. She'd hold her own in such a boisterous crowd with her snappy comebacks. My favorite comeback, which only came once, occurred when I asked about her youth. I was young myself but I will never forget the gist of what she said. It went basically like this:

"The truth is, I came awake one day all grown up and found myself in Schmidt's Market. Mr. Schmidt said since I was there I might arrange the oranges, and the apples, too, if I had the time, into pretty pyramids. I was known as Maid Maeve, Queen of the Nile. Until this Tuohy boy came by one day for a pack of Luckies. The rest is history."

She had no siblings. Her parents owned a local bar, The Shamrock, and both went to their graves early. It was not a successful bar, apparently.

That same summer I graduated, the bishop died. He came out on his porch to smell the day and boom, down he went. Not as smooth a landing as Grandpa Roger's, but quick anyway. Old Hanrahan sat down beside him, Mrs. Gustafson said, and gave out what the bishop used to call "the hound's sweet song of longing."

Frank, as he did with Grandpa, would not be attending any service. He was still almost dead himself, he said, the details of his dolorous days in a wheelchair he would spare us. He sent flowers and a generous sum for Masses to be said for his brother for a long, long time. Frank's lawyer sent a letter turning over to my mother and me the pinkish brick house and adjacent properties. "Well," she said, "it seems Frank owned just about everything except the bishop's Christmas turkeys and Hanrahan."

The ceremony was all right. I kept thinking, though, how much better everything would feel if we could hear Bach's cello suites, if only selected movements, instead of the dismal droning falling down upon our heads from the organ like a thick tarp. Of course I had learned enough by this time to know that Bach's suites were basically dances—and totally secular—so providing them on such an occasion would have called for a considerable stretch of imagination probably not possible for those in charge. I was guessing it was the bishop's successor who had chosen this funeral music, because he presented about the sourest expression that God, if He was out and about, could invent. Moreover, I concluded from such a dyspeptic look that His Excellency really didn't want to be there, swathed as he was in all those vestments in that hot, humid little church named for the famous ascetic Francis of Assisi and the bishop's stated venue for this event. The same church the bishop arranged for Grandpa's little service.

It was funny how my mother and I always called him the bishop when talking *about* him, but face to face we never called him anything. Unless you count the time when we came to tell about Grandpa being gone. I was thirteen and listening hard because the bishop was talking about his brother's wife, my dad's mother. "Thrown from a horse.

Just a young thing, very fair, a laughing girl. Roger was much older, perhaps too old to be left with a boy babe in a house full of gloom. Losing her was the greatest of blows." The bishop patted me on the head. I said, "Thank you, sir." So maybe I did call him something to his face. Sir. Which I continued to do.

He surely had a name, though. Sean. But Sean seemed to belong to a taller, younger man, a man who was not in the church. "Someone," my mother said, "like your father." Which was probably the main reason we couldn't use it for the bishop. We—my mother and I—only rarely used it when talking about my dad. Names. They can be complicated sometimes.

"Why was my dad named after the bishop?" I remember asking Grandpa.

"Oh, he'd been casting those curious eyes around for a few days, and I said to him, 'What on earth would ye like to be called besides Laddie Buck?' And he says, 'Oh well, Sean would be all right.' So we drew up the papers and made it legal. And we let his honor the bishop, who wasn't a bishop yet, baptize him so he wouldn't go round with a long face day and night."

Growing up, it wasn't hard to see that neither Grandpa nor my mother thought highly of miracles and heaven and all the other stuff that excited church people. They didn't carry on about it, not even when Grandpa announced, "It's time to go needle his honor again." That was a joke I was slow to catch up to. They both thought that Joseph and Mary produced a decent man who spoke a lot of good common sense and at times had some very great things to say. But he had that bad luck with the hypocrite Pilate and all those Hopalong Jesus characters down through the years. My mother and Grandpa seemed to admire Mother Teresa as much. And they'd throw in Mark Twain and Dorothy Day and FDR to sweeten the pot. All of which I could not help mentioning to Isabel; she inspired me to say things that truly interested me or puzzled me—things I never said to anyone else. Sometimes I'd stop myself. "This is ridiculous!" She'd say, always so softly, "Nothing is ridiculous when you are searching."

Until it got too cold, we would sit on her front porch in the swing following her sessions with the cello. She practiced for two hours every morning in their living room and I always found something quiet to do in the yard, like dig up a thistle. I could spend those two hours on one thistle. Listening to Isabel was like this: she made me feel a deep satisfaction everywhere inside, then when she stopped a slow, sad need took over, a yearning. I did not easily use the word *yearning* in my major ambivalent period.

The first time I listened to her I tried to explain, in the swing later, the effect that those two hours had on me. Try describing something that touches you but which you can't touch back, without sounding full of b.s. Describing what happens in a willful Irish wolfhound's brain when he sees a small brown rabbit would likely be less complicated. Isabel didn't want to hear anything that included praise for her abilities, frowning the second I started in. I soon stopped, because she was so sincere. She was also sincere about Ramakrishna, reincarnation, and "the indescribable state," stuff that floated in the air like Hanrahan's loose hair when I ran my knuckles down his spine to cheer him up. I told her, because I couldn't lie, that I was probably an agnostic, like my mother and grandfather, and she only looked at the folded hands in her lap and smiled.

She did the same thing one time when I asked her—I couldn't help it—"Why did you drop out of college to come *here*? After only one semester?" I really meant something else, and she knew it. Her folded-hands-and-smile gesture showed me, as if I needed more evidence, how nice she was. Which was why old Raj latched on to her.

Nights after talking with Isabel I'd lie wide awake in the carriage house and thank Johann Sebastian Bach for writing his cello suites, because those were her favorite pieces to practice. And I'm not kidding, I really thought her playing was as powerful, or almost, as Yo-Yo Ma's. At the college library, if you were a music major, you could check out records and listen to them with earphones in a special booth in the basement behind the stacks of bound magazines. I was not a music major, but that fall I signed up for History of Classical Music so I could use the special booth and listen to Yo-Yo Ma play the cello suites. I listened to the entire set one Saturday afternoon when the Honkers football team was playing at home and the library was practically all mine. Yo-Yo Ma was good—very good—but I thought: *She's close, isn't she?*

I was working up the courage to invite her to hear Yo-Yo Ma with me during the Honkers' last home game of the season. I wanted to ask her to help me understand. "Please," I would say, "why is he better?" But the Black Day arrived first.

I was leaning against her house, eyes closed, off somewhere in my head that was wonderful, listening to her and seeing all the possible hues of blue and purple slip around each other in slender sheets behind my eyes. Suddenly I hear, "Good morning, Mr. Tuohy." It was old Raj, who was supposed to be on campus holding office hours. I was so thrown off, I said, "You're not scheduled to be here!" He gave me that superior sniff. "Are you enjoying the music?" That's when I more or less lost my composure. I told him of course I was enjoying the music, who wouldn't? "Isabel's a genius! She's as good as Yo-Yo Ma!" I turned then, and left.

Well, he reported this conversation. In that ironic tone of his, I'm sure. The next time I saw her, which was not soon, she let me know that I must never—*never*—humiliate her like that again.

"Humiliate?" I was stunned.

"I am an amateur, Samson. An amateur." Her eyes glistened. "Yo-Yo Ma is a master. I thought we were friends."

For two agonizing weeks, there was no music, cello or otherwise, coming from her house. Maybe she was meditating or doing her yoga. Or both. Then the house was completely empty.

Since that time, my understanding of musical talent has improved. My wife, Collette, is a big help in this regard. She's one of the violinists in a string quartet here in San Francisco that is "good enough," the *Examiner's* critic says, "to glean sighs of satisfaction from the most demanding of corners." This kind of writing embarrasses Collette. She is a doctor, as are the other members of the quartet, and for them finding time to rehearse may be the most challenging aspect of their musical existence; never mind a performance schedule and satisfying demanding corners.

But they do perform, largely at benefits related to childhood diseases; three are pediatricians, the fourth an anesthesiologist. All four are of Asian descent (South Korea, China, Japan, and Vietnam) and two—Collette and Kyoko—are former gymnasts who almost made the Olympic team in college. They all bring to their music the kind of seriousness I hear in their medical talk, the two who never engaged in organized sports at least as competitive as the former jocks.

One day in grad school I was killing time in a music store waiting to meet Collette for dinner—we had recently started dating. I ran across a CD reissue of Yo-Yo Ma playing the Bach cello suites. A wave of memories nearly drowned me; I had to take a brisk walk after leaving the store. I bought the CD and later, over our spaghetti, I told Collette about first listening to Yo-Yo Ma in the library basement in South Dakota. Her eyes—her whole face—lit up. "Well, then, you were not so deprived, after all." I thought to bring Isabel into my story, but what with Raj moving them across town, plus the baby and all that, I would only be complicating matters.

Three Short Tales

Up North

I wasn't there when Boots kept busy—for weeks—chopping firewood, but I heard about it. All fall, people said, morning to night. They worried, at first. Tried to engage him in conversation, get him to come inside and eat the food they had brought while it was still hot, but he wouldn't budge. Said to just leave it on the table, not to fuss. So that's how it went, they said; you know Boots.

When I was a kid, I thought Boots and Alice were king and queen of the swans—because of the cob and pen that came when they called. The swans lived quietly to themselves on Black River, back in a pretty oval where white birch grew thick as cattails down to the banks on both sides, and where the river began to curl into Bass Lake; but they always came floating out like perfect surprises whenever Boots or Alice stood on their dock and crooned. No one else could do that.

Boots had been in the war and one of his legs was wood. Just like those birch, he told me. He met Alice up in Traverse City, where he had to go sometimes to have them look him over, check his oil. She was Irish, with green eyes, and the first time we met she said, "Now look here, kiddo. Look at this." She held up her hands, turning them slowly so I could see the fronts and backs. She had regular fingers, long and slim, but her thumbs were short and fat and had big nails—and the skin around them was bumpy like the skin on a cow's teat. Then she moved them, and then she laughed deep in her throat. She had lost her thumbs down in Detroit—in a dumb factory, she said—and the doctors performed a modern miracle. "These used to be my big toes, kiddo."

I thought about all that as I drove out to see Boots. He didn't remember me right away; when he did he slapped the side of his head. He'd been thinking, he said, about doing some fishing. I helped him pull his shanty onto the lake. Beside it I started chopping a hole, using his firewood axe. I had forgotten how good it felt to be making a fishing hole on a cold morning, hearing the chops echo like coins dropped on glass and smelling the pine trees all around. I would have been happy to chop the whole thing, but I was glad when Boots poked my arm and said, "Here, give me that. I don't want to lose it."

When the hole was finished, we pulled the shanty over it and went inside. Boots gave me his milking stool to sit on. He preferred to stand, he said, it was too hard getting up anymore. I looked at the bright green, almost tropical light under the ice. I hadn't seen light like that in thirty years. And I had forgotten how quiet it can be in a shanty. Once in a while you hear those hollow-sounding sharp cracks that the ice makes. But you get used to them, as you do the wind rubbing against the shanty. Like your heartbeats, you forget they are there.

The Middleweight

In the beginning Carlos looked magnificent. He shimmered like a star on the water, he rippled, he could dip from side to side and make you believe he was part shark. I had Philip Sand, the sculptor, do his head. I remember that time as one of grace and breathtaking speed and an unexpected giddiness—it was thrilling even to watch him devour a steak, tease him about the moguls on his nose. Then everything changed, to the point where he only looked soupy. It was painful. Especially when he won, which was rare, because then he would say, "Up, Mona. Going up." My god, I didn't care if he won or not!

I begged him to quit. I had a grotesque thought, a vivid recollection, of poor Rex. In desperation I explained how in college my friends and I had adopted Rex because he looked lost, really lost, bewildered by almost everything no matter how much love we gave him. Most of the time he was happy to curl up in one of our rooms. But if we said, "Walk, Rex?" he could hardly stand it. He'd rush outside and make a brave dash, oh you handsome dog, then suddenly he'd stop and jerk his head in the air as if he'd just remembered something. This threw him off balance enough so that most of the walk all Rex did was weave from side to side, stumbling, banging into our legs, shaking his head, trying to readjust. All this I said to Carlos. We were in the kitchen—he was drinking milk. He set down the bottle and only blinked at me puzzled as a child, one eye so viciously mauled and bubbled with scar tissue it was hardly a slit. Then he hung his head. He understood! But no, after a long moment he looked up, smiling. I was only having fun! "A dog? Carlos Alguien?" He flexed his arms. I burst into tears. "See?" he said. "We are okay now. Such pretty fingers. Come."

He had one more fight and was terribly beaten. They had to carry him out. I waited through the night to see if he would regain consciousness. He did. Needless to say, that was the end of his career. I took care of him. I *wanted* to take care of him. He helped Monk and Fonda around the house with the yardwork and shopping, and I think he was happy. I know he was happy when I had my nails done. It was our "date" and he was my "bodyguard." He loved to hear me say those words—also the word *helado,* and of course he loved the actual ice cream. He always chose a vanilla cone, which he would lick while the girl worked on me.

A year to the day after Carlos's last fight, I heard from my stepson Charlie. This was a surprise because Charlie had not spoken to me since that mess over his father's will. It turned out he was suddenly faced with a potentially embarrassing financial problem and would I be interested in buying—"at their true value"—his famous thoroughbred and her colt. Of course I was interested, and I wired Charlie, who was a nice young man, even more than he wanted. Then I left Monk and Fonda in charge of Carlos and flew to Kentucky, where the horses were stabled. I spent ten glorious days in Lexington with my new mare Nola and the stunning Nola's Baby, watching the colt begin his training, brushing mother and son, truly falling in love with these sleek, spirited animals that smelled like new shoes and punky wood! I sent photos to Monk and Fonda to share with Carlos; I said maybe I would bring the horses back to California. Perhaps I should not have said that—it was no more than a whimsical comment—or even sent the photos. But I am only guessing.

Fonda was nearly hysterical when she called me to say that Monk had taken Carlos out for *helado* and an incident occurred at the ice cream shop. Carlos had strangled the owner's very old Irish setter and was now in jail. I returned as soon as possible. Oh, how he looked at me like a confused boy when I asked why he had done it.

"The dog didn't bite you?"

"No."

"It didn't bite anyone?"

"No."

"And the ice cream lady—she wasn't unkind to you?"

"Oh no. She was nice to me, like you, Mona."

"Then why did you hurt her dog? She loved her dog, Carlos."

His whole face whole face seemed to bunch together in the middle, in pain, in an effort to remember why. He pinched at the skin on his upper arms, first one arm, then the other, back and forth, as if he were hugging himself in a jittery embrace to keep warm. We were in a room for mental patients at the county hospital (a transfer my lawyer had arranged while I was flying back), and the room to me was warm—in fact I wished the air conditioner could be turned up—and yet Carlos, trying to answer me, seemed to be freezing.

I held him. I stroked his hair, combing it with my fingers. Quietly I told him to never mind, it was all right, everything was all right. As I murmured these words over and over I began to think of Nola and Nola's Baby, of brushing them, and for a few moments I thought of Carlos in almost the same way. At first this was soothing to me, then it frightened me a little. But he was calm now. I asked if he was cold, and he shook his head. I wiped his tears with my hanky. I gave him a roll of mints. "And look here," I said, pulling a key from my pocket. "This is to the house, Carlos. Hold it for me, okay?"

Then I left. I said I would be back soon. I did intend to return, but one thing or another kept interfering—little things, I think, really, though at the time they seemed important. I had him moved to a private hospital and there he stayed. He stays there still, an old man now, though for years his broken-nosed face oddly kept a certain boyishness. They used to send me a picture every Christmas until I told them it wasn't necessary.

I will be sixty-five this spring. My life, by design, is uneventful. Sometimes I want to cry out to someone, but to whom, and what would I say?

The Moaning

Exactly when Mrs. LaRue *first* heard the moaning is not clear to her. She was outside, as she is now, standing right here beside the garbage cans. She was seeing about that rake the boy had borrowed, whether he put it back where it belonged, yes. She had wakened from an unruly nap that had gone on longer than intended and had come directly outside to see about the rake and—but was it early in the morning, before sunup, or after dark? Yesterday or a week ago? Oh, it's annoying to lose track of time like that. She hates it. Hates to be suddenly in the middle of something and not recall right away how she got there. Damn those roofers! She *told* them not to leave their ladders leaning against the house. What if someone comes along in the dark now and bangs into one? Well, she wouldn't, of course, she can see just fine. But she *knows* the place. I'm talking about strangers! she says firmly—and is a little surprised at the sudden sound of her voice. Though pleased too, reassured.

She holds dead still, listening for the moan. And looking through the lilac bushes toward Mr. Starr's house next door. No lights on that she can see. Well, he goes to bed with the chickens. There! There it is again. And it's not a radio. Not his radio—he listens to what my father always called The Masters. No, that was most certainly not a radio, or a television either. A television in Mr. Starr's house? He'd sooner have a troop of Gypsies, he says, with lots of earrings and pots of boiling toads, eh, Mrs. LaRue? Oh, he's a tease, all right. When he's civil. Well, I must say he *has* been civil lately, not like last summer. Yes, I know, I know, Irma was supposed to be moved out of his house when he came back from Europe, yes he did send a letter from France to remind me again of the date, yes, Mr. Starr, it was all made perfectly clear before you left that Irma was renting the place for one year and one year only. But—

But what, Mrs. LaRue? he says. Here I am, back from a grueling journey, tired, wanting a shower, my bed, and look what I see. I see you and your ward rocking comfortably on my front porch, Mrs. LaRue, as if nothing could be more normal. I see enough furniture packed in the place, Mrs. LaRue, to equip an entire neighborhood. Just from where I stand I can see in my living room alone, for example, one, two, three, four, five, *six* sofas and one, two, three, four, *five* TVs, Mrs. LaRue, and I am made dizzy. Never mind that big buffet-looking thing blocking the fireplace and all those stuffed animals taking up, it seems, every inch of the mantel. Never mind all the large chairs pushed snug together, all the coffee tables riding piggyback to save space—it is uncanny, Mrs. LaRue, how much they resemble miniature Eiffel Towers topped with knick-knacks—and never mind the question of how one actually gets *into* the living room to use any of this treasure. The point is, Mrs. LaRue, I see not the signs of your ward moving out, but the unmistakable signs of someone who has squirreled up a lot of stuff over a long, long haul having settled very much in. In a house, may I add, which, when I left it, contained all the furniture, if *not* all the glittery figurines, anyone could want for a lifetime.

She tried to point out that one of those TVs was an original Muntz that still worked—the sound did, anyway—and was practically priceless, if only for the walnut cabinet, a quality item you didn't see these days unless you paid a king's ransom. But he just stared at her, his face turning purple.

Well, she told him the truth. The truth never hurt anybody, that's her motto, though if she'd had a moment to *think* she probably would have said something more diplomatic. Mr. Starr, she said, we knew you were coming back, of course, but we were hoping you wouldn't.

Oh my, you'd think she'd said something shameful. His face turned even darker. He couldn't seem to breathe. He slapped the top of the highboy that Irma had moved out to the porch to keep some nice shells from Hawaii on, and all of them fell to the floor making a terrible clatter, and that set off Fluffy and Choo-Choo whom Irma and I were holding on our laps—and now had the devil's own time to pacify. Even poor old Hendricks, who never barks at anyone anymore, raised his head from the loveseat and gave a sharp word. I *knew* she should have put that highboy in the kitchen, there was plenty of room behind the table if we moved those extra chairs nobody sat in anyway out to the garage. But she said the garage was full. Well, you can always find more room if you look hard enough. People have been telling me for years that my house is full, but *I* find room.

Now listen! There it is again. Is that someone dying? Or have I lost my mind?

She waits. She looks at the ladders leaning against her house in the moonlight, follows one with her eye up to where it ends at the hole under her overhang—where the squirrels, damn their greedy little claws, have broken in. Into her attic! Now, she *told* John she wanted that hole boarded shut. How many more nights must she listen to them running around up there? Clicking their sharp nails among her rafters, disturbing her insulation, chewing on her wires! He *knows* it's dangerous. The whole place could burst into flames. She'd be lucky to smell the smoke in time—and blooming now in Mrs. LaRue's head is the image of a fat squirrel biting on one of her electrical wires, releasing sparks. She shudders. She sees herself grabbing Tina and rushing out the door. All of her antiques left behind, that gorgeous player piano with the porcelain tiger and the priceless photograph of Woodrow Wilson and the elegant English thoroughbred Gainsborough resting on top. Tina barking, not understanding. The firemen shooting water through her windows, ruining everything! Her China dolls, her rugs, her collection of newspaper clippings—how could she replace those? How? Let John explain *that,* if he can.

The moaning sound issues through the lilacs again and Mrs. LaRue reaches out and grips a ladder. She heard a distinct word this time, too. *Baby.* And it was a woman who said it. On Mr. Starr's property. He has a woman over there, in the dark, and she is saying *baby.*

Mrs. LaRue lets go of the ladder and leans on her cane. She listens hard for a moment, but hears, now, only a little cricket noise around the garbage cans. Of course Mr. Starr may not be over there at all, what with all the traveling he does. Paris, Mexico, Madrid, Istanbul. Adiós, eh, Mr. Starr? But he certainly would have informed me if he'd rented the house again. Or he would have asked—surely—if I knew of any good prospects. Now that all that business with Irma is over . . . and the few things I'd stored in his garage moved out. What a fuss that was—a tempest in a teapot, Mr. Starr.

But, he says, Mrs. LaRue, you must have made a personal contest out of it, to see how many of your possessions you could stuff in there.

Well, I said to him, how did *I* know you'd be bringing a car back from Europe? Maintaining a vehicle is not your style, nor mine. Hired drivers, taxis, that's how we do it. And since that garage was standing there perfectly empty—had been for years—

You couldn't wait to fill it up for me, Mrs. LaRue.

No, I just had these few items I didn't have room for at the moment, nice clean things, you'll notice—mattresses and box springs and those lovely bedroom suites—those are real oak, Mr. Starr—and those chiffoniers and pretty chairs are real Empire quality—and a few—

I see a lot of crusty pipe, Mrs. LaRue, and cracked mirrors and boxes of old magazines and, if I am not mistaken, I see a large quantity of loose roofing shingles. Now what in hell—

Now, now, Mr. Starr, I said, no need to raise your voice. They were tearing down a house up the street while you were away—the old Shuttleworth place—and I told John what with the price of copper tubing these days—

Mrs. LaRue, I haven't had my shower yet.

Well, go up and take it, I said to him.

Irma is still in my house, Mrs. LaRue, and you have said nothing about moving her out.

Moving her out? Now?

Exactly.

How did we come to this terribly sad moment? Yes, sad. Poor Irma, at her age, no relations, only me, really, and Fluffy, Choo-Choo, and old Hendricks. Dignified Hendricks. Oh, I can't bear it. I wish I were a girl again. Or an animal, free in Nature, or a cloud, or—look at my house! All locked up, empty, everything sold, yes, I did agree to it, but I am not happy at Whispering Oaks, Mr. Starr, don't you see? Irma is happy, the dear thing, she fits in anywhere, but I require, I prefer, I mean, Mr. Starr, you have all that extra room and, as I said on the phone, I can pay you, in cash, Mr. Starr, you won't even have to *tell* anybody. Look here, a man doesn't need *three* bathrooms, does he? If you had two and I had one, wouldn't that do, Mr. Starr? I tell you I simply do not sleep well. All night I hear a ticking. It's not loud, it's not even unpleasant, but it never seems to stop, Mr. Starr, on and on it goes, like nothing I've ever known, that's what I've come to explain, that's where I'd like to begin.

Stories Under the Stars

At a dinner party recently on Vashon Island, given by my vivacious Polish friend Agata, everyone was having such a good time that she suggested we all tell a story about having a good time. "A selection from the past," she said. "No—wait. Let's make the subject *living well*, yes? Why not? It's larger. Always—always—we must reach out!" So while the candles burned toward the stars and the stars burned back, we went around the table with our contributions. Waiting my turn, I thought about Lee Duncan.

When I first knew her—she was Lee Fryman then—we taught together in a private boarding school whose students were the sons and daughters of the very busy rich. We generally liked our students but could not help feeling sorry for them; the brighter ones—who often seemed the loneliest—called each other ARLers, a coinage inspired by the mission of the Animal Rescue League. Lee and I felt that we were lucky to have come from blue-collar Detroit and Cleveland—where our fathers worked in the automobile factories—because we knew pretty much where we stood, and what things were worth, and what we needed to do to survive. But our origins were less on my mind than Lee's startling green eyes—I could see them even across the school's soccer field—and that bright expression—explosion, really—of vitality and intelligence in her beautiful face. After a year, she resigned to go back to the university for her PhD. I planned to follow suit as soon as I had saved up enough money; I didn't want to go into debt again with loans. (The truth was I feared debt almost as much as I feared death.) In the meantime, which stretched out longer than I'd planned, she met and married Mac Duncan, and gave him a son.

They had everything, as we would say—fine pictures, first editions, ancient hangings lining their walls—Mac flush in Lee's brilliance, she in his, the son primed for good schools, primed to carry on, all of them confident, scented with grace—the usual heady stuff most of us, maybe, ease into sleep wishing for. A story, of course, that soon begins to bore us unless something bad happens, some catastrophe, some rat that shows up to paw in the sugar bowl and other sweet places when the lights go off. Mac was accused of a crime, theft actually, from the company he founded. The particulars aren't important, they're common enough, likewise his adamant, proud declaration of innocence. The point is how desperately hard he fought to save his name, pulling everything off the walls and the walls down, before he lost the long expensive battle. He lived a year behind bars. When he came out his blond hair was nearly white, his chin sharp as if whittled, his formerly smooth voice (a honeyed tenor when he leaned back with a perfect cognac) turned to an instrument he seemed to have no control over: it could be shockingly shrill or sink in a sludge of self-pity. I remember him saying, "We're like most people now, eating out of cans." But he also said, more than once—and grimly, fiercely—that he knew how to make money. He vowed he would get everything back, the fine pictures, the tapestries . . .

The last time I saw the Duncans, they were living in yet another small apartment complex. This one, called Seven Oaks (there were no oaks), was near the airport. You could hear an almost steady drone of planes landing and taking off. Lee served us tea. Mac soon excused himself, to make some business calls, he said, and disappeared into their bedroom—which was also his office. Lee told me he was working very hard—"like a demon." Their son, she then said, had left home. "He's trying to find himself. He phones from time to time, usually late at night from a booth beside some highway. I always hear traffic hurtling by. And as if it were possible, we both try to explain everything to each other." She smiled. The bright expression I had known was now a brave, sober, workaday look that said *we do the best we can.* She pressed her palms to her cheeks, gazing off—away,

I thought, from everything she had come to. "Lee," I said. "You can leave. You can walk out the door with me now." Those beautiful green eyes met mine, and when I reached over and touched the hands that covered her cheeks, I know they were saying yes. It's a moment I can never forget. I could feel the truth of it as I can feel, right now, the beating of my heart. Then, abruptly, she got up. Mac was shouting. I followed her and stood behind her at a window; she hugged herself, facing a former cornfield out there waiting to become something, while "You owe me! You owe me! You owe me!" pursued us like the mad barking of a dog . . .

But that was not a story I could tell under the stars. I told about the years after I left the boarding school and worked in Europe teaching English, and meeting interesting people—people who treasured their freedom, tasting life—and traveling to Rome, Paris, Prague, Madrid, even Iceland, even Lapland, Skye—anywhere I wanted.

In El Hipo

The first time Keane saw Gloria Morris she was looking out from under a cupped sailor's cap and laughing while serving to a Mexican boy, his smile a mile wide, who scrambled to catch her balls in a fruit basket. This was on El Hipo's one decent clay court. If someone had come along just then and told Keane, as someone did later, that once upon a time she had the biggest headache and sinus problem on American television, he would have said she seemed to be over it now. He asked if she wanted to hit, she said why not, and that's how they started.

They played three or four afternoons a week. The days they didn't play, Keane had longer to sit in the shade outside his hotel and brood over the story he was writing; when his sentences went flat, he often left his chair for a hammock and tried to picture her up in her studio painting what she had not shown him yet, only alluded to—an Indian carving the crucified Christ. While Beethoven, she said, raged throughout the Morris villa. As for her face on TV faking pain and relief, Keane could call up no solid memory of it; he was in his early teens when that ad was running. It was a lot easier seeing Sid Caesar or Ed Sullivan or, leaping forward in time, a couple of very funny *Free Press* guys he used to have a drink with after work who did corny imitations of Caesar and Milton Berle and Red Skelton. And almost always, lying in the hammock he'd see the fixed watery gray eyes of Daniel Morris, Gloria's husband, if only for a moment.

They lived up the mountain overlooking El Hipo, the two of them plus Daniel's ancient golden retriever, Bonus. Daniel Morris never left the villa. He was dying of emphysema. The first few times Keane went there and had to wait for Gloria to come down from her studio, the maid showed him into a big stone-and-glass room where the bone-thin, blue-faced Morris would be sitting in a leather chair listening to Beethoven and gazing at the Mexican sky. The room reminded Keane of an airport control tower, or a large turret. Morris would acknowledge the guest's arrival by raising one hand. Next to his leather chair he kept a tank of oxygen and a glass of beer, and the only time Keane saw him leave that chair was when he moved with great slow effort to change the record. No one else was allowed to touch his magnificent music. Did Keane enjoy Beethoven? Yes, of course. That was the sum of their talk until, many weeks later, Morris made his speech about saving his wife and not building a wall, and asked Keane if he understood.

One day Gloria surprised him. "Daniel," she said, "has suggested I invite you to accompany me to Miami. What do you think of that?"

Keane couldn't think, and said so.

"He seems to have the idea," she said, "that you would protect me."

"From?"

"The gloom of visiting my parents. My moods. Temptation." She smiled, not looking at him. "He thinks of you as my son."

Gloria was fifty-one (this always astonished Keane when he thought of it), twenty years younger than her husband. Keane was just young enough, biologically, to be that son.

On their flight to Miami, when he asked what her parents were like, she said, "Please."

"It's that bad?"

She smiled. "They're like most people who have far more than they need and nothing to do." She removed her sunglasses, lay her head back, and let her eyes slide toward him, their near-flatness saying that the subject was not interesting. She put her glasses back on and turned her gaze to the window. But after a few minutes of silence, she suddenly said, "I was a little girl, hiding behind one of my mother's outrageous plants. There was a party. I was supposed to be in bed. But I snuck downstairs, seduced by all the music and laughter."

From her hiding place, Gloria said, turning to face Keane, she saw a man bow to her mother, bend to one knee, and then cause the rose he had been offering her to apparently disappear in his mouth. Everyone applauded, including Gloria. Then her father, all red in the face—"most probably from alcohol"—thrust a rose in his mouth; he chewed and chewed and everyone laughed, as if he too were performing a trick, only one that was stupidly clownish on purpose. Gloria did not think it was at all funny. This was when they lived in Virginia, she said, and her father made lots of money doing something with land—like Daniel—and she had a horse named Lady Be Good.

"He is not, however, my natural father. That man, when I was a baby, got lost in a snow blizzard on a mountain in Oregon. Mount Hood, I was told. *Years* after it happened. He was a stuntman in films."

Unable to see her eyes behind those dark glasses, Keane focused on the slow lush movement of her lips.

Mr. and Mrs. Hoffman now lived in a large apartment overlooking a stretch of blue-white water and white sand that seemed to go on forever and which, apparently, they had no interest in experiencing up close. When Keane admired their grand view, Mimi Hoffman only said, "Yes, it's nice, all that scenery."

Gloria and Keane arrived in time for dinner. They sat at a table built to accommodate at least twelve, though her parents' days of lavish entertaining, Gloria told Keane, were long past.

"And how is Daniel?" Mimi asked.

"The same."

"So he hasn't shot himself yet."

"Annette," Gloria said to the cook when she came out to see how everything was, "your fish is divine. It's *always* divine."

"But Nettie, darling, please," Mimi said, "your TV, the neighbors will think we've let in half the refugees."

"Thank you," the cook said to Gloria, and returned to the kitchen, a long-striding honey-brown woman whose stack of black hair bore, at the top, a Monarch butterfly fully extended.

Hoffman said, "You're discussing the cook? She could lower her voice when I ask a question, I'm not standing over in Cuba."

"Well," Mimi said, "I would shrivel and die without her."

"And what is your business?" Hoffman asked Keane.

He said he was trying to be a freelance writer.

"A what? What is that?"

"I sometimes wonder myself," Keane said. "But the fact of the matter is, I'm trying to write a book about the last person to see James R. Hoffa alive."

"The last who?"

"The witness," Keane said louder, "to Jimmy Hoffa's abduction."

"The *Team*ster," Mimi said to her husband. "The gangster Nixon let out of jail." She waved her napkin at the air between them, as if it were thick with dust. Like Gloria, she was one of those women who did not show her age. Under the dark brown hair she wore like a helmet, she could produce the bold stare or spontaneous smile of a much younger woman, and appeared completely at home in the smooth white skin attending her face, neck, and fluent cleavage. Keane learned later that, also like her daughter, she had started her professional life in the theatre.

"You'll like this story, Mother," Gloria said. Then to Keane, "Tell her about Kayo."

"I'm starting to wish I'd never met the guy." Keane smiled and sipped from his wine glass.

"Don't be shy, darling," Mimi said.

So Keane told Mimi Hoffman about Kayo Colone (while her husband slowly nodded off). "On the last night that Hoffa was known to be alive," he said, "Kayo saw him get into a maroon car with three men in the parking lot of a Detroit restaurant. The Machus Red Fox. Kayo was a Motor City radio personality. He hosted a morning talk show—actors, authors, comedians, hungover rockers on their way up or down. He had a good following among older women, because he often asked his guests what their mothers cooked for them when they were kids."

Mimi Hoffman laughed, "That *is* cute."

"He got into pierogi, matzo, soul food, and with an Italian he apparently covered the whole kitchen," Keane went on. "As a result he received a ton of love recipes in the mail. Hot dishes arrived at the station by cab, widows sent him their photos. Now and then a rocker would look at him as if he'd just come from Mars. What did my mother *cook* for me? Is this a joke, man? Or like some heavy oldie I should know? The show was goofy and fun and Kayo was doing all right. He was thirty-one, had a sailboat, season tickets to the Tigers, a TR-3, and a fiancée—"

"Beautiful, no doubt," Mimi said.

"And rich. Belinda Wolfe, of Grosse Pointe. A long time later—or to Kayo it seemed like a long time—living quietly in France, carrying a passport that said he was Philip Dowset, he tried to imagine what his life would be like if he hadn't stepped forward and told what he'd seen that night on Telegraph Road. Where the Machus Red Fox is."

"I hope this story won't be grim." Mimi smiled at Keane.

"Well," he said, "Kayo's intense loneliness finally caused him to sneak back home. Or try to. He got as far as Mexico—San Miguel, an hour from El Hipo. That's where I found him and heard what he had to say. Then he disappeared again."

"Tell how you found him," Gloria said.

"Through his mother. It was all . . ."

"Romantic?" Mimi reached over theatrically and touched his arm.

"In a way."

As they walked on the beach later, Gloria told Keane he had got her mother's attention.

"Tomorrow, though, tell more about Kayo and Miss Wolfe."

That night Gloria entered Keane's room and lay down beside him. Her body was cool, then warm. Though he had been hoping for something like this, he was still surprised. She said nothing, made almost no sound except for a little cry of satisfaction. He kept to himself what he wanted to say, savoring for later the words of affection gathered on the tip of his tongue. He also remembered what the director of the American film crew staying at his hotel had told him about her early TV work—that industry-famous headache—and when Keane said she seemed to be over it now, the director said, "Well, then, you should have a good time."

After they returned to Mexico, Gloria took him up to her studio to see the Indian carver—that picture she had been laboring over for more than a year, she said. The carver twisted to look at them as if interrupted, his chisel still planted in Christ's cheek as he hung on the cross. Like his subject the carver was almost naked, his upper body muscular, the body of a man who used it; but his hands were too fine, Keane thought, too delicate to belong to the rest of him. In a picture on another easel, beside him, a woman, a weaver, also turned as if interrupted; she wanted to say something, it seemed, but was unable to, perhaps was too irritated to find the words. The rug on her loom was releasing dozens of small black birds into a clear blue sky.

"So you have two pictures," Keane finally said.

"Yes." She moved the second easel farther away from the first one. "That gorgeous man and the weaver are lovers."

Keane preferred the picture of the weaver—it seemed more realized, at least there were no distractions in it; in the other one the carver's hands were clearly all wrong, and Keane couldn't help wanting to cover them up.

"He has a temper." Gloria smiled. "I have to separate them sometimes. More than once I saw him throw down his chisel and walk off in a rage."

"Why?"

"Jesus was not showing anywhere near the pain *he* was suffering."

"As an artist, you mean?"

"Yes. He felt he was not able to put to a satisfying use the gift his god had given him." She said his name was Tomas. The girlfriend was Alma.

"They worked as gardeners when their money ran low, and one day arrived at the villa. They knew our maid." Gloria said she learned of their real passions, visited their studio—and they hers—and eventually she got them to pose for her. "Though not for a while now. Which, perhaps, is for the best. The girl—who's an American, actually—seems to have developed some jealousy. And then Daniel did not care to have Tomas naked in the house."

Keane and Gloria now returned to his hotel after their tennis.

"Tell me how things are going with Kayo."

"Which part? I'm trying to fix bad writing all over the place."

"It doesn't matter. How about the grim details Mother wasn't interested in?"

"Do you want me to read to you?"

"No—talk to me."

Keane thought a minute. "Okay. Following his testimony to the grand jury, Kayo received an eel in the mail. Then a dead rat, a Polaroid of his father's headstone at St. Leo's cemetery, and a page ripped from the Detroit telephone book that contained his mother's listing. The sender didn't have to circle her name, Kayo got the message. He turned all this stuff over to the FBI. Then Belinda's father, Winston Wolfe, found a canary nailed to his desk at home. Nailed, he showed Kayo in a hastily called man-to-man, where he usually signed his letters.

"Wolfe said something like, 'I am not a crusader, Kayo. I am a businessman. I believe in right and wrong, yes. And in honor. I think Theodore Roosevelt was a great man. Thomas Jefferson. Wendell Wilkie too, though you may find that hard to believe given all his "One World" talk. But—'

"Kayo had been waiting for the *but.* Waiting for Winston Wolfe, citizen, husband, father, and publisher of 'family newspapers,' as he called the string of weekly shoppers, chockfull of ads, that he owned—waiting for the man to come forth with a portrait of his daughter, a description of her education, her beauty, her dreams, all of which he did bring forth and made Kayo feel even worse because the portrait was as true as true could be. 'So you must see,' Winston Wolfe said, his manicured hands bravely folded above the nail hole whacked in his desk by hoodlums, 'that we have to send her away until all this unfortunate business is over—'"

"I love how excited you get," Gloria stopped him, placing a finger on Keane's lips. "Now me," she whispered.

The next time she came to his room, she again asked to hear about Kayo, how the writing was going for Keane. Just that morning he had been struggling, Keane said, with the part about Belinda marrying someone else—a key element in Kayo's decision to leave Europe—but it wasn't going well.

"Then go back to where we were last time—where Mr. Wolfe folds his hands over the nail hole in his desk."

Keane watched Gloria slip off her shift and lie down. Then he said, "So Winston Wolfe summarized his daughter to Kayo. Age? Education? Social position? The poor guy knew how old she was, for God's sake, and *who* she was—the only daughter, only child, etc., etc. Kayo also knew her green eyes, the constellation of freckles above her breastbone. He remembered the walk they took around Cranbrook's statued gardens the day they met, how she stroked the naked bronze thigh of a Greek youth holding up a pan of fire. He remembered the kiss she placed between his shoulder blades when they went sailing, how she smelled, the weight of her sigh, the attention she paid, bite by bite, to a single, sweet peach, and how she tasted afterwards. Yes, Kayo knew the young woman Winston Wolfe was talking about.

"And now he remembered the July night he kissed her between *her* shoulder blades and everywhere else, this girl who possessed a degree in art history from Virginia and smelled like the woods after a rain, when mint and pine flower the air. They were at his place. She said, 'I've never done this before, Kayo. I really can't tell you why. Is that all right?' She also said, 'If I start laughing, please don't stop.' The only thing she would not do was stay all night. Her parents.

"So he drove her home later to Foxdale Farms. His head felt separated from his neck by several important inches, and when Belinda hummed beside him in the car he thought: Can I go back to being what I was before? Will that be possible now? Driving along, he saw himself on the air, on his show, mugging with Ginger his producer, selling dog food between interviews, responding to an actor's practiced remarks as if they mattered, giving his attention, his time, to a rocker's sleepy, strung-out mumbling—it all seemed so pointless now, a poor, dismal joke. His head continued to feel several inches away, like a cartoon balloon, but it was trying to answer a serious question: What could he do now to deserve this beauty? He was of course in love with love. With her fruity nipples and green eyes and that woodsy scent—

"They arrived at her house and said good night under the stars. Her scent and the scent of those sleek horses in the pastures all around, the perfumes of the night and of what they had done and of what richnesses lay ahead—all this filled him and fueled his happiness as he drove back toward the city. And of course as high as he was he got a little lost, if lost in his home town is the best word.

"When he saw the sign for the Machus Red Fox he pulled over. Coffee. He needed coffee to sober up. Everyone in the place looked gratefully fixed to a steady purpose. No great struggle here, they all seemed to say. The fork goes on this side, the knife on that. And later we get to go home and watch Johnny Carson. Who's he having on tonight?

"In the parking lot, walking to his car, he thought, as he spotted him, 'Ah yes, Jimmy's going home to watch Johnny too. Perfectly normal.' And though he seemed angry—in fact he was yelling—Kayo never gave seeing Jimmy Hoffa, and the men with him, another thought until later, when he read in the paper that the Teamster had disappeared."

Keane had gone on longer than he'd intended, but it didn't seem to matter. Gloria was ready for him.

He had trouble now being in the same room with Daniel Morris. When Sésé, the maid, answered the door he said he'd wait for Gloria under the jacaranda tree in the garden. He did not understand why he couldn't just tell Gloria he'd meet her at the tennis court. Or he did understand. "I like how you come for me," she once said. "Like we're having an old-fashioned date." She laughed then, as if she had said something silly. But the remark stuck to him, gave him a prickly thrill. Another time she said, "You're not difficult, darling. So many men are difficult." He said, "Was Tomas difficult?" "Oh my god!" she laughed, and gave him a perfect, spontaneous smile. "Always." This too thrilled him. Her lack of guile. They never talked about what they were doing: it had simply started and now was simply happening, like breathing. Keane was briefly tempted to mention having a drink in the bar of his hotel with the director of that film crew—Hal Hopkins, his name was. They were down from L.A. to do a job that suddenly got cancelled. Maybe she knew him?

One afternoon, waiting in the garden, Keane saw Sésé and the Mexican boy, who used to chase Gloria's serves, bring from the house a sheet-wrapped bundle. It was Bonus, Sésé told him. While the boy dug a hole with a spade under the jacaranda tree, the maid looked anxiously back at the house as if expecting someone to come out. How did the dog die? Keane asked her. But she only shook her head. Then Gloria emerged from the house and told Keane she would not be able to play that day. She wore jeans and a white T-shirt, her hair tied back. Her face was flushed, she looked fresh, alive, and beautiful.

"I'm sorry," he said. "About the dog, I mean."

"Daniel shot him this morning." She glanced at her nails, then at the boy digging the hole. Then she looked at Keane. "I'll let you know—about next time?"

"Is there anything I can do?" He wanted to stay. He wanted to hold her.

"No, no. We'll take care of this."

"Are you sure I can't—"

"Please—just go."

Keane left as Gloria was instructing Sésé and the boy to keep the dog wrapped in the sheet when they buried him.

A few days later the Mexican boy found Keane in the shaded yard of his hotel; all morning he had been crossing out and adding words to the same sheet of paper. The boy said that Señor Morris wished to see him.

When Keane arrived at the villa, Sésé showed him into the turret-like room where Daniel Morris sat waiting.

"Will you drink a beer with me?"

Keane said he would. Sésé brought him a German pilsner; Morris had his usual bottle and glass on the tray beside his chair.

"Mrs. Morris is not here," he said. "She's—" he made a careless gesture with his hand, as if halfheartedly shooing away a fly.

"When do you expect her back?"

Morris took a slow, attentive, raspy breath and slowly let it out. "I was just thinking, before you arrived, that I once considered building a wall around this house. You've seen them . . . ugly broken glass and spikes along the top. But I did not do that." Here Morris began to cough and brought forth a handkerchief to cover his mouth. Keane looked away. He saw Sésé standing by, in a far recess. When Morris finally collected himself, he took a careful sip from his glass. Then he said, "She used to enjoy reading books about the Civil War, especially if they favored the South. It was diabolical, of course, meant to provoke me. That mocking laughter. She always marked her place with a photo of our son, who died young. Nothing could be done. Life," he said. "Life."

He then closed his eyes and folded his hands in his lap. Keane waited. After several minutes he glanced over to where Sésé was still standing, watching them. He wanted to leave, being there was crazy, and Morris had fallen asleep. A son? Dead? From what? Why didn't she tell him? Finally he stood up. He looked at Daniel Morris, waiting for him to open his eyes. Suddenly the man began gasping for air. Sésé came quickly, followed by the Mexican boy. They brought the oxygen tank closer and arranged the apparatus over his face.

After a few long moments, Morris was breathing normally and Keane helped Sésé and the boy put the old man to bed. It was like moving three or four large grocery bags, each containing a few items and stapled tenuously one on top the other. That was how surprisingly breakable Morris felt, how light.

His room, its Spartan furnishings, surprised Keane too. There was the single bed, a crude wooden chair, some books on a shelf fixed to the wall. One window, high and narrow, faced the mountain that continued to rise above the villa. This was the cell of a monk, a prisoner, Keane thought. Then the monk-prisoner began to speak. Often he mumbled. Keane could make out that Morris was sorry he had been "an egoist too," but proud of having saved his wife from "the degradation of selling herself," and of not having built that wall around their home. He wanted to know if Keane understood, and Keane said he did.

Not long after that, Keane left Mexico and returned to Detroit. There was a chance he could get back on at the *Free Press*. One day he went to see Kayo's mother. She still lived in the house where he was raised, still prayed for him daily at Mass, and still believed she would see him again before she died. Keane thought he might try to turn Kayo's story into a novel—using only the part about falling in love with a girl and losing her, forget Hoffa—if he could figure out how.

Pro Bono

I.

Mary Beth pulled her Mercedes into the parking lot of Grace and Holy Trinity Cathedral beside the finned yellow Cadillac. She could see Marvin's blue-jeaned knees sticking up in the front seat, his white cowboy hat covering his face. Nine A.M. She was right on time.

She and Marvin tried meeting in her office at Riley Hamish Woodward Dunne. Once. Almost from the moment he was introduced to Eilis Flynn, a junior associate who was there to take notes, he seemed to freeze. His head barely moved as he looked slowly at the three posters of Milton Avery pictures: "Mountain and Meadow," "Oregon Coast," "Poetry Reading"; at the Stieglitz photo—"The Street"—showing a time in New York City when horse-drawn carriages were everywhere, and here a woman on a snowy sidewalk is hurrying past a line of such carriages toward a horse standing and waiting as if only for her. Marvin glanced at the poetry books and novels and law books on their shelves, and seemed to assess her carpet in which there was nothing to see except the color beige. Finally he shook his head and put the cowboy hat he was holding in his lap back on his head.

"I ain't comfortable here, Mary Beth. I'm real sorry."

What they did was drive around in his Caddie—which was also Marvin's home—and she interviewed him. He said the car had been with him a long time—longer than he'd been with anything or anybody, even his grandmother and the church in Jefferson City she had taken him to as a boy to get him started. "Started on my education," he told Mary Beth. "When she passed, I was eleven years old, on my own. This here mode of travel—I call her Honey Bee—and all that's inside her is my worldly accumulation. Some of it's important, like my last will and testament, my Webster's dictionary, and my grandma's wedding ring.Some's just here cluttering things up."

Mary Beth got out of her car, sliding off the cushion she sat on so she could see better. She knocked softly on the Caddie's passenger side window. Though they were having a warm, sweet-smelling spring, Marvin had all his windows rolled tight.

Slowly one finger raised his hat, just enough to see her. Then he sat up and pulled on his Tony Lamas, surprisingly agile for a big man. He stepped out grinning.

"Oh, my Lord, what a pretty day."

"Good morning, Marvin."

"And a good, good morning to you, Miss Mary Beth." He looked over at her Mercedes. "I see you driving your daddy's car again."

"Marvin, the first time you said that, it was funny."

"*Now* you tell me."

"Did I wake you too early?"

"Can't tease *me*, Mary Beth. I was just lying there cogitating on life and useful words, and now I am closer to wisdom. You get your beauty sleep last night?"

"I was up at four o'clock, Marvin—"

"Goodness, that's early."

"—because a poet tells me you are large and contain miracles."

"Aw, Mary Beth." Marvin jingled the coins in his pocket. "Lemme buy you a cuppa that good Episcopalian java yonder."

The two Cathedral volunteers on duty—wearing matching black French berets—knew Mary Beth from church (and from working this same soup kitchen for the homeless), and now they knew Marvin, who was taking most of his meals there.

Seated at a table with their free coffees, Mary Beth and Marvin opened the spirals she picked up at a drug store soon after she was appointed to try Marvin's case pro bono. Which was a week or so before he bolted from her office. Later, he'd tried to explain.

"A building fulla fancy lawyers makes me feel like I ate something rich and it won't settle. Your office was real nice too. Those pretty pictures and all."

She'd looked at him then, and said, "Marvin, I'm going to believe everything you tell me until my S-detector goes off."

"I won't try to slip anything past if I can help it." His eyes had been down when he said this, but immediately they came up and met hers.

"I'm not working for Riley Hamish now, I'm working for you," was all she'd said, though she might have said—but never would—that pro bono lawyering was more satisfying to her than any she would ever do for the wealthy poobahs of Riley Hamish.

At the Cathedral, Mary Beth got down to business. "I think I did okay this morning. Served two subpoenas—Rachel Andrews and Olive Washington. They corroborated everything you told me."

"Good folks. Known those fine women forever."

"The subpoenas scared them a little."

"I told them don't worry. Said you were a genius with paperwork, a eru*dite* genius. Like that word erudite?"

"I do, thanks. But I couldn't rouse Mr. Timmons."

"Probly sleeping over with some tender sweetie. Leads a very heavy romance schedule, ole Sammy, even at his advanced age."

Mary Beth paused and looked at Marvin until he said, "Now what?"

"Nothing."

"Come on, ain't nothing."

"How am I going to say your name in court and not swoon?"

"Here we go again, *damn.* I was Marvin Gaye *long* before that rooster opened his mouth and I can *prove* it."

"'*What's going on?*'" Mary Beth sang.

Marvin slumped back in his chair as if exhausted by the subject of sharing a dead singer's name. He pulled his hat over his eyes. In a moment, though, Mary Beth—and the two ladies serving at the food line, plus a large woman in several layers of clothes selecting a doughnut—heard Marvin croon softly under his hat, "War is not the answer / Only love can conquer hate."

Marvin's lawsuit against Towers Trucking for racial discrimination would be heard in Federal Court on Mary Beth's birthday, Judge Ambrys Tucker Maas presiding. Judge Maas, a conservative of the first water, was near retirement and Mary Beth dreamt one night that he leaned down from the bench and kissed the top of her head, saying, "Lord knows I need to leave something decent behind."

Judge Maas was a classic growler and scowler, with great bushy eyebrows and a bumpy red nose, which may or may not have been the result of dedicated drinking; a dream-kiss gave her no confidence that he would be the least bit kind. A jury trial gave her far more confidence. She was good with juries and despite defendant's counsel rejecting all but two of the eight African Americans who had been called, she felt pretty okay about the final seating. She managed to save a high-school history teacher by giving the woman a sour look that she didn't see—but which Mary Beth's opponent *did* see, at exactly the right moment; and she also got a part-time county librarian seated. When the Towers Trucking side let those two join the party she could have raised both arms in triumph.

That night she bought herself a bottle of champagne on the way home and drank almost half of it over a chicken breast and Emily Dickinson. "Success is counted sweetest / By those who ne'er succeed." True enough, but by God she was planning to succeed; and contrary to her usual pretrial insomnia, she fell asleep beautifully by ten o'clock, not waking until five when a cardinal started blowing his head off outside her window trying to impress some female.

Studying her eyes in the mirror, brushing her teeth, she made a face—"That's for you, Judge Maas!"—and then she winked—"Happy Birthday, lawyer person."

She put on the most conservative tucked-in suit she owned, a sparrow-brown wool gabardine that she bought anticipating days like this one. A portion of light green blouse-ruffle appeared under her chin like a small reminder of our Puritan past—or a small salad. No jewelry except for very plain gold earrings the size of BBs, a wire-thin wedding band (juries preferred their women lawyers grounded), and her watch with the black leather strap. Her tan shoes carried more than a hint of sleek overdrive, but a girl can batten down only so far. The heels were a sober medium. On the Beaufort Scale she was traveling between zero and one—closer to zero—her smoke rising almost perfectly straight up. That slight waver, a tad snaky, was to remind people that wind speed can shift without warning. So be careful, boys.

Applying a lip blush the color of rust, she tried curling a snarl. Which made her laugh. She drove to the Federal Courthouse listening to Louis Armstrong—

Just direct your feet
To the sunny side of the street

She pushed the repeat button three times, driving with the window beside her down and the warm Kansas City morning air brushing her hair dry. She did not want gold dust at her feet—no, not even metaphorically would she care to be rich as Rockefeller—and Louis knew it! What she wanted was far, far simpler. Meantime she had a trial.

Mary Beth did not fool around with the jury. One by one she looked its members in the eye as she laid out her statement. Mr. Gaye had driven for Towers Trucking for nine years without incident. He picked up and delivered the goods on time. Not one speeding violation, not a single infraction while on the job. Yes, he had some warnings—two, to be exact—related to parking. Who hasn't been warned about something? He was a man doing what Towers Trucking hired him to do, keeping his part of the bargain. One day he comes to work and finds a note under his windshield wiper. A nasty note. Calling him the kinds of names that make every decent American feel funny.

"You know what I mean by funny," she told the jury. "Shocked, sad, sorry, embarrassed, disgusted, angry, small, afraid. We are a long, long way from Lincoln's Emancipation Proclamation, even a long way from the Civil Rights Act of 1964 and Doctor King's 'I Have a Dream' speech that applies—by the way—to everybody, not just people of color. Mr. Gaye finds more notes. He can't believe it. He shows them to his close friends Rachel Andrews and Olive Washington, both of whom you will meet in a little bit. Mr. Gaye approaches Mr. Rust Mills, the union representative. Shows him the notes. You would expect help from your union, wouldn't you? You would expect help from your *employer*, wouldn't you? Did Mr. Gaye receive help? No, he did not. In fact, after he complained to these proper offices, the notes and their vile, threatening, hateful language increased. Increased, ladies and gentlemen. And that, I am sorry to say, is why we are here today."

Marvin, wearing what he normally wore—jeans, boots, a flannel shirt—took the stand. He spoke evenly in a pleasing baritone. Mary Beth had advised him to not even *think* of cracking wise, and no new polysyllabic words he wanted to try out—or any old ones either. "Plain speech, Marvin, is the bedrock of real communication." He promised he would try to be bedrock plain and winked at her.

On the stand he responded to her questions pretty much as they had practiced, adding only one important detail that she hadn't mentioned in her opening statement: scattered on the driver's seat of his rig the next time he came to work following his complaint to the Towers manager were six spent rifle-bullet casings. Mary Beth introduced these casings, holding them up in a plastic bag for the jury to see.

In their prep talk, Mary Beth had also advised Marvin—while on the stand—not to look at anyone from Towers Trucking who might show up to watch the proceedings: to look only at her, the jury, or the judge if he happened to ask a question. But when Marvin started telling his story she saw that he couldn't help glancing at the half dozen beefy Towers toughs who had not only showed up and sat together in a row but wore, to be extra-visible, their varsity-letter-jacket-style windbreakers: bright blue satiny garments with *Towers Trucking* in yellow script across the front and their names in the same yellow script across the back. They sat like wrestlers before the match, their flushed facial expressions saying they were itching bad for the ref to get things going.

When Rachel Andrews and then Olive Washington were sworn in, they couldn't have been more dignified and outraged and cool all at once. In turn, they listened to Mary Beth read aloud from the notes Marvin said he had found under his windshield wipers, and then holding them, they acknowledged that these were indeed the notes that their old friend Marvin Gaye told them he had found on his windshield; then the witnesses sighed in ways all their own that required no more words from them, not one. Mary Beth could see that the jury understood the wickedness that the women on the stand—and everyone else in the room—had just been exposed to via this evidence and that neither Rachel Andrews nor Olive Washington cared to get down in it any further and thrash around like the fools who had written such garbage. The mother of two high school boys active in student government and bound for college, Rachel Andrews had worked twenty-four years in the state's driver's-license bureau. Olive Washington supervised a cleaning crew at Hallmark Cards and Sundays sang solo in her church choir; her only child, Georgia, was a senior at Cornell College in Iowa. When Mary Beth finished with these women she whispered in Marvin's ear that today was her birthday and she wanted an ice cream cone.

Towers Trucking had four attorneys at the defense table, all men, and all of them dressed uncannily alike. Blue suits, reddish ties. Which made Mary Beth smile and want to say something clever about it to Marvin. Hoods and their uniforms. If only it wouldn't sound so damned self-righteous. One of these attorneys—Manfred Lintz, the lead guy—now whispered something to his colleagues and they all nodded as if they had just chewed on a piece of meat that had been grilled exactly the way they liked it. Yeah-yeah, Mary Beth thought. But along her collarbone she was heating up.

She called to the stand Rust Mills, a beefy man wearing a dark blue pin-striped suit and red tie, his hair combed back in perfect iron-gray moguls.

"Did Mr. Gaye bring his complaint to you?"

"He did."

"Did he show you the notes that the court has entered as evidence?"

Rust Mills sighed as if this conversation were a total waste of his time.

"He did," Rust Mills finally said.

"And what was your reaction?"

"To what?"

"To those notes, Mr. Mills."

"Not much," he said.

"I'm sorry—would you mind clarifying 'not much'?"

"Nothing much?"

"Did Mr. Gaye also show you some spent bullet casings?"

Again the bored sigh. "Yeah, he did."

"And what was your reaction to those bullet casings?"

"Not much. Excuse me—I mean, nothing much."

Mary Beth stepped over to the evidence table trying not to stomp, and held up the notes in one hand and the casings in the other. "Are you saying, Mr. Mills," she raised her voice, "that your reaction to these threatening notes and bullet casings left on and in a Towers Trucking vehicle scheduled to be driven by Mr. Gaye, a Towers employee and a member of the union you represent, was *not much* or *nothing much*?"

Rust Mills leaned forward aggressively. "I thought—and still do—that Marvin Gaye—the one that's still alive"—out slipped a smirk—"was a complete whiner and good riddance!"

"Your honor," Mary Beth said, "I ask that the court certify Mr. Mills as a hostile witness." She could see Lintz stand, no doubt ready to object to her leading questions.

"Denied," Judge Maas growled, saving Lintz the trouble of opening his mouth. "Continue, Mrs. Urquhart."

She knew right then—*boom*—that they had her. She'd held out for a chance—a dinky-ass chance—to compete, to get her story to the jury for *it* to decide, but that wasn't going to happen, not at this trial. Judge Mass' growl housed the sound of doom. Turning down her request to certify Mills eliminated a real examination. She couldn't push him now, bear down, make him sweat, bolstering her case-in-chief. All she could ask were who-what-when-where questions and he could pull back and slide by with *I don't know* until lunch or the end of Western Civilization, whichever came first.

She had nothing, really. She hadn't been able to depose a single Towers employee, so there was no point in calling any toughs to the stand in their bright jackets just to hear them ape Mills by professing ignorance. And Towers management could lie through their smiles and get away with it. None of this was Marvin's fault—nor should it have been in a Republic that claimed fiercely to be civil—even though he did make a big mistake early on in trying to represent himself and taxing Judge Maas' not generous patience; the court calling her into the case in the middle of it wasn't even a Band-Aid: the knife was firmly placed and the blood-letting all but let. She had tried to warn

Marvin when they took their first drive in his car, but he was clearly so happy to have her on his side—and in addition getting a good foil for his wit and vice versa—that she couldn't press their puny, if that, chances. She *did* like occasional long shots, don't ask her why, but today was not eligible.

She rested her case.

Manfred Lintz then asked the judge—as she knew he would—for a directed verdict on the grounds that plaintiff had failed to make a prima facie case.

His eyebrows moving up and down like caterpillars with approach-avoidance problems, Judge Maas asked Mary Beth what she had to say. She cited Federal law—to at least get that on the record—but she could see the judge fast losing interest: it did not matter what she had to say.

During the break for lunch, Mary Beth and Marvin sat in Honey Bee and ate the trail mix and drank the carrot juice he'd brought in a cooler, and gazed at the untroubled blue sky out their windows. They knew they were only waiting for the drive to the cemetery.

Marvin suddenly broke the silence. "You know why Episcopalians don't get themselves involved in orgies, don't you?"

She looked over at him, and waited.

"Too many thank-you notes."

"That is so bad," she said.

"Just trying to cheer you up."

When court resumed, Judge Maas gently twisted the knife. He said, "Mrs. Urquhart, I want to commend you—you've done a highly professional job here today." Should she jump up and down, clapping? Or curtsy? Or just salute? "But I find that as a matter of law your client cannot establish a prima facie case of race discrimination, and I am therefore dismissing this case." Gosh, that little Latin phrase does get a workout.

He told the marshal to bring the jury back in so he could explain his decision to them. While he was explaining, Mary Beth glanced at Marvin: she shook her head to let him know she was sorry; he leaned toward her and whispered, "A little blood don't mean I'm dead."

Then Judge Maas banged his gavel—just like one of those fake judges on TV, she thought.

II.

The following spring Marvin was notified that his suit against Towers Trucking was in line to be heard by an appeals court, and that summer a truck he was driving across South Dakota almost ended up in the Missouri River. Monkey business had been performed on the truck—he suspected Towers—and he called Mary Beth in her office.

"They *seem* detasseled about my case going up on appeal."

"If there's a connection," she said.

"If?"

"I know, I know. But the main thing is, Marvin, are you *okay?* You weren't hurt?"

"Naw. Too stubborn-boned to get hurt. But I *was* wondering: will I need legal representation in this new assault on my person?"

"It wasn't your truck?"

"You know I can't afford no truck. I was driving for a small outfit."

"Well, their insurance company will be interested in the matter, we can be sure of that. I'd say, call your appellate attorney in St. Louis, tell him what you know, then stay cool, see what develops."

"Cops say the jiggerations on that vehicle a long way from professional. Hacksaw quality."

"And really, you weren't hurt?" she said.

"Tiny bump or two, nothing to manifest a departure from looking good."

"I see you are still working the English language."

"*Got* to stay in shape, Mary Beth, you know that."

"Where are you?"

"Back in K.C. Living in Honey Bee."

"At the church?"

"They *like* me. Especially since seeing me on TV. I made the national news."

"Well, congratulations, I guess."

"Mary Beth, you got to mix more with the hoi polloi."

"I do?"

"*And* you got to get to church more. Ladies there shaking their heads."

"'I am a little church, no great cathedral.'"

"Hey, that's nice."

"E. E. Cummings said it."

"Frienda yours?"

"You might say so."

That night she got a call from Charley Finder, an attorney she'd known since law school but hadn't seen or talked to in a while.

"Charley, how *are* you?"

"I'm okay."

"And Nancy?"

"Well, she left me, Mary Beth."

"Left you?"

"Walked out three weeks ago tonight. But I'm okay, pumping iron, painting the bedroom a bright blue—a quite *loud* blue, actually, with stars." He laughed. "I'm calling, Mary Beth, to see if you'll have dinner with me. No soft cries of self-pity, no moaning, promise. Just a fun dinner. Say yes, if you're free."

She liked Charley and said yes. They met the next night at an Italian restaurant. Before their veal parmigiana and angel-hair pasta with clams arrived and not halfway through their first glasses of a good chianti, he took her hand, kissed it, and confessed that he'd loved her since their first meeting—that torts class with Professor Trueslow—did she remember? When he had to move his big feet in the aisle so she could get to her seat? Then he started to cry. She said, "Charley, stop it." The waiter brought their food and left. Charley said, "Marry me, Mary Beth. Make me whole again."

The really sad part of their date was leaving that plate of pasta and clams. She was starving and really wanted it, the white sauce smelled divine. But Charley Finder couldn't stop sobbing and she couldn't listen to it any longer.

This was the third year in a row that Mary Beth had turned over writing her firm's annual Christmas poem to Eilis Flynn, the junior associate who worked for her. Eilis was pregnant, with twins, the due date nine days away. She was an ample young woman to begin with—six feet tall, big-boned, buxom, a volleyball star at Notre Dame before law school—and filled out, now, to what appeared the bursting point, nearly everyone at the party, it was fair to say, joined in holding a collaborative breath as she made her large way to the Kansas City Country Club's portable stage to read her poem.

It was also fair to say that very few actually followed the poem's clever story line, which was shaped around the Supreme Court acting as Santa and giving George W. Bush a present of the Presidency. Al Gore got a new telescope. The lawyers and secretaries laughed when their names came up, they laughed at the rhymes because Eilis, having studied Mary Beth's former efforts, filled them with as many syllables as possible—*interlocutory order / sock it to 'em billing-wise longer not shorter*; but there was too much anxiety in the room to just relax and enjoy, too many thoughts of water breaking, babies wanting out, and who-knew-what-to-do? Eilis' husband Dunston, a linebacker for four years at Nebraska, now sweating bullets in law school at Kansas, was dressed as an elf; as his flushed, ladened, perspiring wife read her poem, he stood behind her and tossed handfuls of paper snowflakes into the air. To many in the audience, this seemed to make a highly tentative situation somehow more tentative.

After Eilis made it safely back to her table, Mary Beth quietly slipped away to the Ladies, and thence to her car. Before starting the Mercedes, she sat for a few moments and gazed at the stars, the half-lit moon, and wondered what her teenaged parents' first thoughts were when they knew she was coming, and what they immediately did then.

On St. Patrick's Day, after the parade, all of the single attorneys at Riley Hamish Woodward Dunne—and many of the non-single—joined the mob of revelers downtown to buy large paper cups of keg beer from the nuns. Not too many years ago even Woodward waded into the crowd, but not since his gallstone operation. The surgeon said the number of calculi in his sac rivaled the seeds in a pomegranate probably and this image stopped Woodward from eating and drinking most things with flavor or pleasure attached. The sisters wearing old-fashioned habits, their sleeves rolled up, beer foam sliding over their knuckles like lace, were Mary Beth's favorites. Turning from one after getting her cup filled, she saw Marvin Gaye. He was leaning against a beer truck, drinking a Dr. Pepper.

"I can't believe this! Marvin!" she sang out.

"Why, gracious me, *who* do I behold rubbing shoulders with the hoi polloi?"

"And *you're* drinking *pop*!"

"My delectation for beer is not keen, Mary Beth. Besides, on duty tonight. Driving. *Good* to see you. Been a while."

"You working for the Pope now?"

"Naw, just Sister Sarah, who poured that cuppa brew you holding. Old frienda mine."

"That right?"

"Did some marching with Dr. King. Arm in arm. You too young to remember any a that."

"Haw."

"By the way, I hope you ain't drinking and driving your daddy's big car tonight."

"Straight to Gates' for some barbecue later. Interested?"

"He makes it too peppery. I favor Mr. Arthur Bryant's culinary savories."

"Okay, let's go there. In a cab."

"Can't. Gotta keep tapping those kegs, earn some credits."

"You're a good man, Marvin."

"You're a good man too, sister. Be careful."

To officially line herself up as Marvin's pro bono counsel in the new trial—scheduled to start June 25—Mary Beth first had to clear things with Woodward, then send a written request to the court. Though he looked unhappy when she met with him, Woodward said, "Fine, that's fine."

"Are you sure, Henry?"

"I can't eat shellfish. Fiona and I were invited out last night—the Halls—and Adele served a lobster-something. I should have passed. Now I'm paying for my timidity. Never be timid, Mary Beth."

The court also said fine. The judge would be Brice (Ace) Reiser, another conservative, but a colorful one. He'd played baseball at Yale with George H. W. Bush, coached the team at Davidson for several years, then flew Panther jets in Korea in a Marine reserves call-up. Ted Williams and John Glenn were in his squadron. He started law school in his thirties, at UCLA, and while there occasionally worked as a film extra; he was famous among his fellow students for having had a date with Marilyn Monroe. ("I just called her up," he claimed.) Ronald Reagan appointed him to the Federal bench. He was now 77 and engaged to a former Miss Arkansas who was 38 years his junior. Mary Beth was delighted to have drawn him.

A week before Marvin's new trial Mary Beth invited her old friend Sam Green to lunch. Sam was an Assistant U.S. Attorney in Kansas City. He and his wife Tillie were two years ahead of Mary Beth in law school and had fed her Spaghetti Delux—they called it—every Sunday night, plus during exams. Sam's strong tenor voice could and often did overpower his fellow choir members at Grace and Holy Trinity; he was a big man, physically, a former high school All-State fullback, and he once offered to kick the shit out of Todd Urquhart when Urquhart was Mary Beth's husband and his infidelities had become known.

Over their grilled salmon, Mary Beth told Sam about Marvin Gaye's discrimination suit: how Judge Maas had thrown it out and how the appellate court in St. Louis had sent it back. She would be representing Marvin again, before Judge Reiser. She told Sam about the spent shells and threatening notes, how Rust Mills had sneered on the stand, the gang of Towers drivers in the courtroom contributing their sneers.

"Check this, Sam. Last summer, mid-June, Marvin is driving a load of FEMA generators from here to Washington State. For an outfit called Cornhusker Delivery. In South Dakota his steering suddenly fails—on a big bridge over the Missouri River—"

"That bridge near Chamberlain?"

"The same. Marvin's rig crosses the centerline—he's going 75, the limit—and crashes through the guardrail. His tractor ends up hanging over the river's deepest channel . . ."

"Whew."

"The tractor is totaled, bridge mussed, but nobody's killed. Marvin really lucks out, just some bruises. South Dakota investigators *and* the insurance guys find that a tie-rod to the steering arm had been weakened—almost certainly with a hacksaw."

"Whoa," Sam shook his head, smiling. "First," he took a sip of his cranberry juice, "a silly question: when did St. Louis reverse Judge Maas?"

"February."

"*If* your civil case is related, why would Towers be so dumb as to go courting—sorry—a criminal case? With large ripples?"

"Maybe you've already answered that."

"They think Maas' word will be final and can't help twisting the knife—for the pure dumb joy of it?"

"Not nice people can be *so* slow, Sam, it's disappointing, really."

"Trust all the subpoenas are lined up?"

"Yup."

Sam Green stretched. "Maybe I'll slip in the back and observe. Maybe invite Willie McGee from the FBI to join me since our cargo was FEMA goods. Generators for what, by the way?"

"Does it matter?"

"No big flood?"

"Just getting ready for one, I guess."

III.

Among the potential jurors for Marvin Gaye's new trial were an artist from Hallmark, a secretary at Russell Stover Candies, a retired high school baseball coach, a bartender at a well-known jazz lounge, a grandmother with big dimples who worked in obituaries at the *Kansas City Star*, and—this one made Mary Beth's heart go faster—a professor from the University of Missouri at Kansas City who specialized in poetry from the Romantic period. He wore a gray mustache and wire rim glasses and his voice was chocolaty smooth. She would never get him seated, nor the black bartender, but she had high hopes for Ms. Twila Mayberry the artist, Ms. Jennifer LaVasseur from Stover, the grandmother—Mrs. Groeth—and the retired coach. Coaches tended to be conservative, but this one, Hoot Cubbage, wore cowboy boots and a breast cancer lapel pin, and he gave Mary Beth a friendly smile that he did not, she noticed, give to Manfred Lintz.

In the end, Lintz and his crew (Towers had the same four attorneys as before) bounced the poetry professor and the bartender pronto; nor did they care for the grandmother from the *Star*, no great surprise. Mary Beth got the Hallmark artist, the Russell Stover secretary, Hoot Cubbage, and nine women with kids growing up. Eight of these women liked staying home, cooking and cleaning and watching the paper for sales; the one who didn't like staying home drove a taxi after dropping off her two preschoolers at her sister's house.

Mary Beth put Marvin on the stand first thing and they got his story out, as before, straight and simple. She introduced the rifle shells and the threatening notes. She also asked him to tell what happened when he was driving a load of FEMA generators across South Dakota on June 15, 2000. He told how his steering suddenly failed and he found himself heading for the Missouri River.

"Where did you spend the night of June 14, 2000?"

"In Sioux Falls, South Dakota. In that big truck oasis—Siouxland."

"Did you sleep in your truck?"

"No. In the motel there at Siouxland."

Rachel Andrews and Olive Washington followed Marvin to the stand and gave their testimony. Mary Beth called Rust Mills to verify that Marvin had made a formal complaint of discrimination to him in 1998 regarding those rifle shells and the racially hostile, threatening notes.

"And then you did what with the complaint?" she asked Mills.

It was at that moment, as if she'd choreographed it, that Willie McGee, the FBI agent whose office was in the same building, entered the courtroom and took a seat beside Sam Green. McGee was African American, six-feet-four—he'd played basketball at Creighton—and Rust Mills saw him and worked to find a more comfortable position in the witness chair. He fingered the knot in his red tie. Lintz and his colleagues also took note of the agent's appearance. (They had already seen Sam Green come in.) Mary Beth let all this settle a moment, then raised her voice a notch.

"I said, Mr. Mills: after Mr. Gaye made his formal complaint to you, how did you respond exactly?"

"I reported it."

"I'm sorry, Mr. Mills, can you tell us *to whom* you reported Mr. Gaye's complaint? And speak up, if you would, please, so we can all hear you."

Rust Mills labored to clear his throat, then said, "I reported Mr. Gaye's complaint to management."

"That would be Towers Trucking management?"

"Yes."

"The spent rifle shells, the threatening notes left in and on Mr. Gaye's truck—all this was in your report to Towers management?"

"Yes."

"Thank you. You've been very helpful."

Mary Beth called a South Dakota State Police investigator and an investigator for Cornhusker Delivery's insurance carrier. Both testified they had no doubt that a hacksaw had been used to weaken the steering mechanism of Marvin's truck. "An astonishingly crude sabotage," the insurance investigator said.

Then she called a Towers driver named Lance Lang and asked him where he was on June 14 and 15, 2000. He said, "On a run down to Texas with a load of batteries."

"Thank you," Mary Beth said. "That's exactly what the Towers log says you were doing."

Next she called a driver name Buster Flemke, a big-shouldered crew-cut man in his early thirties. He had been one of the satin jacket-wearing toughs at Marvin's first trial; now he wore a dark blue suit and a pinkish tie that seemed to be choking him.

"Is Buster your legal name, Mr. Flemke?"

"No. That would be Francis."

"How long have you worked at Towers Trucking?"

"Proud to say ten years in September."

"Do you remember your first day?"

"Sure do. September 1, 1991. Just finished truck driving school. Hauled a load of cow feed out to a lot in west Kansas."

"Where were you last June 14? The Towers log, unfortunately, is not helpful on this."

"Right here in K.C."

"All day?"

"All day?"

"Yes, from morning to night. It was a Thursday. Flag Day, actually."

"Shoot, I don't exactly remember."

"But you *were* here, you said."

"Yes ma'am. I slept in my own bed that night."

"Could you have taken a trip that day, out of town, and returned late to sleep in your own bed? You'd remember if you took a drive, wouldn't you?"

Manfred Lintz objected with a weary sigh. "What is the relevance of this questioning, your honor?"

Judge Reiser looked down over his half-glasses at Mary Beth. "Mrs. Urquhart, what's your point?"

"Your honor, I plan to link up this line of questioning with evidence and testimony from other witnesses."

"Proceed."

"Could you say, Mr. Flemke, that you did *not* take a drive out of town on June 14?"

The witness looked in his lap. Then at the table of Towers attorneys, where Lintz at that moment was reading a note that the attorney beside him had just written on his legal pad.

"I can't remember," Buster Flemke finally said.

"Were you on a personal vacation possibly?" Mary Beth asked.

"I can't—no, I wasn't."

"So you can't account for what you did during Thursday June 14, 2000, except sleep in your own bed."

"No ma'am. Not at the present time."

"Tell me this. Have you ever been to Sioux Falls, South Dakota?"

"Yes ma'am, lots of times."

"Do you know of the truck oasis Siouxland?"

"Yes ma'am. It's a good place to stop after loading up here in K.C."

"Might you have been there on the night of June 14, 2000?"

"Well . . . I just can't remember."

"How far is it from K.C. to Sioux Falls, would you say? In miles."

"Oh, four hundred, maybe four-fifty."

"According to Triple A, it's three hundred seventy-two. Could you drive that far in one day?"

"Sure."

"Could you drive twice that in one day?"

Lintz stood up. "Your honor—"

While Lintz searched for his phrasing, Judge Reiser said, "I'm going to let this line of questioning continue."

"Could you, Mr. Flemke?" Mary Beth asked.

"If I had to."

Lintz leaned back, took a deep breath, then stood and declined Mary Beth's offer of Buster Flemke. Lintz also declined Harold (Booty) Bender, a Towers mechanic in his late twenties. Mr. Bender, like Mr. Flemke, was not mentioned on any Towers worksheets for June 14, 2000, and he himself could not recall anything he did that day except sleep in his own bed in Kansas City. But he did know what a hacksaw was and what it could do to a tie-rod if rubbed back and forth on it just so deep. A redhead like Mary Beth, he blushed fully and bright when he had to agree with the insurance investigator's opinion that a hundred miles down the road would likely contain enough bumps and turns to snap it.

Next came Lester Driscoll, whose rounded shoulders and large head seemed to join without the benefit of a neck: he was another of those satin-jacketed Towers drivers from the audience of the first trial. Mary Beth got the same response from him that she got from Buster Flemke and Harold (Booty) Bender: he couldn't recall what he did on June 14, 2000, except sleep in his own bed. She trusted that the jurors were starting to tap their feet to the rhythm of this mantra.

Finally she called Trish Bloom, a secretary for a road contractor in Kansas City who had previously worked at Towers Trucking. Back when Mary Beth was preparing for the first trial, Marvin had mentioned Trish Bloom as one of the few people in the office who always had a nice word for him. "She was nice to everybody," he said. Prepping for the new trial, Mary Beth looked up this secretary.

Miss Trish Bloom was a native of Kansas City, in her late twenties, and she was wearing—Mary Beth had no doubt—a scent called Clinique Happy. Also a tad too much makeup. They met for breakfast at a popular Westport café.

"I'm curious," Mary Beth said, "if you'd ever heard any talk about Marvin at Towers that was negative, over the line."

"Well, you know how guys are sometimes. I mean, sure they talked a little rough, laughing at jokes they'd pulled or planned to pull, you know."

"Jokes?"

"Oh, once they left some bullets—the empty shells, I guess—under Marvin's seat cushion."

"Seat cushion?"

"For his back? A support thing?"

"These were other drivers?"

"And Chew Wrigley, in the dispatcher's office. *He* loved a good joke. So did my boss, Mr. Junior Towers."

"Ever hear Mr. Wrigley or Mr. Towers or any drivers refer to Marvin's race?"

Trish Bloom hesitated. "I don't work there any more. I sort of feel funny talking about them, even though—" She stopped herself.

"May I ask why you left Towers?"

"Better job."

"How so?"

"Oh, the people where I am now are actually more polite. You've noticed how big I am? My bust? Well, at Towers I had to hear more than I cared to, if you want the truth."

"Inappropriate language can hurt."

"Sure does." Trish Bloom's eyes narrowed. "They said Marvin was gonna squirm for acting so smart. Sweat and squirm. He really got under their skin—you know?—when he sued them. Even his union was mad. Least Rust Mills was."

On the stand now, Trish Bloom took a deep breath after telling about the jokes—the notes and bullet shells—and the threats she heard at Towers "to put Marvin Gaye in his place."

"Thank you, Miss Bloom."

Lintz stepped briskly to the podium. He asked Trish Bloom where she went to high school in Kansas City.

"Paseo."

"Were you popular?"

"I had many nice friends."

"White *and* black?"

Trish Bloom looked toward the ceiling. "Probably more African American friends. As you know—"

He cut her off. "Yes, we know that Paseo has a predominately black student body."

Where, Mary Beth wondered, was Lintz going with this? He was digging himself a hole!

"Did you graduate from Paseo, Miss Bloom?"

"No. But I got my GED."

"Yes, you did. Congratulations. That was *after* the birth of your baby, wasn't it?"

"Yes." Her eyes were starting to tear up.

"Are you married, Miss Bloom? Some professional women, though married, continue to use *Miss.*"

"No, I'm not."

"Have you ever been married?"

She began to cry. Lintz said, "Your honor, may we allow the witness a moment?"

Judge Reiser said, "Yes, fine. But now would counsel please approach the bench?" Mary Beth and Lintz walked up. His voice lowered, Reiser said to Lintz, "Counselor, unless you can tell me where this line of questioning is headed, I'm going to stop it. In any event, it's getting late." Then he recessed until nine o'clock next morning.

That night, Lintz called Mary Beth about a possible settlement.

"You know, Manfred, I couldn't figure out, at first, where you were going with my witness today, beating her up like you did, committing suicide."

"Suicide?" He laughed.

"At the moment we're not interested in a settlement."

"Do you really think you have the jury? Or are you just listening to your own emotions?"

Now she laughed.

"What's funny?"

"You know what—the weepy woman lawyer card you're trying to play."

"We did win the first time."

"And *then* Towers tries to kill my client!"

"Is that why you got Sam Green and Willie McGee in the courtroom?"

"Jesus, Lintz, they *work* in that building. Do I control their movements?"

"Anyway, an attempt on your client's life hasn't been proved."

"Darwin's theory hasn't exactly been proven either. Look, Towers is in deep doo-doo and you know it. Beating up on Trish Bloom was cheap and dirty, and Towers couldn't care less—they want Marvin Gaye. They probably didn't even notice how fast the *Star* reporter was taking notes during your shameful performance. You're trying to end this trial, before you lose it, to eliminate big punitives against your client."

"Oh, come *on*, Mary Beth."

"You come on, Lintz. Towers is out of control they're so pissed at Marvin."

He called an hour later. He'd talked with his client, he said, and strongly recommended settling.

Mary Beth snorted. "Of course you would."

"So what does your man need? What will he take?"

"Are you actually trying to get me to bid against myself? I *used* to think you were smart, Manfred."

"I'll have a figure for you in the morning."

"Please don't embarrass yourself further."

Mary Beth got in her car and drove to Grace and Holy Trinity's parking lot. Marvin's Caddie was in its usual spot.

"Smells like a pizza parlor," she said, sliding into the rider's side.

"Needed a snack—with anchovies. They high in omega three's."

"Why don't you look for a nice house, Marvin?"

"On *my* salary?"

"Or get a cell phone?"

"And be like everybody else—always jumping like Hollywood calling when it rings?"

"Well, it appears Towers may want to settle. You could have some decent money soon."

"Settle?"

"Lintz called me tonight. Figured he might, after that crummy thing he did to Trish Bloom today."

"Knew you were mad, the way you packed up and scooted."

"Went for a necessary jog. Sorry I didn't share my thoughts."

"So how come he treated her so mean?"

Mary Beth sighed. "Lintz has lost control of his client. All Towers can think of is punishing you, doing really stupid things like hacksawing your steering."

"And slashing Honey Bee's tires that time."

"Those—" her lips tightened, remembering.

"Watch out for swearing."

"Okay, okay. Anyway, he—Lintz —is afraid that if we get to the jury and he loses, you'll be awarded big damages. The jury could take Towers Trucking down *and* out. Lintz put on that show today to give us the idea he's vulnerable—and to give his client the same idea. I'm not sure Towers understood the commercial: that settling would be the sure, cheaper way to go. Of course, we might not *get* to the jury. Lintz knows we haven't forgotten Judge Maas. And Judge Reiser *could* be a problem—he did give Lintz a break today by cutting him off—though I don't think so. The question right now is: are you willing to settle if they make an offer?"

"Don't know."

"Said he'd call in the morning with a figure."

"Hmmm."

"Marvin, settling is not selling out."

"You know that old Episcopalian fable about the man asking the pretty lady if she'd canoodle with him for a thousand dollars? She says, 'We-l-l, maybe I would.' He says, 'Would you do it for twenty dollars?'"

"I know, I know, she gets all huffy and says, '*What* do you take me for?'"

"And he says, 'We already established that—now we just dickering over price.'"

"Why is that an old Episcopalian fable?"

Marvin laughed. "You mean it ain't?"

Pulling out of the parking lot, she realized she hadn't eaten dinner and was hungry. She drove straight to Winstead's, the burger joint on forty-seventh that her dad took her mom to on dates.

"Cheeseburger," she ordered at the counter. "With onions grilled in, tomato, pickle slices, and mustard. And a sack of fries"—in case she stayed up late—"and a chocolate malt. All to go."

She slid into a booth to wait. Almost nine-thirty and the place was more than half full. Wasn't it always? She wondered what they talked about, her parents, how they sounded? Were they afraid? Surely they were: eighteen, no money. In the next booth a young couple—high schoolers—sat bent over their glasses of water with nervous flushed smiles. Were they doing it? Unable to keep their hands off each other when they parked in his car on a dark street? Did they just come from one of those precious-few, hot, hurried, passionate embraces? Was she happy for them? If she had a daughter, how would she advise her? The girl's blond hair was awry. The boy sported a few bright pimples, the scraggly beginnings of a mustache. But it didn't matter how they looked to anyone else, not right then.

Her takeout arrived. She decided to eat it there but forced herself to eat slowly: she was not that eager to get to her office any sooner than she had to. She hoped Lintz's offer would be respectable.

"Mary Beth!"

She looked up from her plate. It was Charley Finder.

"Charley—nice to see you."

"I'll bet," he grinned. "May I?"

"I'm actually about to leave. Work awaits," she rolled her eyes.

He slid in opposite, blocking out the young lovers. "Till you go, then? Okay?"

"So how are you?"

"Full of remorse. Can you forgive me for—"

"Forgiven," she said quickly. "Look, let's just bury that night, okay?"

"You look beautiful."

"Charley, I've got a tough night ahead—if you don't mind."

"Can I help it if you look so great?"

"Charley, Charley." She took a breath. "At five o'clock I ran five miles, trying with every step to erase from my mind the faces of a certain attorney and his client. Then this attorney phoned me, interrupting my amateurish attempt at profane meditation. Then I sat with my client in a parking lot. I haven't showered. I'm eating my dinner at ten o'clock. I do not *feel* great. But thank you. Now, *if* you don't mind, I have neither the energy for nor the interest in flirting."

"It's me, isn't it?"

She had to laugh.

"*That*," he said, "makes you even prettier."

She chewed for a minute. Then sipped her malt.

"I do like you, Charley. But you're right—it *is* you."

"I'm not your type."

"You're not my type."

"May I ask what is?"

"*Type* is not the best word. But trust I'll respond if and when he comes along. In the meantime, I'm not *that* horny, if you get my drift."

Marvin Gaye sat sipping carrot juice in Honey Bee and gazing at a two-story red brick house that had a For Sale sign out front. He liked this house. He liked that long slope of yard, all those big old leafy trees; and inside the house he could picture high ceilings and solid oak floors that he would also like, rooms that allowed hefty persons such as himself to mosey through with ease. He also liked the big sun porch on the side. A man could host his friends out there in cool, natural comfort on the hottest, stickiest day. He himself could invite Olive and Rachel. Old Sammy too. He'd tell Sammy to bring along his latest cupcake if she was of legal age *and* he wasn't afraid of having her meet a truly handsome man.

The truth was, Marvin had been courting Olive Washington discretely for some time and now he could court a little bit louder. She was a woman of many fine attributes, including a voice that floated his heart all the way back to his youth in Jefferson City when he sat in church with his grandmother—sat and stood—and they clapped and sang and reached for the sky, full of love—mellow, thunderous, and all ways in between. And Olive, bless her tasty lips, had kisses to accompany that voice, believe him. And the more he thought about those kisses and about sleeping in a real bed and stirring his breakfast oatmeal on a real stove and reading his *Star* on that grand porch, the more he was flexing up to sing. And then he did sing.

Tiger Lilies

For the annual Spring Frolic, Lila wore what looked like a lampshade. To fit a six-foot lamp. Her parents drove her to the school gym and left her at the door. Inside, she fixed her cape on a wire hanger on the coatrack. The only garment hanging there. She stood against the wall watching her schoolmates dancing and laughing and felt so graceless and empty that she needed to hide. In the girls' restroom, she entered a stall, locked the door, and sat on the toilet for over two hours hugging her knees, terrified someone would discover her. Then she went outside to be picked up at the entrance, as planned, by her parents. Her mother asked if she had had a nice time. She said she'd had a wonderful time. She pronounced "wonderful" the way the girls in the restroom pronounced it, kind of breathless.

Two years later, her parents drove her to a small Methodist college in Missouri. Her mother said she would make lots of new friends, that she would blossom. Lila heard "blossom" the way she had heard the girls in the restroom say "wonderful." She was ready—eager—to blossom. She had not grown much taller, thank goodness, but she *had* grown nicer looking in the face, hadn't she? Her skin was unblemished, milky. Her green eyes were bright, her hair a long rich brown. When she arrived at her room in the dorm, the girl who would be her roommate, Marie Johnson, gave her a spontaneous hug. Lila said, breathlessly, "This is . . . this is all so wonderful."

Her parents stood together just inside the doorway. Lila's mother asked Marie where she came from (northern Iowa) and told where they came from (upstate New York). She believed that the girls would turn their room into a lovely little nook. Three times she exclaimed: what a scrumptious view they had through those cute windows. Lila's father finally said, "Those are called mullion," jingling the change in his pocket. "Yes, of course!" her mother laughed. It was a high-pitched, almost cartoonish laugh, and everyone looked at her. Lila's father said they had a long drive ahead and ought to get started.

Lila said she would walk them out to the car.

"Abso*lute*ly not." Her mother smiled at Lila and Marie in turn. "This is *your* life now. We've had our fun." She burst into that laugh again; this time everyone looked down. She opened the purse hanging from her arm, found a tissue, and began to worry it into a fuzzy ball. "So, little missy, you stay put." Stepping forward, she gave Marie a hug. "Be good, study hard." Then she embraced Lila, kissed her on the cheek, turned dramatically, her head thrown back, and went out. Lila's father, left alone for the moment, smiled awkwardly at the young women, nodded, and followed after his wife.

Lila stood at the window to wave; she had her hand ready but her parents walked from view without looking back—her father giving an arm to her mother, who seemed to be having trouble with a heel. Turning from the window, she took a deep breath. "Gee, I'm sorry I didn't get to meet your mom and dad."

Marie said she had come down from Iowa by herself, on the Trailways bus. "My mother offered to bring me in the car, but we just don't travel well together. If you know what I mean."

They began to unpack. Lila thought to tell how *her* mother had dressed her up like a lampshade for a school dance in tenth grade, but she stopped herself because she didn't want to be disloyal to her mom—who really did try her best—and because she didn't want to tell the rest of that sad story, or confess that she'd never attended or cared to attend another school dance. Ever. Which wasn't quite true: if Bobby Dee Tackett, their handsome quarterback, had asked her, she would have said yes. Of course that was as likely to have happened as for her to have been named Miss Universe. So instead she told Marie that in tenth grade she made a really important decision: to become a special ed teacher.

"Kids with problems need help," she said.

Marie said, "Big year for me too, tenth grade."

"Really? Did you make an important decision?"

"No, no."

"Oh."

"My father died. So . . ."

Lila came and took her hand; her eyes watered.

"It's okay . . . it's okay."

"Gee."

Marie shrugged. "He was forty-four. Heart attack." She gave Lila's hand a swing. "So, hey, do you have siblings?"

"I'm the only one."

"Me too. Funny. My dad was one of seven—two boys, five girls—and he was the only one to marry." Marie smiled. "So far anyway. I come from that strange tribe called The Swedes. Plus a German mother."

"I'm sorry about your dad."

"Thanks, I am too. I miss his jokes. Not that they were belly whoppers. Belly whoppers? Anyway, he brought me back from despair more than once."

Marie patted Lila's hand by way of thanking her again, then let go of it. She slid open the closet door.

"Which end of this space do you want?"

"Gosh, no dif."

"So what's upstate New York like?"

"Well, the part I come from is so small I've never been able to even find it on a map!" Lila burst out in a high-pitched laugh not unlike her mother's. After a moment, Marie, hanging up some flannel shirts, laughed too. Then she turned.

"If you're going into special ed, you'll want to hear about my bus ride today. Talk about a kid needing help."

Lila said she hoped this wouldn't be a sad story, and smiled.

"Well, you decide."

They sat cross-legged facing each other on one of the twin beds. Marie found a pack of Winstons in her backpack. She offered it to Lila.

"Gosh, no. I'm afraid if I start, I'll smoke like my mom—in secret—every chance she gets. My dad *still* doesn't know. He'd have a fit."

Marie lit up.

"Okay," she blew smoke out the side of her mouth, "there was this girl on the bus with a puppy, both of them skinny as jerky. Called herself Star. Called the dog Jo-Jo. Said she was eighteen, same as me, but that was clearly a lie. Fourteen, tops. Said she found the puppy two stops back, in Sioux Falls, in a cardboard box in a dumpster."

"What kind of person would do that?" Lila said.

"Exactly what this Star said." Marie inhaled, nodding rapidly, then blew smoke out the side of her mouth again.

"Throw away a little dog like it was trash." Lila shook her head. "That's not right."

"Well, it was lucky for Star, finding this dog, because she needed a friend." Marie looked out the window a moment. "She was running away from home. She didn't say this, but you could tell, you know."

Lila nodded as if she did know. The truth was she had never known anyone to do such a thing. She remembered one time her mother shouting at her father that she was leaving and he could go to hell. Her mother never talked like that. But she didn't get past the front door; she sat on the floor and broke into terrible sobs. Peeking around a corner, Lila saw her father sit on the floor beside her and put his arm around her shoulder. "There, there, Helen," he said. "There, there." This surprising tenderness made Lila feel so good for her mom—her dad too—that she cried.

Marie had been tapping ash in her palm; now she hopped off the bed and deposited the ashes in a wastebasket. She brought back the Pepsi can she'd emptied just before Lila and her parents showed up. Resettled on the bed, she said, "Yeah, Star said she was heading for the Osage Indian Reservation in Oklahoma. Said, 'I'm gonna find me one Native American I can understand.'" Marie inhaled smoke and blew it out, Lila now thought, like a gangster in a movie. She had never seen a girl smoke like that, that she could remember, and was almost as fixed on Marie's smoking as on her story. Though one thing was for sure: she preferred not to hear about anything bad happening to Star.

"I think"—she produced a hopeful smile—"that Star will find what she's looking for in life."

Marie shrugged. "She said to me, 'Am I crazy?' Before I could say anything, she said, 'Well, I know I am. In fact, I'm schizophrenic.'" Marie looked hard at Lila. "Hey, is a fourteen-year-old girl who says she's schizophrenic really schizo?" Marie answered her own question. "I do not think so, doctor."

"She's pretty brave," Lila said, looking down, pushing at the cuticle on her thumb. "Just taking off like that."

Marie dropped her cigarette in the Pepsi can and swirled the can several times. She suddenly pointed the can at Lila. "Said to me: 'I give up, totally, on wasters. I can't even *look* at them.' Said she'd tried. Said she'd hung out and listened and *listened.* 'And know what?' she said. 'They don't even make human noises. They don't laugh or cry or even swear with any feeling. They made other noises. Like mechanical toys. Like *robots.*' Which was why she was heading out for that Osage reservation."

Lila was still focusing on her cuticle.

"Know what I think?" Marie finally said.

Lila looked up, waiting to hear.

"She is one mature kid."

"Oh yes," Lila agreed. "Completely." She was glad the story of Star had taken on a positive note.

Marie shook her head. "Isn't it a shame, though, that *she* is made to feel crazy?" Marie looked into Lila's eyes with such intensity that Lila began to feel uneasy, began to feel that her roommate might be somehow blaming *her* for Star feeling crazy.

"Gosh, yes," Lila said. "I mean, of course it's a shame!"

"We ought to get on a bus and go down there and see how she's doing. See if she needs help." Marie said this so sincerely that Lila felt a little dizzy.

"You mean now?"

"I don't know what I mean." Marie lit another cigarette. "Look here." She removed from her jeans a wrinkled piece of paper. She kept the cigarette in her mouth while she smoothed it out and handed it to Lila.

Lila read:

If you really
really care
you can't worry
all night long
my love beware

"Wow," she said.

"Star wrote it, I think. Can you believe it?"

"It's really . . . wow."

Marie took a long drag and blew smoke straight up. "I know," she said. "I know." She gazed at the glowing tip of her cigarette. Finally she sighed deeply. "Isn't it all so damn sad?"

Lila didn't know what to say. The story of Star—its meaning—was eluding her. But she didn't want to say so and sound stupid in front of her roommate, who was clearly very smart, on their first day together. She wanted Marie to like her. At length she hung her head and said, "Sad."

"Just before I got off the bus—I mean *just* before—Star read it to me. I said something like, 'Man, did you write that?' She said, 'Do you like it? Don't say you do if you don't. I hate insincerity.'"

Marie looked at Lila as if waiting for *her* response.

In almost a panic Lila blurted out, "Gosh, yes, I do!"

"Well, dumb me. I said, like, 'It's very sweet.'"

"What's dumb about that? It *is* sweet."

"I don't know," Marie said. "I just don't think *sweet* went down very well."

"No, no, I believe she was happy to hear you say that. *I* would be."

"How come she threw the paper out the window then? As if it were junk?"

Nine years later—almost to the day when they first met—Lila sat at her father's kitchen table in upstate New York reading Marie's letter, which had been forwarded from Kansas City. She read it three times before she noticed her father in the doorway staring at her. She wiped her eyes with a dish towel. He was wearing his bright blue track suit; he had slept late again, his hair wild, his face unshaved.

"Is there something I can get you?"

He took a raspy breath, scowling, and cleared his throat. "I was going to make myself a bowl of hot oatmeal."

"No, no, I'll make it."

"Don't forget the raisins."

"I'll remember this time. Promise."

Lila folded the letter and put it back in the envelope. Her father took a chair. He sat with his head at an angle, looking at his hands folded on the table with a mildly surprised expression, as if his thumbs, twiddling, were performing a mildly interesting trick.

Standing up, Lila noticed Marie's return address—she was using her maiden name. Lila blew her nose. She put water on to boil; watching it, she suddenly remembered she needed to call her son. After that, she would call Marie.

In her letter Marie said she had just heard on NPR of Ken's death in Iraq. She'd tried to call, she said, and learned that Lila's number was no longer in service. "My heart goes out to you, Lila. You know that. You know I feel bad for everybody who has lost somebody over there. I can only imagine how you are taking this. But please let me say how fortunate you were—both of you—to have had Kenny and those precious years together." She closed by asking Lila to let her know—please—where she was now, if she had left Kansas City.

Writing even that short note had been hard for Marie. She wanted to scream out, throw something. Her hands were trembling. After sealing the envelope, she put her head on her desk and cried.

The first time Marie met Ken, shortly after the baby's birth, she'd exploded in his face. "Those people in the White House are maniacs! And maniacs follow them!" There was more—too much more. She didn't know that he was in the Reserves. He'd said nothing; Lila waited until he was on his way to Baghdad to tell her.

She told her in that childlike hand that always made Marie think of her cursive lessons in fourth grade, and then of those days when Mrs. Nelson was ill and her mother would substitute, and how Marie was *never* to call her mother "mother" in school. She remembered going to bed that year praying *please* do not let Mrs. Nelson be sick tomorrow. Now all of this got churned up with the painful memory of her rant at Lila's. Ken did not interrupt her in any way; he simply looked at the floor. When she was finished, spent, he said—shyly, as if the baby's name were the subject all along—"I wanted to name him Jack—after Kennedy?—but Lila wouldn't let me. You know how stubborn she can be."

Stubborn was not a word Marie would ever use to describe innocent Lila. And she was sure that Ken would have agreed if he was serious. How lucky Lila had been to find him! Through four years of college she'd had very few dates, all of them blind. With guys from the university up the interstate who never called for a second date. The boys at their little school apparently weren't interested in a six-foot-plus girl wearing bangs and a perpetual smile. A blessing as far as Marie was concerned. They tended to be either Bible-quoters or business majors bent on building their pile, or both. The few odd exceptions—and they were odd—were the jocks who seemed to arrive on campus with girlfriends already in tow. Ken Kilinski was so different from that history that Marie found herself becoming happily distracted around him.

Now he was among all those dead in a war that she felt chained to like a prisoner, a dog. She could no longer finish a meal or pay proper attention to her clients at social services. Almost daily she debated quitting and getting a job where she didn't have to see people at all. Who was she kidding? Comfort the desperate? The old? Those teenage mothers? Wrapped in her fury, how could she comfort anyone?

When NPR said his name she fell back against her kitchen counter and knocked a bottle of olive oil to the floor. She stood in the mess of spreading oil and broken glass as the reporter finished his brief biography of yet one more U.S. military casualty: ". . . in partnership with his father and uncle in a Kansas City veterinary practice."

Why didn't he tell her he was in the Reserves? *Later*? When they looked at each other. Would that have been so hard? But she knew the answer—or enough of it to feel rotten. Why strike a match next to a woman soaked in her own gaseous stink? That was pretty much what Roger had said. "You're bitter about almost everything anymore,

Marie. I can even smell it on you." Before she could tell him what she thought of *that*, he picked up his briefcase and said he was going to the library.

Her first response—which she came to regret—was to phone his chair at the university and ask her what kind of PhD candidate in history runs away from serious debate about government policy? Is he a *viable* candidate? Not to mention a responsible TA?

The chair, who had heard Marie's views on Iraq at faculty parties—and who shared them, though not so passionately—liked the young woman and tried for a little humor. "If by any chance you are referring to our own Roger Joyce, Marie, I shall ask the dean's office to behead him, how's that?"

"Don't patronize me, Martha."

"Now, now, my dear, I'm sure—"

Marie hung up. Then she gathered up every picture of him in the apartment—except one—and ripped it to shreds. The exception was framed on her desk: besides Roger with his arm around her, it showed Lila broadcasting her big eager beam at one of those blind dates he had arranged when they were all seniors. It was the year, immediately after finals, when she and Roger got married before a justice of the peace in the heart of the Ozarks, with Lila and a retired dentist living next door their witnesses. It was also the year Bush was running against Gore—the same year her Uncle Hermann died and her mother was especially nasty—really a bitch—to his sisters. In retrospect, introducing her new husband to her mother at her uncle's funeral—where her mother did not wish to be anyway—was probably not the smartest thing she'd ever done.

The following year, teaching special ed in Kansas City, Lila began to date the man who gave her mutt Matthew his first examination and shots. She kept him a secret such a long time, she confessed to Marie later, because she wasn't sure he would continue to like her—and then because of his military connection. She didn't want to cause any more unhappiness. You know?

Yes, Marie did know. So she missed the small wedding at Ken's parents' house that Lila described for her. Lila's parents drove down from New York. Her mother's drinking was now out in the open; she wept so loudly during the ceremony that the minister stopped twice to try and soften things for her. Lila started a case of hives that day that lasted for several weeks. Ken wore his uniform because his father, a former Marine, asked him to.

"Can you forgive me for not inviting you?"

Forgive her? Oh, Lila, Lila.

So not quite a year after the wedding, there was little Kenny napping in his mother's arms, and there she was feeling her cheeks heating up before a man she'd known only a few hours . . . and whose blue eyes she felt looking inside hers.

One night, in bed, she said, "Sometimes, Ken, I think I should just run away."

"It's Roger, actually," her husband said.

At first she didn't know what he was talking about. Then she did, in a blaze, as if a noon sun were suddenly everywhere. She should have said something right away. Instead she lay awake a long time seeing Ken's shy smile, then Lila's beaming from the photo on her desk, Ken's again, and how sweet he was to her afterwards. Finally she said, "I'm sorry, Roger, a stupid—stupid—it doesn't mean anything."

But he was asleep—or chose not to respond.

About two weeks after she called his chair (yes, yes, making a fool of herself), Roger left a note on her desk. He said he needed—they both needed, he thought—a separation, some peace, time to think. Specifically, he needed tranquility in order to finish his dissertation and prepare for his orals. After that he wanted to leave Iowa. "I still love you," he said. "The other you."

Now it was her move. But she felt more tied up than ever. When the phone rang beside her, she was staring at a sheet of stationery she couldn't even write *Dear Roger* on; finding the paper and a pen had nearly exhausted her. Lila's voice seemed so small.

"Marie? It's me—"

"Where *are* you?"

"In New York . . . at my dad's."

"Oh, honey. You got my letter about—"

"Yes, I did. Thank you so much."

"I'm just—"

"I know."

The details seemed to come from Lila's small far-away voice as if from a child who had lost something—a trike, a favored doll, a pretty button—and didn't know quite what to do. She was sorry about her Kansas City number, but strange people kept calling and calling. Twice Marie had to ask her to repeat something. Why wasn't she angry! She'd lost him, for God's sake! And her mother too, yes, that sad woman. Hoarding her sleeping pills until she had enough. Sitting down at the dining room table as if to a feast, all dressed up, wearing her pearl choker, eating them off the Noritake china she'd brought into her marriage. It happened the day before the government notified Lila about Ken. Back-to-back funerals. Back and forth between Kansas City and New York. Her father falling on the casket. Ken's mom keeping Kenny for her while she looked after that poor man, trying to figure out what to do.

"Why didn't you call me?"

"I was going to. Then . . . "

Neither one said anything for a few moments.

Then, "He was getting ready to retire. They had a ceremony planned. That same week. In Albany? Where his company's offices are? So they just mailed him a plaque. Now he sits in front of the TV for hours. Do you know what, Marie?"

"What, honey?"

"He doesn't have anybody but me."

"Let me come help you."

"Oh, that's okay. You have—"

"I'll fly up as soon as I can arrange things here."

"Gee, that's awfully—"

"Hey." Marie almost added *What are friends for?* and immediately felt dishonest, wicked, guilty.

On the drive from Iowa City to Minneapolis, for a direct flight to Albany, she remembered arriving with Roger at Johansson's Funeral Home, where her Uncle Hermann lay on view. Mr. Johansson, who greeted them, said he would go find her mother. "She and all your aunts have been expecting you." He sounded short of breath.

"My poor aunts," Marie sighed after he walked away.

Roger made that long hum that meant he was off in his head.

"What?"

"Oh, just thinking how your father and his siblings—all farm people—produced only one kid."

"Sex."

He raised his eyebrows.

She shrugged. "Wait till you meet my mother."

Did he smile? In her car driving past fields of corn and beans everywhere, she shook her head. What a dumb joke.

After a few miles she could see her mother coming into the reception area all over again, as if late to an appointment, clutching her purse, her eyes behind those thick glasses syrupy and black, like olives in a jar. A small woman, really, but making up for her lack of size with energy, a fierce motion: here came the old teacher, the disciplinarian fueled by German blood, about to pounce on malingerers, the unkempt, the out of line.

But Marie stopped her, cold.

"Mother, I'd like you to meet my husband, Roger Joyce."

For just an instant the woman's eyes flared even larger, blacker; then they closed. They stayed closed it seemed for several minutes. Her breathing was audible, hard.

They waited.

Finally, she looked at Roger, briefly, up and down, then said to her daughter, "Well, you surprise me." She might well have said *you disappoint me,* for that's how her tone weighted the words emerging past her stretched lips.

Turning to Roger, she thrust out her hand, declaring, "Anna Flueger Johnson." Her grip, he told Marie later, felt astonishingly like what he and his pals called "a cow bite" when he was a boy—that same kind of five-fingered pinch. "Well, you came to see Hermann, of course." And she led them as if to the principal's office to where her five sisters-in-law were keeping watch over their brother.

One by one they greeted Marie—Ingeborg, Helga, Ingrid, Olga, Nora. Five maiden ladies with pearl blue eyes and mostly white hair and tiny carnations of pink blush in their cheeks. Ingeborg, the oldest, the most reserved, hesitated a moment—to read Marie's expression—before taking this lone niece into her ample bosom. "We knew you'd come," she said softly.

Helga, the next oldest, followed by Ingrid and Olga, the twins, all hugged her and thanked her in a rush, as if they hadn't been able to breathe freely until now. When it was her turn, Nora, the baby—who became a nurse and ran the county's Women's Center—only needed to smile.

Marie understood all of this: she would deflect, simply by her presence, much of her mother's ill will toward them.

From her earliest years—five, six—Marie could see that her mother made her father's sisters nervous and not a little sad. She didn't understand of course, but who couldn't notice how their chirpy talk, their spontaneous giggles, fell suddenly away when Oskar's wife entered the room to instruct them sharply about this and that as they tried to prepare or set out the Thanksgiving or Christmas or birthday meals.

She almost had to pull the car off the road when the famous "dip" incident came back to her. Pulling up the bottom of her T-shirt, she wiped one eye, then the other. Her aunts were attempting to make a surprise birthday party for her dad. How did they think they could get away with that? Her mother, when she learned what was going on, was outraged. *She* had already taken the time, despite her demanding teaching responsibilities, to make a special treat for his birthday. Which she was planning to celebrate "quietly at home." Which meant just the three of them. Plus the treat.

Her mother had opened a can of Hormel chili, mixed an equal amount of Velveeta cheese with it in a pot, heated this glob on the stove until all the cheese was melted; then she stirred everything up to the consistency of baby shit. For her dad to dip his taco chips in. That was it—the party food she'd gone to all that trouble to prepare. (And continued to make for years after, not because anyone liked it—her dad was the only one to take a polite bite—but because it was so different from anything her aunts put on the table.)

Well, it all worked out, the party. They gathered—everybody—at Hermann's place, as always. He was the oldest, the first to come over, to find and buy land in Iowa and put in seed and see it flower, and then to send for his brother Oskar. Get the boys settled first. Get the land churned up good and paying out. Then bring the girls, whose futures in the old country held such small promise.

"And what did they end up doing?" Never mind Nora—her work with women unable to help themselves somehow didn't count. Oh, her mother was relentless! Sarcastic, angry, bitter, hateful—and why? What did those kind women ever do except keep a warm, friendly house and tend to their gardens and orchards and bees? Their jewel-like jams, their fruits and vegetables and honey were famous for counties around—people even drove up from Des Moines. And, yes, they cared for their brothers—not to mention any number of neighbors who were suddenly hurting or sick or just plain lonely. Her mother resented them for all of it, accusing them of behaving beyond their positions, their place. Somehow *babying* that big Swede Hermann was the worst. No wonder he never married, never learned English, never left his precious farm. Why should he bother! They treated him like some kind of stupid king! And the same thing would've happened to Oskar if she hadn't come along.

In Johansson's Funeral Home they stood before her uncle's ample remains lying in a modest wood casket and told Marie that he had gone peacefully while taking a nap.

"No pain."

"He even had a little devilish smile. See how Mr. Johansson kept it there?"

"He told us: No fancy box. Don't waste money."

"Yes, and quite firmly."

"You know how he hated showing off."

Their comments came as if from one—it didn't matter who said what.

And off in a back corner sat her mother who might have been Mr. Johansson's assistant, if he'd had one who went into mortuary science as if into taxidermy, no real difference, since both were concerned, finally, with shaping a body up.

There was, however, more going on that Marie didn't know about. She soon learned of it.

"Hermann"—in a whisper—"will be laid to rest in a beautiful place."

"On a slope shaded by a giant oak."

"In the Fjord City Cemetery."

"Room"—the whisper dropping lower—"for all of us. In time."

"Our brother's wish—his hope—and ours—"

"—that we all be together."

"By and by."

"All the Johnson family, Marie."

"Everybody."

She said, "But my father—"

"We"—the whisper now at its lowest—"can move your dear father."

"It is possible."

"Isn't it?"

Marie glanced back at the mortician-taxidermist in the far corner—the corner opposite from Roger—where she clung to her black purse and wore, staring straight ahead, her familiar clenched jaw. Move this woman's husband to a new location, never mind, when the time came, that she could come too? What were they thinking?

At the Fjord City Methodist Church next morning, she sat in a back row, and at the cemetery she stood apart, almost hiding behind the giant oak. Marie's aunts had not yet brought up The Family Plot proposal to their sister-in-law, but from the frown of disapproval fixed on her face, the tight wrap of arms across her chest—ready for any approach to her heart—it would never happen; he *and* she (and Marie too, if she had her way) would ride out eternity together in the Lutheran cemetery in Martinsburg. Under a black granite slab bearing some words from Luther himself—though they might well have come from her mother, appearing to warn any and all to stay back from: *A safe stronghold . . . A trusty shield and weapon.* Luther was actually referring to God, but, hey, that was her mother, far more stubbornly on target than any Swede could ever hope to be.

The fact that she included Marie's name and birth date on the slab—without telling her beforehand—did not surprise Marie a bit. Later, when her mother asked if she liked the tombstone, Marie looked at her and said nothing. Its color, the legend, all their names—and only *their* names—struck Marie as beyond sad. She simply walked away. You didn't contradict the woman. You kept your thoughts to yourself. In college once when Roger had quoted to her Thomas Hobbes' grim observation that the life of man was solitary, poor, nasty, brutish, and short, she mused, privately, that you could substitute long for short and have a perfect description of her last two years at home.

Was she a snot about her mother? Well, what was a snotty daughter? Someone who got all *A*s, never had a boyfriend or a messy room, never went to parties where beer might be consumed (never mind the other stuff), never spent a dime of her babysitting or corn-detasseling or yard-work earnings on anything foolish, and still received lectures on all the ways she could improve her thrift, her position, her future, and still kept her mouth shut, did what she was told, and *still* felt guilty? She felt guilty that the girls she ate lunch with at school were Catholic, that her aunts bought her a pair of Levis and she *wore* them. She even felt guilty that her mother crossed off Luther and Wartburg from the list of Iowa colleges she might attend, even though their dismissals were based only on rumors her mother had heard about wild parties on those campuses, nothing that could be pinned on her.

Plus—*plus*—she never challenged the clear lie about her mother's birth date on the tombstone. Five years had been subtracted from her age. So that the widow could not be accused of robbing the cradle? This was not the stonecutter's error; her father had revealed that he was only nineteen when he married the twenty-four-year-old schoolteacher in a quick, quiet ceremony before a justice of the peace. "We drove all the way down to Polk County. You know your mother—worried what people might say." He swore Marie to secrecy, a promise she remembered not long after his funeral as she lay sleepless in bed puzzling over *what* had attracted him to this woman.

How they'd met—when he told the story that time—was sweet and romantic, she thought. Or could have been. One August at the county fair he simply walked up to her in the brand new white shirt his sister Helga had made and tipped his hat and offered to buy her a cold lemonade.

"Isn't that so, Anna?"

They were eating supper, the three of them, and the fair was coming soon, which no doubt reminded him of the story he'd just told.

"I never would have accepted a lemonade from a stranger."

"Not even a nice cold one?" Her father winked at Marie.

How she wanted her mother to smile for him, bend a little, blush! But there was nothing; she continued eating as if her husband and daughter were fools from the moon.

Did Marie *ever* see the woman warm up? Hug him? Put a kiss on his cheek? No. Nor could she remember a single time when she and her mother had hugged. Forget kissing.

Maybe the difference in their ages and running off to get married had something to do with her mother's treatment of her aunts. But how, exactly? Marie had neither the courage nor the heart to ask them. Nor did she wish to break the promise to her father.

The week before she left for college, she bought her first pack of cigarettes and vowed to enjoy it. She also bought a one-way bus ticket.

On the flight to Albany, she fell into a deep sleep and dreamt that her aunts were kneeling about their brother's grave, removing from coffee cans the tiger lily bulbs they had dug from his front yard. They took great care with each bulb—loving care. Why did they bother so? You could sink your shovel into a bed of tiger lilies and come up with enough of a chunk of a bulb that would most likely thrive like blazes almost anywhere. It was impossible to hurt them. Her spying mother, close to the giant oak, resembled the crooked shadow of a leafless limb. Where was *she* in the dream? Why wasn't she there helping her aunts, who were beaming with happiness, their fingers stained brown from the lilies' long velvety brown tongues?

As the plane began its descent, she woke with a dazzling headache.

Lila met her. They embraced, awkwardly; Marie's mouth was dry, almost gritty, as if she'd been eating dirt. Lila had gained weight, her shoulders rounded in that hunch that some tall women develop. They both had tears to wipe away—on meeting, while waiting for Marie's luggage, and again in the car. They couldn't seem to find the right place to begin. Was Kenny's first birthday really the last time they'd been together? And now he was almost *two?* Marie's throat hurt.

She said, suddenly, hoarsely, "I loved Ken."

"I know you did."

"I couldn't help it."

"I know."

Did Lila understand what she was saying?

That night they sat with her father, who wanted to watch an *I Love Lucy* video. Several times he would say, "Isn't she a pistol?" and wipe his moist eyes on his sleeve. They all sat before TV trays and ate cold cuts and potato chips. Lila took from her pocket a slip of paper, many times folded, and unfolded it. "Oh," she said to Marie, as if disappointed, "here it is. That number I told you about?" Earlier, in the car, Lila had said she needed to call a Mrs. Kelly about looking after her father, and had misplaced the number. She hated to do it, she really did, she told Marie. "But it's better than a nursing home, don't you think?" She had tried Mrs. Kelly's number three days ago—no, four—and it was busy. She needed to get up the courage to try again. Her eyes had bruise-colored pouches under them. She mainly gazed at the rug covered with roses in front of the TV set and twisted her wedding ring round and round.

Marie could have told Lila that her life would come to heartache. She could have told her this in college. She could have told her aunts that their hope for a family plot that included her father was futile, pointless. She could have told them while they all knelt and planted tiger lilies on Hermann's grave and on the spaces beside it reserved for everyone else. The world was off-center, out of whack—not to mention cruel and greedy. That girl, Star, running away with her skin-and-bones puppy to find one Indian she could understand, made as much sense on this subject as anybody she'd ever known. She could have told Roger on their wedding day that their marriage would be difficult and probably fail.

All of this was clear to her now as she sat with Lila and her father, watching Lucy and Ethel working frantically at a conveyor belt: chocolates came to them to be boxed—came faster and faster—they couldn't keep up, all these chocolates, what to do? So they began shoving them in their mouths, their faces smeared browner and browner. The audience loved it. Lila's father loved it. "Isn't she something!" he cried, wiping his eyes. "Wouldn't you like *her* for a mother?"

Marie had to smile. Bitterly. Lucy and her mother were so different, it was ludicrous housing them in the same thought, comparing them in any way. Her mother would have somehow *willed* those chocolates into their boxes, no ifs, laughs, or buts about it.

She saw Lila looking at her, frowning a little. Trying to recognize her? Place her? What was Marie doing there? Then Lila's dog came and laid his head on her chair, and she smiled; no more mystery. For a moment Marie saw her old roommate telling her about a good grade she just got on a test; she saw her greeting another blind date, hopeful as always; and looking up, so contented, when Ken came into the room, and then turning back, lovingly, to the baby in her arms.

Lark

That fall when Jerry and Jacki became the owners of Sacred Heart Church, it was really, they said, the result of a lark. They were looking for a nice solid house in Spring Lake that they could use for a getaway or rent out, maybe a little of each, they weren't sure; the main thing was, they wanted to put the forty thousand dollars Jacki had inherited into real estate, and they liked Spring Lake because it was small and leafy—all those majestic oaks lining the streets, their brilliant colors simply took your breath away—and it was close enough to Minneapolis without being too close. It looked and *felt* to them, fans of old films that they were, like a college town from a 1940s Mickey Rooney movie in which Mickey and his pals say Gee Whiz a lot and put on variety shows and the girls wear bouncy short skirts but are wholesome.

There was no college in Spring Lake. It was a community largely of retired farm folk and escapees from city life who found ways to make a living on their computers. Main Street, you could fairly say, was comatose, except for Saturday night when The Hot Spot sold cheap twofers on tap and Howie's Big Table featured all-you-could-eat buffet suppers. Settled on either side of these establishments were S. L. Water & Electric and the Knit Nook; the chiropractor, the post office, and a mail order seed concern held sway across the street. As for the lake, it was weedy and shallow and therefore not much good for recreation; but looking down on it from Willow Peaks Park it had a certain dreamy charm, especially at sunset. In pleasant weather many of the older residents could be seen strolling over there to sit on wood benches in their sweaters and gaze out at the rosy water, maybe peeling an orange. Jacki's Aunt Norma had been one of these strollers. Never married, she taught for thirty-seven years in Spring Lake School, saved her money, and died at ninety-two working the *Star Tribune*'s daily crossword puzzle.

No, Jacki told friends in the Twin Cities, she and Jerry didn't feel they had to invest in Spring Lake because of Aunt Norma's legacy. They really did take to the town. Why else would they have made that offer for Sacred Heart when no other property they liked presented itself? Yes, of course their offer was for fun more than anything else, surely the bishop wouldn't accept it: the property, which included five empty lots, was clearly worth a good deal more. But the bishop apparently had waited long enough for a buyer, and the handful of parishioners who had fought him to keep their beloved church were either dead or had gotten used to driving—or being driven—twenty miles to Redemption, which was still holding on.

Life had been good to Jerry and Jacki. Following the advice of Jerry's brother Louis, an investment counselor, they bought and sold their tech stock all at smart enough times and now, in their early fifties, were retired—basically had been for almost a decade, could that be right? They hadn't made a killing—they didn't wait quite as long as they might have to sell—but they made out just fine. And they didn't go crazy, suddenly buying a bunch of things they didn't need. They were conservative that way, and thank God. Poor Louis, unable to follow his own advice, got greedy and lost his balance and now was paying dearly. Jerry and Jacki had to force themselves to go see him in that St. Paul duplex that was falling apart—all three hundred-plus pounds of him raising his voice and slamming his fist—and always came away depressed and frustrated in ways they found hard to articulate, vowing never again. Were Louis' losses, both personal and professional, their fault? Did they pick out the kind of woman he married? When his son Lance left the U. his freshman year after getting Brenda, still in high school, pregnant, didn't they contribute to that ridiculous business their nephew wanted to start? What was it, anyway? Some kind of jazzy gizmo that kids could install in their cars to give a certain sound to, what, their radios? their engines? both simultaneously? Didn't Jerry once try to have a heart-to-heart with Lance only to have the boy say his uncle was a stingy jerk? And stomp off? What was happening to kids these days? Not all kids, of course not, but the ones who'd had advantages and should know better?

Jerry and Jacki could not have children. Well, they *could*—once upon a time—but it would have been taking something of a chance, what with Jacki's history. She'd had rheumatic fever as a girl. Not a really serious case, but rheumatic fever is rheumatic fever, isn't it? Affecting the heart so? And look how petite she was and how big Jerry was—what if the fetus turned out to be unusually large, a real threat? And don't forget the heart problems in Jerry's family—both his dad and grandfather keeling over like *that*, and his mom's sad end. Anyway, they opted not to risk having a baby. Which, at certain times over the years—Christmas morning especially—they regretted, to be honest. When their financial ship came in, they talked about maybe adopting a child from Honduras (they'd been sending a check down there for a while now, to support little Eugeńio, who always wrote a note of thanks in his own hand that the Fund-A-Kid agency passed on, with its thanks), but they finally decided that adopting at their age—over forty at the time—wouldn't be fair to a growing child.

Now they were putting their energy and imaginations into giving Sacred Heart a new life. Lark or no, it was turning out to be a smart little investment (knock wood, but they *did* seem to have a knack for picking winners) and great fun besides.

The church divided up neatly into four spacious apartment sites—two of which they had ready to show that summer and rented out right away. These were adjacent spaces in the walk-in basement, where the parishioners had held their potluck suppers and played bingo and gathered—the ladies mainly—to fill boxes with donated clothes for the underprivileged here and overseas and to stretch their muscles in novel ways to improve their waistlines. Plumbing was there, partitions in place, so Jerry and Jacki had no trouble garnering off the church a quick and steady little income to use in sprucing up the third apartment—the old pastor's office and living quarters. This one went even faster than the first two and was rented before the new paint had dried. Now they had enough church money coming in, they figured, to cover the taxes, normal repairs, and a good portion of what they needed for improving the sanctuary, where they would live. An idea that appealed to them more and more. They would put in a big bright bathroom, a kitchen with all the cupboards and elbow room they'd ever need, an elevated family room, complete with fireplace, utilizing the former altar space, and—the topper!—they would build a loft above where the pews had been. Oh yes, they said, clinking their wine glasses, planning it, they would sleep up there the sleep of the just and wake in the rich colors the morning sun sent through the stained glass renderings of angels and shepherds and those perfect burros and sheep.

And so they set to work. A year went by with almost no hitches in their plan, their swelling dream. They found a seasoned carpenter in town, a really capable man who was about to retire, and coaxed him into leading them, as they put it, in the grand design. Pete then found them, as they figured he would, other good inexpensive workers—plumber, electrician, and an old German mason, Max, who was collecting social security but who agreed to give them three or four hours a day to erect a fieldstone fireplace on the spot where Sacred Heart's pastors, one following the next, had bent to their golden chalices, murmuring Latin and, later, English, to turn water and wine into the body and blood of their Savior. Jack and Jacki had no affiliation with the Catholic faith, but they had had enough Catholic friends over the years to learn how the Mass basically worked. Also, in her youth Jacki had been best friends with a neighbor girl whose brother was an acolyte at St. Mary's up their street. She went to Mass with them a few times—well, more than a few—and to tell the truth she rather liked it, the singing, the colorful vestments, how the church smelled. And didn't she have a big crush on the brother, too? She seriously considered joining, taking lessons, getting baptized—the whole thing—but what happened? It's sort of vague to her now. Seems that when she started working at the store after school, and meeting Jerry—a college man—and really wanting to get away, things just changed for her, you know? And then when Jerry's dad had his fatal heart attack, and Jerry quit the U. to manage the store, because his mom certainly couldn't, and Louis had no interest in selling clothes—haberdashery, he would sneer, nada, and pretend to shiver—well, there it was, all pretty much spelled out for her.

She was eighteen when they married, Jerry twenty-one. They were lucky that her folks and Jerry's mom were still alive to help celebrate. After honeymooning in the Bahamas, where a fraternity brother of Jerry's was assistant manager at a resort and got them a deal, they returned to Minneapolis to run Off the Rack and More pretty much all by themselves. Well, yes, they did have Phyllis, the longtime bookkeeper, and old Roberto in the tailor shop, and Stevie in shoes. And Jerry's mom helped out at Christmas and Easter. But Louis would not come near the place, which hurt Mom, it really did. Then when his Las Vegas wedding to Pammy included none of the family, well, that was probably the arrow that pierced her, causing the stroke. To Louis' credit, however—and Pammy's—they came to see her every other Sunday, alternating with Jerry and Jacki. Always brought flowers or candy in a cute box. She and Jerry gave that to them. And only the one time—at their annual family dinner—was guilt ever mentioned, which Jerry immediately apologized for, putting out his hand first. And yes, they gave Louis all the credit in the world for his financial advice, though for a while Jerry was very reluctant to take it, knowing Louis' wild flamboyant side as he did. (It had *nothing* to do with Jerry being younger.) But Jacki quietly kept pointing out how well Louis and Pammy lived, and how slow things were at the store—really, they were just barely staying alive—so Jerry said okay, they'd buy some of that sexy new stock, as Louis called it. The rest, as they like to say, was history.

Or they used to say it. People. You have to be careful around everybody these days. Take when they finally sold Off the Rack and More to a condos builder. Yes, they made a little on the deal, but look, they did it mainly to pay for Mom's last couple of years, which were not cheap, plus pay off the cemetery plots her folks were constantly fretting about and chip in on their meds. They also wanted to give Phyllis, Roberto, and Stevie something for their faithful service.

Oh my, you never—never—would have thought that Phyllis could be so nasty. Claiming that the store was holding its own and could have done better if Jerry and Jacki had put a little more into advertising, kept up with fashions just a tiny bit, spent a few dollars on *paint.* Nothing drastic, she all but shrieked. Mousy Phyllis in her gray cardigan, go figure. Jerry responded as anybody would have: Phyllis, calm down, you are throwing a fit. Oh, she said, oh, well, *you* don't have to worry about *your* old age. And burst into tears. It was not a fun scene. As for Roberto, he looked at them with such a sour expression, such a bold stare. God knew they didn't have a thing against Puerto Ricans as a race—if they had tempers, even at seventy-seven, so be it. Luckily for everyone present, Roberto finally turned his not very friendly eyes to the floor and kept them there. In a way, you had to feel sorry for him, losing control like that. Little Stevie took the whole thing in stride, bless his heart. Actually performed a curtsy when they handed him his envelope, and smiled. Don't ever tell Jerry and Jacki that all gay persons get snotty over the slightest whatever, looking for a catfight.

What was no surprise at all—none—was Louis. *Now* he had something nice to say about the store. How his grandfather founded it during a grim time in our history, then how his dad, standing up to the big chains trying to kill him off, worked himself sick, blah blah blah. What a hypocrite.

That's why Spring Lake and the church have been such a comfort to them. It is tranquil beyond belief—civilized, really—because people definitely know their place. And you should have seen their sweet old neighbor lady next door, Sarah, who used to clean for Sacred Heart, choking back tears when she stood inside the former sanctuary, looking and looking at their conversion of something just sitting there, collecting dust, to something stunning. How different it all was, she finally said. Jerry and Jacki could barely hear her, the tiny bent-over woman, crippled by arthritis, was so moved. But this gave them a real feeling of pride. Yes, the church was different. The old movie posters, the streamers, those wonderful trees you don't have to water, the gorgeous antique brass bed piled with silk pillows, the full-color walls in peach, plum, neon lime, fleshy orange, chilly blue, on and on. And their renters down below and off to the side couldn't be better. Of course, over a lifetime of dealing with the public, you learn how to size up people, spot the good bet, right away.

The New People

It was Riverside's keen-eyed birder, Blanche Bell, of the Sylvan Bell Timepiece family, who announced that new people had appeared on our beach. A woman with two young boys. "Frisky towheads, teenagers, could be twins," Blanche reported. "They play catch with a ball—racing all the way to Lighthouse Landing and back. The woman, however, seems lost in a dreamy stroll, her face mostly hidden by a big white swirly hat."

A face, it came to pass, that was very pretty, I might add.

The boys would burst out of the old Bastion mansion and spill down our famous dune morning, noon, and improbably just as the sun hovered on the horizon, when the late May day turned decidedly chilly and we Riverside veterans, trying our best to be comfortable, were about to enjoy the cocktail hour in front of a cozy fire. "Dashing about"—Blanche again—"like they hold immediate title to every inch they touch, kicking up sand and howling as they plunge into our icy waters!" Goodness.

Lillian, Doctor Rick Rockwell's last wife, said she wouldn't even consider donating to the hospital's thrift shop a single thing those people wore. If the clothes they wore were hers to give, that is.

True, the woman's diaphanous coverings looked literally thrown at her slender frame, barely finding purchase, and when she drifted and whirled around in her spontaneous little dance (silly little dance, Lillian called it) you did think every stitch might peel away and fly off on the wind—which I myself, before I met her, rather hoped to see. But raiment not good enough to donate to St. Joseph's? Come now.

Swimming in our splendid Saguenay (not to be confused with the Canadian river of that name), the boys kept their oversized Hawaiian shirts and shorts on and came out looking, in our Lillian's trope, "like creatures covered with gaudy seaweed." Better, of course, than teen boys naked as jays, which was what she most feared might rear up before her. She said. The woman continued to be lost in herself, weaving and twirling on dry land, and Lillian declared—Blanche seconded, although she seldom agreed with any of Lillian's observations—that the newcomer must be on *some* kind of medication, at the least. Lillian was glad her Ricky wasn't still with us to see such abandon. "You know," she said, "that he would be concerned and want to help, good neighbor, caring physician, and connoisseur of youth and beauty that he was." One marveled at how the always youthful Lillian, who'd had to put up with Rockwell's wandering eye, could render both pride and bitterness in the same breath.

It transpired—no huge discovery—that those frisky towheads were not the dancing lady's issue at all. Yes, yes, anybody could see, using binoculars, that she was indeed too young to have children that big. "Unless she's an Amazon!" said old Merl Hurst. But whose boys were they? And why weren't they in school? More to the point: who was *she*? Most Riversidians quickly reasoned she must be a nanny—engaged by the family who bought the Bastion place and hadn't shown up *in toto* yet. Wasn't that hideous For Sale sign gone? One novel opinion—held by Lulu, Charlene Brown's niece—fancied the woman a fashion model on a working vacation. Blanche said, "What in hell does that mean!"

Merl said, "Oh no, she's an Amazon! Check her out!" Merl of course was losing his marbles—and some days he knew it and cried; poor man's money couldn't stop the flow.

Lulu was the second among us (after yours truly) to venture down the dune to the beach's cold sand and introduce herself. And then was tight-lipped about it. Hooray for her! And her big eyes and brave tiny feet. Naturally no one could pump Charlene for information—not any more: She hadn't spoken a word on Riverside since the suave Bruno left her that last time. She obviously communicated with Lulu about things, like food, but we veterans heard nothing of the ditched aunt's opinions and fears unless Lulu cared to share—and that was rare and so clipped she might as well have been an orange and purple bird that had lost not only its flight feathers but its tongue as well. Charlene could win the lottery again and probably shy Lulu, who had come to her rescue, would utter nary a peep. Which would have driven Blanche and Lillian and many others up the revetment we'd had to build to keep Riverside from sliding down the dune into the Saguenay—and which the private school hooligans tried to outdo the public school hooligans in defacing with such vivid vulgarities against each other that we had to pay Gert Gottschalk's handyman Leroy, a native Mississipian you never could understand, a regular retainer to wash them off.

Anyway, did Lulu think *we* might come sheepishly to Charlene's door like Bruno? For a *handout*! Of course some of us had loved it when in record time Bruno once more said, "*Arrivederci*," and drove away in the custom canary yellow vintage Corvette the unlucky lady bought him with her lucky win. "It's easy to see," said Lillian, "why Char is struck dumb. Who wouldn't be after a man like that?" Dear Lillian, having negotiated her adult way via nearly translucent skin and a firm, lyrical derriere, understood such woman-man matters better than most. "What tickles me is picturing her sneaking out at night to that trashy beer and pop place to buy her ticket," Lillian laughed.

O let me leave these insular views and my dull attentions to them, at least for a while, and turn to the lovely Florence Ford and her stepbrothers Giles and Quinn, called Buzz and Buster by Florence's father. The boys were indeed twins—fraternal but almost identical. They were twelve. Florence was twenty-two and I, God help me, was smitten. That adjective may be excessive, but I can't think of a better one. She opened up to me immediately and I felt revised, refined, and responsive to, by, and in her generosity and innocence. Yes, innocence, though she was not innocent in the conventional sense. I wonder if I am good enough to share this attractive angel. Her mother, an athlete, had been killed in a spring avalanche in Oregon—"Mt. Hood, actually"—and her father, retired from the diplomatic corps, married the widow of Senator Daryl Terrill. Hildy, her stepmother, who had money, bought the old Bastion mansion "for fun, something to fix up," where she and Mr. Ford could rendezvous summers with Florence and the twins. Where the boys, especially, so exuberant, could be boys, running and jumping. Florence had hoped to be in New York by now, with the American Ballet Theatre, but that had not worked out. Nor had Hawaii for Giles and Quinn; they would be heading to their new school in the fall, in Switzerland. "We are so scattered," the young woman sighed, "and it's all so sad." In my usual mode I might have said something patently cheerful. But I could see, in those few minutes of our first meeting, that she was deeply lonely and I said only that I was sorry.

For several days I debated visiting the beach again. I know who and what I am—much of the time, anyway—and I did not trust myself. It was one thing to have consensual therapeutic sport with Lillian and to flirt with sweet, overweight Lulu and patronize Blanche and the others—I mean to say it was very easy living in the comfortable house my grandparents had built and letting my neighbors inspire me, but I felt it would have been going too far, a seamy violation, to behave similarly with Florence. The boys were off in their own world of robust juvenescence and I was happy to participate around its edges now and then by throwing a football with them and even dipping in the still-too-cold river when they suddenly commanded *we must*. My own son Quill would have been their age by now, about a year older, actually, and it was not just Quinn's name or Giles' left-handed throws that reminded me of the boy. And yes, I accepted several invitations to join them and Florence for another of their cook Juanita's tasty suppers, especially when an invitation provided an excuse for me to tell Florence that we shouldn't linger longer in my studio. After her dance on the beach, she liked to stretch out on my sofa, reading or just gazing off, while I typed away at another breathless installment of "The Ridge," the TV series once wildly popular, now struggling, that I could not try to pretend to her I hated. Of course I despised myself for being one of its authors, but I also enjoyed too much, I suppose, the easy self-pity it allowed me to take on in place of some drive toward real writing. Florence might come lay her lips to my neck and sigh and then return to the sofa and I liked it. If the boys had not been waiting for us, she might say, "Well, then . . ." Nor did I stop her those shameless times she called Juanita to say that Mr. Newhouser had a change of plans and that she herself would eat warmups when she got home. In no way, in other words, was I entirely passive. I let her hang two photos on my wall, which hang there still, and I allowed her more sleepovers than were prudent. But I never, not once, succumbed to using her for material, even though I was tempted.

One afternoon she asked me for pen and paper and began on "something" that I could see, she said, when it was finished. "*If* it's finished," she said. "This will probably take forever. I hope you can stand it." We both smiled. Meantime she would store her "scribbles" between the covers of Milton Avery's collection of pictures she was elated to find on my bookshelf. She loved Avery's art, especially the picture on the book's cover, "Tangerine Moon and Wine Dark Sea." It was painted in 1959, the year, she said, of her mother's birth. Her mother was thirty when Florence was born, and I can turn to the sofa where Florence used to lie back in her chiffony sheath and see, above it on the wall, a photo of the mother—Fredericka—only hours before she delivered her baby.

Fredericka, whom most people called Freddy, Florence said, was tall and lean and you can't really tell that she is pregnant under her ski sweater. She is standing on the side of a white hill, her poles stuck in the snow on either flank, smiling into a brilliant sunlight. Gazing out my window at the sun going down, Florence said, "She is—or would be—very nearly your age. My father is considerably older, actually. Hildy is—well, I don't know Hildy's age for sure. She won't say. But she doesn't mind revealing that she's had her face done twice already. Isn't that a little strange? My father says he loves to hear her laugh. Giles and Quinn nearly killed her when, as she puts it, they first met. 'Tangerine Moon and Wine Dark Sea' hangs in the National Gallery in Washington. That's where *we* met, Mr. Avery and I." Florence turned from gazing at the sunset. "Where are your parents?"

Where *were* my parents? I could have said oh, probably this minute leaving the Arizona wilds, where they seem to be wintering lately, and heading out, following their democratic noses. Toward what I can only guess. They now drive a rather spiffy Mercedes-Benz

RV, which seems both anachronistic and normal. They long ago told my grandparents to please leave the Riverside property to the Salvation Army, to the Nixon Library, to Planned Parenthood, to Mother Teresa, or even to their only grandchild if he grew up to find it amusing, but they had no wish to be there beyond a night or two. Lou, my father, told me once that he'd had to live on Riverside for eighteen years—and eighteen years was more than enough. When he met Joy at Reed College he found, he said, the part of his heart that was missing; and she let me know the feeling was mutual. "We were a pair of sooty terns in a pond full of auks," was how she put it. From the beginning they encouraged me to call them Lou and Joy, and later, if I was puzzled about anything, to consult the dictionary.

They never planned to have children, they told me, but when the pregnancy happened they were "curious enough" to go along with it. By the time I arrived they were sufficiently engaged in the experience to include me in all of their thinking. I am not sure I ever discovered exactly what that thinking was. They were not rebels, not conservatives—in fact no good label fits them even now. They could quote Thoreau, Mae West, Seneca, Wendell Wilkie, Shelly, Twain, Eisenhower, Groucho and Karl Marx, and Thorstein Veblen, among many others, with ease and apparent pleasure. They made their modest-to-sudden-windfall living in the world of freelance magazine journalism and an occasional partnership in a movie script at a time when you could do that and still go, as they put it, round and round on the track. They had taken tap water with the sons of Julius and Ethel Rosenberg, warm beer with Fidel Castro, and coffee with John Glenn. They were disappointed when Senator McCarthy did not call them to testify.

Growing up I lived in California, Connecticut, Nevada, Florida, New Jersey, at Churchill Downs and Saratoga, and once, when Lou and Joy were flat broke from bad bets, in a barn on the Pennsylvania farm of an old radio actor whose name means nothing now to even the most rabid fan of popular culture. A rather nice barn, I thought. Around which I rode an old pony named Mr. Jackpot. Lou and Joy could and can be as happy in a Hollywood bungalow-with-pool as in an oil-hemorrhaging Winnebago in a Walmart parking lot. I came to prefer steadier comfort. As I said, I could have given this history to Florence, but instead I told her my parents were dead. I don't know why I lied—and so easily. It is possible I needed to compete with her story, for one night, after she'd gone, I peeked at her "scribbles."

Dear Mother,

There is a large-ish photo of me in Mr. Newhouser's studio in which I am wearing a green velvet dress. I loaned him the picture so he can see me from an early stage in my development. It's a portrait, of course, by your dear friend Victor. I remember that green dress—the lace cuffs brushing my wrists, how the dress made me appear so smart. Didn't we buy it at the store where the little old man always had his tamale cart outside on the sidewalk, and every time we passed him the air smelled so good and I wanted a tamale and you, always careful about my diet, never let me buy one? Didn't you have to return the dress after Victor took my picture? I can't possibly remember all the things you have done for me. What I do recall, though, is vivid. I can still feel the fabric on all the dresses you made or bought for me. I can remember picking out the fabric. My very favorite was the pearl-white damask with hydrangeas in several shades of blue—lavender, periwinkle, robin's egg. And the bow in back tied with light blue grosgrain ribbon. So many clothes. So much patience. How did you manage juggling all that with your training routine and keeping dad happy? I know he wanted you to win a gold medal, I did too, so please, please—

And there Florence's writing broke off. Days, weeks went by. She would arrange herself on my sofa, pen in hand, and I would type away at "The Ridge," which was dying; the latest ratings, in fact, declared it postcomatose. Now and then I would glance behind me and see her gazing off—for inspiration? Lost in nostalgia? This was when I was tempted to work her into a script. I began by typing a few lines and erasing them. Then I wrote an entire page. I felt excited. I wanted to rush to the sofa and take her in my arms. But I didn't even dare look at her right then. Each night, after walking her home, I peeked at her pages. Nothing new. One afternoon during this period Florence took my hand and led me to my guest room, which we had not used before. Afterward she said, "I fear I am only your guest, aren't I?" I could say nothing. "But let's not worry about it," she sighed, embracing me. "It doesn't matter." My whole emotional system went haywire and stayed that way for hours.

Then one night I read:

> *You were often so sad. Or sadly quiet. I remember one exquisitely vibrant spring day, very sunny, and how you threw open all the windows! Somewhere The Fifth Dimension was singing "Up, Up, and Away" and I thought I actually spotted a red balloon high in the air. I wanted to say, "Tell me. Tell me. Tell me." Young as I was, I suspected something was terribly wrong with your life, that winning anything, at your age, was going to be so difficult—*

I say it's possible I had a need to compete with Florence. I remember—in this context—Lou sending me a short note. "Why," he wrote, "do you include your business card whenever you send us one of those inane Father's Day or Mother's Day things? Is that a joke we are not getting?" Of course it was a joke. Or mainly a joke. Were they, like Merl Hurst, losing their marbles? Or was I? Or was he turning the joke around on me?

On July 4th I set up a grill on the Bastion deck so that Juanita could cook our burgers and corn on the cob out there. The Fords were planning to arrive the night before, but something came up at the last minute to keep them in Paris. Later I built a bonfire on the beach and, against Riverside Association rules, the boys and I sent some rockets and flares downriver toward Little Spit Island, where nobody lived—the ground there, happily, was too wet for houses but perfect for turtles and snakes. Blanche, instead of complaining to the Association, joined us and even contributed a shaker of iced gin. Lulu also came round, with a bag of marshmallows. Lillian strolled past and waved, calling out, "I'd *love* to join you all but I have a silly engagement!" Giles and Quinn and Lulu went swimming and

Florence, looking especially beautiful and flyaway, danced along the wet sand. I tended the fire. Afterwards we all sat around it and roasted marshmallows on twigs. It may have been the best time I ever had on that beach. Juanita and Blanche got into a discussion of old movie stars. "Of course Rita Hayworth had Spanish blood! That's why she was so beautiful!" "But how could she marry that shrimp Mickey Rooney?" "Did she?" Florence and I took a slow walk under the stars to Lighthouse Landing, and ended up at my house. She gave me a part of her wispy wrap to hold, then slowly twirled away from me until she stood naked. I was about to fall on my knees and tell her I loved her when she announced that she would be leaving Riverside in August. "Where are you going?" "Oh well, we haven't got that far yet."

Some time after Quill and his mother took that wrong turn, which they did not know was wrong, I told the producers of a project that eventually came into being as "The Ridge" (which title I can claim credit for) that, yes, I would be delighted to sign on. I knew I would not be delighted and remember laughing until my eyes watered. This, too, is a joke: Lillian especially enjoys watching her taped copies of "The Ridge" in preparing for our sport. Now that I am available again.

Beáta

So. Here I am with this American book to translate for Triomphe, the French publisher. Fate, how funny. Yes, yes, I had a choice. There were other projects. But I picked this one. I hate short stories! I don't even read them for pleasure. Except now and then, to pass the time. The somber stories of Bruno Schulz, for example, when I feel moody. Okay—and Isaac Singer if I want to be charmed. Jean Rhys if I think I am attracted to a man who is no good and I need a bitter laugh.

Now, a different laugh. My old friend G., through this book, returns to Paris, and he has *me* to make him presentable! The truth is I am still a little angry with him. Yes, after all these years. I wanted to visit America. But how, without a visa? They won't give me one at the embassy because—enormous fear!—I will go to New York and no doubt find a fabulous job paying thousands a week and prevent some poor American millionaire from adding to his pockets. And of course I will want to stay forever, yes? Perhaps the poor millionaire will starve! All because Beáta Wnuk, the Polish refugee from Paris, wants to earn a dollar and buy a nice pair of shoes on Fifth Avenue, maybe a hat as well, like Garbo's. Ah, never mind.

So, okay, I choose G.'s book. Work is work. Also, I admit it, the dedication—*To B.*—intrigues me.

Foreign Stories, he calls it. Not an especially attractive title. I read the first story. It's about this Slovak poet, Pavol Hudák by name, who is a pickpocket. I have known a few interesting Slovak guys—well, maybe two—anyway, this Pavol seems appealing. Not stuck on himself, not look at me, the *artiste*! I have to laugh at how he goes gaga on the street stumbling into the beauty, Slavka. Who picks *his* pocket. Her technique, he discovers, is as good as his own! Okay, they get together, become a team. They also become lovers, of course. They make so much money stealing from rich tourists that they buy an apartment and marry. Now listen to him. He says they decide to have children—they will teach them all they know about picking pockets and retire into a nice old age, letting the kids do the work! Bah, he is turning foolish—I smell a stupid fairy tale.

So, Slavka becomes pregnant. Little Pavol is born. But something is wrong with this baby—he won't open his left hand. They caress him, bathe him, sing to him—nothing will induce the child to open that hand. They consult a hag of a country woman who is said to have old wisdom. She tells them to dangle a piece of gold over the boy. Pavol does this—one of Slavka's earrings. The baby's eyes fix on the earring. He reaches for it, slowly opening his clenched fist. Guess what's in that fist already? The midwife's wedding ring! Hah. Some joke.

At the end, Pavol the poet recites one of his poems.

Really. You saw a hawk there
swooping without mercy
on yellow hens…

That's life
diving head down
on to childhood.

As a poem, I suppose it's okay. But how does it relate to the silly story? Never mind, I am no literary genius, only a simple translator.

The next story is about a party in the Rue Dufoin, near the Place des Vosges. I was there! I recognize everyone—why not? He doesn't even bother to change their names—G. himself, Mel, the model Bibi, and of course our bold thief Gimenez who was crazy for her—all of them, yes, yes, Gwenna, too, that tall Venus from the Lido, who met her rich husband at the party—but they are not interesting, those two plastic actors, forget them. As for Gimenez, who strongly resembled a real actor, Charles Aznavour—I can still hear him apologize to Bibi for being late. Saying he had to find a prostitute for his nephew. Someone *suitable*. "It's the boy's sixteenth birthday, you see. He is visiting from the country, is quite innocent of course, so I must first determine that the woman will be sympathetic, yes? After all, Bibi, I have a duty as the boy's uncle." Bibi understands. Poor thing is crazy in return for this Gimenez, who only weeks before breaks into her apartment, sees all the nude photos of her on the walls, and must return, when she is home, to introduce himself! G. is very good, I admit, at capturing them. Me, however, he does not even mention in this story. Perhaps I was cool to him that night. I can be very cool, it's true. What absurdities we are sometimes—so full of desire, so bloodless.

Will this be a book devoted to thieves and their beautiful women? Thieves bore me. Beautiful women, too, if they are stupid.

Contrary to expectations, the third story has my interest at once. It's about a woman who wears her hair exactly as I do, shaped like a helmet, is very particular about her bath, her lotions, and whose lover is a blind composer, a man with weak lungs. All of these details belong to *my* life. But does G. say so? Does he say this is Beáta? No, he calls her Mona! A woman who hides behind her rouges and powders. He didn't even know my Alonzo!

I throw this hateful book down. If I still kept birds, I would tear out the pages and line the cage's floor with them. But I gave up birds when I lost Alonzo. I had to. The songs were too sad.

Now I am sad. Why does G. do this to me? He, too, is a thief. Yes, of course I have some vanity. Who doesn't? But I also have some good things inside. It was in my heart where I was hiding, nowhere else. This Mona, whoever she is, simply wants to dress up in black silk and gaze at herself in the mirror. What does she want!

I wanted to go to New York only because Alonzo wanted to go there, to play his music where the great Ellington played. "Beáta," he would say, "this is my desire, to take the A train—yes?—and to smell Fifth Avenue, Harlem." When I listened to Alonzo play, I was not aware of a man playing a piano, only of being alone. Of course he loved Ellington's "In My Solitude." I am talking about a music that is part of your breath, that can breathe *for* you. No, no—no one can put this feeling of solitude into words. But I could embrace it with

Alonzo's music. We were alike, he and I, dreamers, orphans. If I was particular about my hair, my scent, it was for him. Such small gifts, really. As for Mona, after *her* lover dies, she goes almost immediately to her bath. Surrounding herself with candles and incense. It's a hideous ending to a hideous story.

Why I pick up G.'s book and read the next story, I don't know. It's called "The Proposal," and my god, I am stunned. He hides nothing. A Pole named Beáta, living in Paris, wishes to visit New York, because her dead lover Alonzo, a Gypsy, had wanted to go there. But she can't get a visa. Then she meets Mel, an American, and sees an opportunity. After all, Mel declares he loves her, and she thinks he means it. Yes, I thought he did. He says he will find a way.

Time passes. Mel is very clever, a man so smooth with his gestures, his pearl-gray eyes. What does he do for a living? She doesn't know. But one day he tells her, "I mentioned to G. your interest in coming to the States with me next summer." Mel looks at his hands. Then he says, "He has offered to marry you." She says, "What are you talking about?" He says, "You know, just to get the visa for you—as a favor to me, nothing more." She says, "Have you lost your senses, Mel?" He says, "It will work, Beáta." She says, "It will *not* work." He says, "But why not?" She says nothing. She is too angry to speak. She thought he knew her at least a little. She gathers up her few things from his apartment and stuffs them in her bag. As she is leaving, he says, "If I could be sure the authorities would not look into my business, *I* would marry you. But they *will* look." She slams the door behind her.

The next day Mel finds her at her friend Estelle's. She has no word for him except "Vanish!" His eyes are penitent, but she is a stone. He goes. Good! He was a big mistake after Alonzo.

G. shows up. With flowers. Oh my god.

"I don't want your flowers."

He stands there. Is he touched in the head?

"You are such a cold man, you give me chicken skin."

"I didn't mean to insult you, Beáta."

"What then?"

"I meant to be useful."

"Useful. Like a notary? A shoe?"

He looks ashamed. Good! Now maybe he will take his flowers and his false proposal and leave her be. But standing there in the doorway he is telling her that he was recently divorced, by a woman he lived with for almost fifteen years. One day she confesses she has taken a lover and plans to go away with him. She moves out. A week later she returns, saying she made a mistake. G. tries to take her back, but something, a mean spirit, a smallness, prevents him. He looks at Beáta and says he wronged his wife. Beáta is confused, wondering what this story has to do with her? The next thing she knows she is accepting his flowers. He turns away. That is the last she sees of him.

I put *Foreign Stories* on my shelf. I go out. To breathe. To calm my heart. I feel naked, exposed, robbed, and mixed up. But finally I know one thing for certain: what happens afterwards belongs only to me . . .

Mel is gone. G. is gone. Spring comes, thank god. I can feel hopeful again. But I don't. Everywhere I step, on the boulevards, in the *bois*, it is sad. Often I think of Alonzo at his piano, of the birthmark on his back shaped like a wave, and with each memory I almost drown. Why is cruelty so effortless?

One afternoon as autumn approaches, I can't believe my eyes. There, on a bench in the Tuileries, is Gimenez! He looks so terrible, so wretched, I forget my troubles a moment. I stop. His eyes are like a dog's without hope.

"It's you," I say.

Finally his eyes focus.

"I know you," he says.

"Perhaps recognize. You don't know me."

He shrugs. He needs soap and water, a shave. Bah! He needs everything, this bum, this *clochard*.

He gestures for me to sit down.

"No, thank you."

"As you wish."

But why don't I leave? I don't know. It is astonishing to see a man formerly so confident now so reduced.

"You are none of my concern," I say. "In fact, you disgust me."

Again, he shrugs. "What does it matter?"

"You make me furious."

"I'm sorry."

"Why don't you clean yourself?"

"Perhaps later."

"You probably have no money."

"That's true," he admits.

"You probably wish only for wine—to forget everything."

He looks toward the flowerbeds lining the walk. Soon the flowers will be lying down.

"No," he says. "I wish to remember. My memories are my . . . life."

To be honest, his condition affects me in a curious way. I sit on the bench, but not too close to him. For a long time we are silent. What happens to people that they should fall apart? Finally, I say, "So—you have memories. But where are you? Look at yourself."

He sighs. "I am rescued during those moments."

"Rescued, how romantic."

"Recalling a loveliness. A certain woman . . ."

"Bibi, for instance."

"Ah, Bibi . . ."

He remembers stealing into her empty apartment. Being so overcome by the photos of her on the walls, he had to take off his clothes and lie in her bed, smelling her scent. "But later, when we met, I apologized. We grew close. Everything became—I don't know the word. Wonderful perhaps."

I point out that his appearance suggests otherwise.

"Life is tragic," he says. "I wished only to be with her and to be happy. Alas, I went out one night, to my old trade, and was caught. I had lost my nerve, distracted as I was by . . ."

"By what?"

"Who can say exactly?"

"A pity."

"Yes. I lost Bibi as well. This was far more painful than jail."

"You went to jail?"

"She sent me a letter. To say she was with a painter now, Danosi the Hungarian, a well-respected figure."

"So you get what you deserve," I say.

"No doubt."

"A waste. You are still not very old."

"I feel ancient."

I tell him if he cleaned himself and got a decent haircut, maybe things would improve.

"You torture me."

"A few things are possible."

He looks at me with those sad-dog eyes. The truth is, they are quite beautiful. I say, "Come. I know a good shop where you can begin."

He protests, but when I make up my mind I am difficult to stop.

At the shop they shave him and cut his hair. What an improvement! The girl there whispers to me, "Aznavour! Do you see it?" I whisper back, "A little, maybe." I take him to another shop, for some new clothes, then to the apartment I share with Estelle, where he bathes. Estelle comes home just as he finishes dressing.

"Oh, la-la, what have we here?" she says.

"Charles Aznavour," I say.

"My god, it's true!" she laughs.

Gimenez bows, kisses our hands. "Angels!" he says.

So. Life continues. One thing leads to another. The heart opens again. He is very tender, almost shy. It is like I must teach *him*!

While Estelle and I are at work, he cleans the apartment, brings fresh flowers, prepares our meals. One night he gives me a gorgeous pearl necklace.

"It was just waiting for a neck, for skin, like yours."

"But how?"

"My strength, Beáta, has come back, thanks to you."

It's true, I am delighted with the pearls. But I also feel strange by them. My heart is nervous. Nor is the necklace my only present—he brings me a gold bracelet, exquisite scarves. Estelle receives nice gifts, too. Soon he is talking about a separate apartment for us—"so poor Estelle can breathe a little."

I say to him, "Please, enough." I tell him I go back and forth between happiness and worry. "For months I am like this. You must stop stealing. Look at my fingers, this new rash."

He says, "Beáta, Beáta," like he does . . . like he really is Aznavour, singing.

"I don't want these gifts!"

"But what can I do?" he says.

What can he do? He can do many things.

"You can be a waiter. A lovely waiter."

"A pimp perhaps."

"You are handsome enough to be in films. Why not? Everyone says so."

"Don't be foolish," he says. "I am what I am."

"But you can be more!"

"More? Look at me—I am full!"

"We can always be more."

He embraces me. Says I am his little cabbage.

"What if I suggested that you would make a very presentable father?"

"No, no, I would make a terrible father. Anything but that."

"But I have seen you with children, how you charm them. In the *bois* on Sundays, everywhere we go. You charm the parents, too."

"Only for a little amusement. Also"—he takes my ugly hands, looks at me with those pretty eyes—"it presents an opportunity."

"An opportunity?"

"Of course. Don't you see?"

He winks, and in a moment I do see. My god, I have been with him when he steals.

Now he is all smiles. "If we put a small cushion under your coat, perhaps the situation would be even better."

I am dizzy. He is laughing. "Or perhaps you really are pregnant and we don't have to pretend. Are you, Beáta?"

I tell him no.

"Oh, well," he says, kissing my cheek.

And a week or so later, it *is* true, I am not.

Now? All these years since? I am approaching fifty. I live with my present companion, the happy Leo, in our decent apartment full of light. We can see the Eiffel Tower in the distance, though I see it more than he does because he travels so much. Which may be just as well. An honest businessman like Leo, to tell the truth, is quite predictable. But I welcome his company, and he does not put bruises on my heart. Almost every day I wake up knowing how I will proceed. There is much to be said for this kind of life.

I am sorry G. is not here to see how this is so, and perhaps to write one more story for his book, if he could find it in his heart.

My Mother's Story

On the morning of September 1, 1901, a Polish youth named Jacek Prus arrived at Ellis Island, moved quickly, miraculously through the procedure for immigrants that same day, and pausing in the city only long enough to sharpen his hunger by admiring the sausages and hams hanging behind a window, boarded a train not for Buffalo, his original destination, but for Detroit. He was sixteen. He was led by a woman named Eva, in her twenties, also an immigrant, who promised him a good job. She possessed written directions, dollars, icy blue eyes and a letter of invitation to America from a captain on the Detroit police force. But the woman wanted everything clear: she had befriended Jacek Prus on board the ship which brought them from Europe for only one reason: his large, fearless presence would keep away wolves. At first he thought she meant this literally. He had been trained as a blacksmith in the country and knew about wolves. And after all, they were heading for the American West. She herself was an actress, she told him, and carried two photos to prove it. One showed her in the folk costume of the Tatra Mountains; the other showed her as a sprite before a curtain. In a play by Shakespeare, my mother said.

Of course neither Jack Prus nor this Eva was officially Polish. Their papers said Austrian, because Austria ruled where they had been born, the southern part of what had *been* Poland; but if any stranger on the train had persisted hard enough, and if Eva had felt like telling, she would have said, as she did once, fiercely, that they were a son and a daughter of Polonia! She knew a little English and was speaking for them both, which was fine with Jacek. He had Polish, German, some Hungarian—that was it. She also knew a little French. She was very clever, and very strong inside, though physically quite small, and Jacek considered himself lucky. When the train stopped periodically, they bought bread or apples or cheese from station vendors—once pickled herring from a Polish Jew; this last, for Jacek, was an important moment somewhere in Pennsylvania, because suddenly here in the morning sun, eating a delicious fish, Eva was looking up at him as if for the first time, her face flushed the color of apricots. He thought that life—his life—was now beginning, that he would always be rich in ways like this moment, and he was ready.

This was how my mother's story usually began. I remember the first time she told it. I was in my forties, she herself almost seventy, and I was stunned. Because Jacek Prus and this Eva—whose last name my mother never knew—were my real grandparents, she said. Not Antoni and Eliza Pisarek. "Dear Eliza and Tony, they only saved me as long as they could from the fire," she said, looking off at nothing, and finally turning her large unblinking eyes on me. Her eyes were blue—and yes, rather icy, but not so cold as that word suggests. Then she asked if I would please bring her a certain leather box from the bottom drawer of her vanity. I did. She opened it on her lap, slowly, caressingly, and brought forth, from under a lace hanky, the two brown photos of her real mother, the actress Eva with no last name.

I sometimes look at these pictures now resting on the shelf above my desk and see in them very little, if anything, of my mother; other times I see her in them completely—a woman possessing a costume, directions, money and a last name no more important than a flower that, once its bloom is gone, needs to be thrown out.

My mother, also, was an actress. And there was a time—my early boyhood—when I thought she was a real actress and any day I would see her in the movies. Musicals. With Fred Astaire, with George Raft, her idols. How she whirled around in a new dress, how she smelled! Then a kiss on my cheek and out the door, and that night returning to our apartment to wake me with chocolate, T-bone steaks, nylons, flowers. And more—the story of her huge success. "They *loved* me, Jackie. They couldn't applaud loud enough. Oh, I tell you, soldiers are the best. The best!" The Second World War was on and so was my mother, singing and dancing at the USO on Woodward Avenue, at the Eagle Club in Hamtramck, anywhere she was needed. "They do need me, Jackie. Next month, next *week* they could be dead. They need to have fun!"

My mother was in her twenties then—her glory time—and carrying around what she waited more than forty years to tell me: that Jacek Prus showed up one Sunday on the Pisarek front porch and wept, and went away, and a week later returned to change her life.

"Grandpa Tony slapped him. Oh yes. Knocked him down, this strange handsome man in a fine suit, and cursed him in Polish, and then, oh Jackie, he got down on his knees and embraced him. Grandma pulled me into the house. We had just come from church. She had a chicken on the stove. I didn't understand what was happening, and she said to me, 'Helen, please sit. It's time to eat.' Can you see it! This handsome well-dressed man on the porch who was back for a second time, who all week they had been telling me must have been drunk, and now Pa is slapping him and hugging him, and poor Ma is telling me to eat my chicken."

The way my mother told her story was not orderly. She would begin orderly enough, with the arrival at Ellis Island, the train trip to Michigan, then she would suddenly leap years ahead, or go off to the side, or stop in the middle of a sentence, look at me for a long moment, then ask, "Jackie, what would you do if you had *enough?*"

On her seventieth birthday she would not answer her phone or open the door. The best I could get was an almost bodiless hand waving from her bedroom window upstairs—a hand waving me away. I knew this gesture. It meant she was fine, leave her alone, she was busy, didn't I have anything better to do than stand down there like a fool? Any of these—or all.

She was either fourteen, fifteen or sixteen (she was not consistent) when Jacek Prus showed himself, and although Tony Pisarek embraced him that second time and walked with him to the sidewalk and lingered with him there, both their heads nodding as if in agreement, weeks went by during which neither he nor Eliza would acknowledge they knew anything about him. Finally, getting nowhere with her timid questions, my mother made a bold move. She said to them that she had seen the man waiting for her outside school. Not only seen him but spoke with him. It was all a lie, but it got results.

"Tony exploded," my mother said, "and called him a gangster, a hoodlum, a no-good bum. Was *that* what I wanted? To know someone like Jack Prus! Who stole from decent people! Then he took off his belt and let me have it, Jackie. But as God is my witness, I never felt a thing. Poor Tony, *he* suffered though. He went right away to the priest to ask forgiveness, then he asked mine.

"I said I forgave him. Then Tony looked at me as if I might strike *him*. 'What did Jack Prus tell you?' My God, I was caught. What would such a handsome, nicely dressed man say to me? Suddenly I knew. I said, 'The truth.' Meaning that he was not a drunk—and that's all I meant. But what a brilliant answer! Tony and Eliza sat together on the sofa, their heads so low I was delirious. I felt sad, yes, because they were sad, but the mystery surrounding my sadness, surrounding everything, thrilled me.

"Drama, Jackie, you should have studied drama in college instead of that other thing. Mathe*ma*tics. I hated all those cold numbers. Multiply, divide and carry. I'll tell you the truth, honey, whenever I think of numbers all I see are the sisters at Holy Redeemer, those pale little faces in all that coarse brown wool. Chalk on their fingers, sour breath. One after another saying Helen this and Helen that. No, no—where's the music, the romance!"

The first man in my mother's life who meant anything to me—and he meant a lot—was Oskar Rau. He was a mounted policeman. He patrolled his beat on a big chestnut gelding named Buck. How could I ever forget Oskar and Buck and riding up and down our street, me holding the saddle horn and later feeding Buck apples? And putting on Oskar's tall boots?

"Oskar Rau?" my mother would say toward the end of her life. "What made you think of him?" Then she'd wave her hand as if a fly were bothering her.

"He let me try on his boots."

"Jackie, don't be foolish. You were a baby when Oskar was there. Why you keep bringing him up, I don't know."

But what she *did* know in those last years was that Oskar Rau never uttered a bad word about her father. Not one. Everybody else hated him, she said. How could a man who had made something of himself—educated himself, learned refinement, became what you were supposed to become in this country—how could he be so despised that almost no one came to his funeral? she wanted to know. And then would answer her own question. "Jealousy, Jackie. Plain and simple. Your grandfather had style."

"Money and clothes, you mean."

"Of course!"

"How did he die?" I asked her once.

She changed the subject.

I should make clear that this story about my mother's true parents was one that *she* hauled out over the last dozen years of her life. If when we got together I would try to initiate something about Jack or Eva, she'd say oh Jackie not now, or please let's just have a nice dinner, or she'd simply ignore my questions and tell me about her day at the health spa she belonged to. And when she did feel like hauling it out, the timing was always crazy: I was either getting up to leave or only stopping by for a minute on my way somewhere else. And when I say she *hauled* out the story, I am referring to the more recent tellings, when it really did seem as if she were carrying forth something physically heavy. Of course every time she told it, there was always a new detail or two, or at least a serious amending of previous information.

I should also mention that she started telling her story soon after Eliza Pisarek—whom I never stopped thinking of as my real grandmother—passed away, at ninety-four, peacefully in her bed at Our Lady's Rest. Grandpa Tony had been gone for years, buried when I was eight and only a vague memory to me—mainly that of a nut-brown man at his butcher's block, cutting meat, or in a dark suit kneeling in his front pew at Holy Redeemer, fingering his rosary. I was very fond of Eliza, at whose house, before she got too old for it, I spent many a Sunday eating her baked chicken or roast pork or the very special duck with plums at Christmas time and answering her eager questions about school, summer camp, college, my work. My mother almost always had something else to do on those Sundays, but would give me a plant or a bouquet of flowers to deliver. When Eliza moved to Our Lady, however, my mother would find the time to go see her, especially after the poor soul lost her sight.

In all those years, Eliza never once indicated that my mother was anything but her daughter. "My busy Helen," she would say. "Always on the go—even as a little girl." Smiling proudly that "her whirlwind, her miracle" had produced such a fine son—a teacher!

On my mother's seventy-fifth birthday I took her to dinner at the Roostertail on the Detroit River—her choice. Some boisterous yachting types gathered at a large table not far away got her attention, particularly a lobster-colored man in lots of silver buttons and gold braid who seemed to be their leader. She started off on how a man in uniform, especially a *blue* uniform, always raised her spirits, and asked if I would please go over and tell the gentleman in the beautiful jacket how much she admired him. She was drinking her second or third glass of champagne; we hadn't been served our meal yet, and because she was always watching her weight it was likely she hadn't eaten much that day so she could splurge that night. I said no, I would not, and passed her the plate of breads and cheeses. Inhaling deeply, she looked at me over her wine glass for about a minute, perfectly still. It was a pose she used to indicate a package of emotions—shock, disappointment, hurt, glamorous bravery in the face of insult—and finally she said, "You are just like Oskar. Stiff as a board. No wonder you can't keep a wife."

I said nothing. In her convoluted way she really meant that Oskar couldn't keep *her.* My wife Emma, she well knew, had been killed years before in a car accident. After a long silence, during which we sat there like strangers, she reached over and touched my sleeve, her expression—I knew it like a book—saying she was sorry. As I always did at such moments, I nodded and smiled for her.

Toward the end of that evening, however, at her door, while she searched in her purse for the key, I wanted to say something. I didn't know how to put it exactly, but it had to do with some very old business, and with telling her, once and for all, that it didn't matter to me who my father was; if she still insisted he was a "a handsome pilot killed in the war"—a man about whom she could not really talk because it hurt too much—which is what she told me when I was eleven, and repeated once more, in tears, when I was eighteen—fine, that account was good enough for me. I wanted her to know that I only thought it was Oskar Rau because he was nice to us over the years, or tried to be, even showing up at my high school graduation sick as he was—and no, I never asked him if he was really my father, as she accused me of doing, and no, he never went behind her back to give me that idea. When she turned to kiss me good night, thanking me for the birthday party, I wanted to say what was on my mind, then, with an accompanying jaunty bow and tip of my hat, with some little playful move—her style—to show that I could take this ancient subject or leave it, I wanted to add, "So, all kidding aside, kiddo, you're off the hook. We're both off it—and good riddance, no?"

But I only said, my style, "Good, I'm glad you had a nice time."

In a life almost too full, she had taken five husbands, counting Oskar Rau, but not the pilot, and God knows how many "companions." I received none of their names. I was christened Jack Prus II, and according to her, Jack Prus I was the first person, after the doctor and nurse, to see me. (She herself was "out like a light.") And he was present to witness my first step, first Christmas tree and first birthday. Moreover, he gave me, as he had given my mother, the fabulous story of his life, though I wouldn't remember a word of it, she said. Then one wet, miserable morning his body was found on Belle Isle; he had been shot several times and his hands chopped off.

It's true, he was handsome. In his photo on the shelf beside Eva he even looks, as my mother insisted he did, like a prince. Head imperially up and tilted slightly back, dark eyes giving you a moment of his valuable time. He made his money in real estate, she said. Though if you listened to Marty Myron, her next-to-last and shortest-kept husband, Jack Prus made his money breaking fingers. Marty himself had had to knock a little sense in certain people now and then—but years ago, not recently, he was quick to add—"so I guess I know what I'm talking about." Marty Myron—he cut down the last name form Myronovich—was a man who shaved twice a day and filled up a room with his cologne. He had a tailor, a bookie, a new car every six months ("smell *this* one," he liked to say), and every winter he took my mother to Florida. When she divorced him after three years, her only comment to me about it was, "Yes, it's true, as he said, your grandfather's hands were missing. It's also true that you can find someone like Marty Myron any day in the comic books."

Why she married him in the first place is anybody's guess. But here's a good one: he was just the opposite of her previous husband, who was a nice guy. That was her pattern: a man like Oskar Rau followed by a man like Marty Myron. There is no point in describing all five—or any of those in-betweeners, who were basically like chauffeurs. The last husband, of course, was a sweet fellow—a widower named Tommy Marshall—who had owned some hardware stores, retired, and spent a lot of time building bird houses and elaborate model sailing ships for his grandchildren. (He gave me a gorgeous schooner.) Though my mother made fun of this, and of Tommy, it was mainly good-natured fun that he seemed to enjoy. He called her "my Geritol fix," and took her dancing. He *was* a good dancer, she said. And I'm pretty sure that Tommy was the only husband she ever took to see Grandma Eliza. She was with him for almost a decade, her longest marriage. I think she was truly sorry when he died. I was too.

Then—it seemed to start the next day—came that period in which there was just the two of us, plus her revelation. I never knew how to feel about that story. For lots of reasons. One had to do with the way she hoarded it all those years, and then released only parts at a time, often changing details, or even, at the last minute, changing them preposterously. Like the night she said, "Oh yes, he was an educated man, your grandfather. An engineer. Trained in a university in Europe, not some podunk city college." "I thought you said he was a blacksmith," I said. "Don't be ignorant, Jackie. Look at his picture. Is that the face of a blacksmith?" Or the night she said, "Your grandparents were like Romeo and Juliet—running away together like teenagers, like flames! My God, Jackie, can you imagine? Vienna, Paris, New York, all those bright candles in the windows lighting their way!" True, she was taking some pills—for high blood pressure, a touch of arthritis—but otherwise, her doctor told me, she was still sharp as a tack.

On the night of her eightieth birthday, which we spent quietly at her house, I said, "I wonder what became of Eva and that police captain who had sent her the letter of invitation? You don't have to tell me."

"Cops. Show me a good cop and I'll show you a miracle," she said.

"Oskar was a good cop."

"Oskar was a little boy in big pants."

"Why have you always been so hard on Oskar?"

"He was dense—he didn't get it."

"Didn't get what?"

"Jackie, the way you keep harping on that poor man is pathetic. Please, don't be a math teacher with me. Go home or take the guest room, it's late. We need our beauty sleep—who knows what tomorrow will bring."

At my mother's funeral mass there was the priest, an altar boy, Mrs. Witucki, who cleaned her house, and me. There was also, in the back pew, a bent little woman in black who, the priest told me later, came to all the funerals at Holy Redeemer. But only the four of us went to the cemetery. The leaves were starting to turn color; as the priest murmured his farewell Latin over the casket, I thought about not getting it—whatever *it* was—and had a moment when I wanted to call out, "Tell me!"

I buried her beside Antoni and Eliza Pisarek. However, Jack Prus' plot is not far away. Nor is Oskar Rau's and my Emma's. Tommy Marshall lies, according to my mother's wishes, beside his first wife across town. I have no idea where Eva the actress is resting. It's bizarre and sad to think so, but possible of course that she never existed, or never quite existed. The brown photos above my desk could be of anyone who put on a certain folk costume and a certain gauzy shift and stood still long enough, gazing straight ahead, to have her image captured and admired and held close.

One In a Million

Came out of a deep doze seeing two large white houses connected by a kind of cage. Felt weighted down. Didn't know where he was or whose car he was sitting in all alone. Had a funny dream that wasn't so funny. Adele was mad as hell at him for pretending to be her first husband Chester, who flew fighter planes in the South Pacific and wore a chest full of bright ribbons in the framed photo on her bureau and then came home in a box. "Take the cake, God damn fake!" *Then* she got mad at him for stealing her second husband's job at the college. Didn't steal anybody's dumb job, got it on his own, thank you very much. No wonder the second husband keeled over. Waxing floors, scrubbing toilets. Worst thing was, that wasn't no dream. What a crummy job. But he did it or she'd kick him out. He didn't want to be out in the cold. Liked her warm Kansas City house, liked her too, those nights they'd have a few and she'd get all flirty and let him sleep in her bed. Then when he learned that his boy had grown up to be a phenom rookie pitcher for the Chicago White Sox, making out like a bandit, well! So long, my black janitor friends. And you, my friend Adele, better be sweeter to me a little more often.

All of this crowded the old man's head and then a space cleared: he was sitting in Mary Beth Urquhart's Mercedes in Peculiar, a little spin from K.C., come to see Edith. Why did he ask Mary Beth to bring him here? It was nuts. But his boy was dead. And big shot Freddy Boylen said that he—the blood-true father!—was not welcome at the ranch anymore. The old man's head hurt; things were falling apart fast. He got out of the car. Boylen would see to it that Daryl's money would never come to his lawful father. Nor would crazy Edith's, even though she took his name, so why was he here? And Adele would finally kick him out. As he walked up one street, down another, such thoughts hounded the old man, their hot breath on his neck as if they were mad, hateful dogs. Did he deserve this?

A cemetery. It would be quiet in here. But moving among the old stones, he heard the raspy outraged cries of crows, followed by thunder, by rain. His head kept pounding. Now he was in a new part of the cemetery: headstones with fresh-cut names, grass bright green—almost unreal—no ancient trees with fat wild roots pushing things over. Then he saw their names, side by side: *Edith Penney Onstott 1909— . . . Daryl James Onstott Jr. 1950—*. He began to cry—he was truly alone, not a single real relation available to him—sobbing, wiping a rain-soaked coat sleeve across his eyes. He cursed them, especially her. She'd seduced him! Taken his freedom! His youth! As he shouted, he knew in a small cold corner of his head that this was not entirely true, but his partial confusion angered him even more, sent his fury to greater and greater heights. He had screamed himself hoarse, was bent over, brain blackened, when Mary Beth rescued him.

He sat in the Mercedes wrapped in a blanket. She was explaining: he'd fallen asleep on the ride down from K.C., and she found where Edith lived by calling somebody on her cell phone (he wouldn't mind having one of those gizmos himself), and that's where she was, in the place, actually talking to people about him and Edith, when he stumbled off. He hurt less and less, now that he knew he wouldn't have to go see the sick old woman, who wouldn't know him anyway, would she? But what did Mary Beth mean about the people in there talking about Edith and *him?*

"So under the circumstances," Mary Beth was saying, "this is not a good time to visit."

"No."

"Edith is having an especially rough day, and you, my goodness, how lucky I *found* you."

"Think nothing of it."

"We can come back next week perhaps."

"Or even later since she's sick."

"The young assistant I spoke with, Miss Gillespie, says that you have been so good about visiting."

The old man jerked his head at her. Hell was she talking about? He'd never stepped one foot in that dump. But he kept quiet, trying to think. Then he said:

"Those tombstones. For Edith and my boy . . ."

"Yes, they're new. That's where Miss Gillespie thought you might be when I saw you weren't in the car."

"I mean . . ." What did he mean?

"She also told me that Mr. Boylen, executor of your son's estate, has been in touch with them. I've actually met Boylen. It was very brief, of course, just a few hours after the . . . the terrible incident. Has Mr. Boylen contacted you yet?"

"He's in charge of my boy's will?"

"Well, he's in charge of seeing that your son's will is carried out. You do understand what an executor does?"

"Sure, sort of. Don't you?"

Mary Beth smiled. "I should. I'm an attorney."

His eyes narrowed. Then, "No kidding? Gee, and you're so . . . nice too."

Mary Beth laughed, she couldn't help it. "Thank you."

"I'll tell you another thing"—he felt revived, replenished: something really good could come from this—"it's a lucky, lucky day, Mary Beth."

Back in K.C. she dropped him off in front of the red brick house on Walnut Street. It was still raining. She gave him her business card. She also offered her umbrella, but he said, "No, no, I wouldn't think of it." He got nimbly out, remembering just in the nick about flying Mustangs and getting shot down; he took a few limping steps, turned, tipped his boater. Her heart went out to him.

Driving home, she remembered the conversation she'd overheard in Volker Park, between him and the woman he called Adele who wore a fox on her shoulders. She also remembered what Miss Gillespie had said about his faithful visits to Peculiar.

Adele was not happy.

"*Where* have you been?"

"Out."

She glared at him. "Am I stupid?"

He slipped into the bathroom, had to piss like a racehorse. But sitting down—sitting made it easier for him these days—he could produce only dribbles, hearing Adele haul out the usual names when she was drinking.

"Scumbag! Fake! Dirty old—"

"Give a man who's hurting some peace, for God's sake!"

Hateful pain suddenly raced through his rectum. He groaned.

"Oh, stop it!" Adele said in disgust. "You make me sick!"

Sharp at first, like a knife cut, the pain was now a steady burn. Like that time years ago in Chicago when they caught him in an alley, those rats, and ripped away his good shirt and cut him with razors across his chest. Because he hadn't paid up. Fouled his pants too, he was so scared. Next time, they said, his thumbs came off.

"Adele, please."

"No, no. Please is all done with. I want you out of my house tonight!"

The vodka was talking. He needed a drink, himself, ached for one. Another knife into his rectum, taking his breath. His mouth went dry. His knees—how bony and blue veined they were—began to tremble.

"Did you hear me, useless old man!"

He dialed Mary Beth's number.

"May I tell her who's calling?"

"Mr. Daryl W. Onstott Sr. Of this city."

He waited. Then her cheerful voice:

"Mr. Onstott, how are you today?"

"Well, can we talk sometime? In private? The truth is, I don't know where to turn."

A little after five, they met at the fountain in Volker Park. He was wearing his usual colorful sport coat, straw boater, and spectators; his face, however, seemed drained.

"Oh, Mr. Onstott—" Her sympathetic voice brought tears to his eyes.

"I'm sick, I guess."

"Yes, I can see you're not your usual—"

He cut her off. "I mean, it's complicated."

"Tell me how I can help."

With his problems on the toilet? With Adele? Boylen?

"I miss my boy."

"Yes. Yes. Of course—I know you do."

"They won't let me come to his ranch in Wyoming no more. And what if"—his eyes jumped—"he *left* it to me?"

"Who won't let you go there?"

"I don't know. The management."

"Has anyone put anything in writing to you?"

"No. Absolutely not."

"Then why do you say they—whoever they are—won't let you go there?"

"I—I mean—it's just a, you know, in my gut." He was wringing his hands.

The poor man: his son's murder, his wife's illness. No wonder he was feeling sick, confused.

"Mr. Onstott, where can I call you tomorrow?"

"Not at home. Oh, no. My landlady gets upset when people call me. Could we meet here again?"

"Is your landlady Adele?"

"She's not feeling too hot either these days."

"Let me drive you home."

"No, no—fresh air, the walk—I feel better afterwards. In fact, I'm feeling better all the time."

Next morning Mary Beth phoned the Big Win Dude Ranch. Red Barber answered.

"You may remember me—Mary Beth Urquhart? My sister Alice and I and her two teenaged daughters were guests that terrible week when Daryl was shot. We in fact witnessed—" she stopped herself.

"Good God, yes. Your sister, those twin girls—how *are* you?"

"Fine, thanks. How are *you* holding up?"

"It's not easy, being closed, feeling lonesome. Right now Flo and I and Clint—and the boy who helps Clint with the horses—are the only ones here. But we've got a memorial for Stotty coming up, getting ready for that gives us something to do."

"When exactly is it, the memorial?"

"September second. We're crossing our fingers for a good turnout."

"This is why I'm calling, Mr. Barber."

"Please—Red."

She told him she had met Daryl's father, who lived very near her in Kansas City, and who had become a friend. (She hesitated at saying "friend," but used it, instead of "acquaintance," because at that moment it felt truer. As for the improbability of their meeting—first, overhearing him in the park cry out to his companion, "*Daryl Onstott Jr. was my son, Adele, my only son…*" then days later stopping her car and introducing herself when she spotted him walking alone on Walnut—well, she knew of stranger things.) She believed that he was under a great deal of stress brought on not only by his son's murder but also by his wife's Alzheimer's. She told about the recent story in *The Star* that reported how Edith slipped into a parked hearse, fell asleep, and went missing for thirty-six hours. She did not mention Daryl's drunken cries of grief in Volker Park, out of shame for having listened in as long as she did.

"All of which," she came to her point, "has led him to a confused feeling of being banished from the ranch. Which I'm sure isn't true, is it, Red? Especially since a memorial service is being planned?"

"Well . . ." Red hesitated.

"Let me just add this: you may remember that I'm an attorney. But I am not representing Mr. Onstott Sr. in any way other than as a friend who would like to reassure him that he is not unwelcome up there. Indeed, I assume he would be most welcome at a memorial service."

Red got Freddy Boylen on his cell in Chicago. He didn't sound good.

"You okay?"

"Little bellyache, it's nothin'. What's up?"

Red told him about Mary Beth's call. When he finished, there was silence at the other end.

"Freddy? You still there?"

"God *damn* that old fuck!"

"What should we do?"

"Break his legs. Believe me, I'm tempted."

"I think, Freddy, we should do the right thing here."

"Which is?"

"You *know* I know how you feel. The way he treated Stotty—calling him a quitter—how Stotty took it and took it. But, Freddy, to be honest, we should invite him to the service. Hey, he might not even come, you know?"

"Did this Kansas City woman—you say she's a lawyer?"

"You met her. She was a guest that week. In fact she saw the shooting. Small, nice looking woman. Redhead. Went fishing a lot."

"That old fuck can spot a free lunch, can't he, Red?"

"Born to it."

"She really say she was a lawyer *and* his friend?"

"Makes you wonder."

"Oh hell, tell her the bastard's invited. It'll make Seeley happy too. And, Red—"

"Yeah, Freddy?"

"Haven't had a snort all day and feel rotten."

"Keep it up."

"We'll see."

Mary Beth followed the same route across Nebraska that she and Alice and the girls had taken earlier that summer. Woodward saw no problem in her taking the time off, especially since her vacation had been cut short and so shockingly. (On returning, when she told him of the shooting, he said, "My goodness, Mary Beth, you certainly didn't need something like that on your holiday.") Passing the sign for Cozad, she remembered Sarah and Della debating the dangers in marrying a man named Cozad, how the debate led to the story of Sarah's friendship with a classmate named Manny Mansour. The anonymous notes she received saying her boyfriend was a dirty Muslim. A *man-sewer.* Then seeing Daryl shot. But Alice said both girls were okay now. No bad dreams. Alice was okay, too. Mary Beth wished she could say the same about no bad dreams.

The little man beside her was snoring, and her windshield wipers raced at their fastest speed. When eighteen-wheelers passed, sending more water into her vision, she had to slow way down. At one point she pulled under an overpass to catch her breath. Mr. Onstott, the straw boater fixed to his head, slept on. He had to be exhausted, poor man. He'd started their day full of excited chatter—about the trip, seeing the ranch again, his son's great record of winning twenty-one consecutive games for the White Sox—imagine, his *son*!—and wondering which great old ballplayers would be at the memorial service. Then his head fell back against the seat. She couldn't blame him, not after his hurried exit on Walnut, frantically dragging that big suitcase, the landlady behind him shouting, "Don't ever come back! Not *ever*!" Mary Beth didn't have the heart to ask him about it, beyond a polite, "Are you okay?" "Sure, sure, she's just unhappy I'm going on a nice trip."

In Sidney she stopped for the night, bone tired. Unlike the trip with her sister and nieces, she was doing all the driving. (Leaving Kansas City, she'd casually mentioned taking turns at the wheel. "Oh," he said, "I don't drive. Never learned." She said, "And still you flew airplanes during the war." What he *meant*, he said, was: he never learned to work the clutch so good after his leg got all shot up.)

After dinner at a Mexican restaurant, she ordered two rooms in a Holiday Inn. Falling asleep, Mary Beth began to doubt the old man's war story, but she chalked up his fantasy—if that's what it was—to stress, unhappiness. This seemed to make some crazy sense to her. On the other hand, she was very tired after battling all that rain.

Next morning when he joined her in the motel's breakfast room, pale, gripping his coffee cup with both hands to hold it steady, she felt a surge of guilt at doubting his war service: though unlikely, it was perfectly possible to be able to fly an airplane but not drive a car—or certainly not wish to drive one after suffering painful wounds. Seeing his hands tremble as he tried to butter his toast, she wanted to give the man every opportunity to survive according to his own designs, starting with that ever-present straw hat, sport coat of many blocks of bright color, two-toned shoes, and that strong—not good—cologne.

"Did you sleep well, Mr. Onstott?"

"To tell the truth, I'm nervous."

"About what?"

"Seeing all those people without my boy there."

He looked warily around the breakfast room; his eyes stopped at a table where an old man and old woman were being helped by a much younger woman who turned out to be their granddaughter. She brought cereal and toast and juice to them, fussing over them, keeping up a cheerful patter that verged on song. Despite her sweet attentions, the old pair wore expressions so sour and fixed it was clear that nothing she did, here or elsewhere, would ever be good enough. They poked at their food as if it might harbor maggots. Something terribly wrong—a whole history of wrongs—had been done to them, their faces said, and it was unforgivable. Daryl turned to look at Mary Beth, biting his lower lip, chewing on it. He grabbed a napkin and covered his mouth to hide this shameful embarrassing behavior.

In the car, he stared down the rainy road, his life jumping back at him, gray and jerky as an old movie. When he ran away from Chicago during the war, away from his hateful job at that old people's home, but also from Roosevelt who wanted to slap a uniform on him, get him killed, he rode the train to Kansas City where nobody knew him. Not many knew him in Chicago—orphan that he was—but he was taking no chances. When he met the shy, heron-like Edith Penney he found a very nice—and easy—way to disappear and eat and get a little pussy now and then too. All over again Daryl could see the ancient aunt who looked more like a turkey than turkeys did, and always squawking, who needed looking after in her big old farmhouse in Peculiar, which Edith was doing when he stepped off the train in his bow tie and straw boater and bought a bag of apples from her on one of those days she put up her fruit stand in the city. Edith was a good decade older than he was, took long striding steps in long old lady skirts (nights when he crawled into her bed and got past the many wraps she wore, he called her "Granny," sweet-talking, which made her laugh), but man oh man could she bake pies and fry chicken. She kept him a secret until the war was over and she wanted to start a family. *"Feel him, Daryl?"* The baby grew in her kicking and rolling almost without stop and came forth at a whopping thirteen pounds. He was a quiet thing out in the world, made hardly a fuss, and nursing him Edith was so red-faced happy she might have exploded. All of this allowed Daryl W. to slip away, with some traveling cash, absolutely free again.

On a gravel road called Big Win Trail, they followed a red sports car convertible containing a man and a woman wearing matching wraparound sunglasses; and then a pickup came up behind Mary Beth driven by a man wearing a tan cowboy hat.

The vanity plate on the sports car said DIRTYBB. The driver wore a yellow shirt whose long silky sleeves billowed and flapped; the woman, considerably younger, wore a white bikini top and dark tan. At one point she got on her knees, waved at Mary Beth, and found a makeup case in the back seat. (This movement revealed that she was also wearing white shorts.) Reseated, she opened the case on her lap and selected the necessary items to attend her cheekbones and lips.

The man in the pickup had tilted his cowboy hat back and whenever Mary Beth glanced in the rearview mirror he was smiling at her as if he knew her and couldn't wait to arrive at their destination.

"We're almost there, Mr. Onstott."

He nodded.

"How do you feel? Better?"

"So-so."

When the sun had finally come out, a while back, he barely noticed. He had been so fixed to the rhythm of the wipers, the rain, the blurry road, it seemed that that was how it would always be from now on: waiting for a way clear, needing to be careful. And seeing Freddy Boylen and Clint Masters and Red Barber and how they looked at him would only make matters worse. Well, not with

Red so much; Red at least talked to him. So did Flo. So did Seeley. And Mary Beth was an ace. Still, a big weight held to his belly, like something living in there; if he could just open his door and roll out, find a place behind a tree to heave his guts, he would, so help him. Better yet, a good snort from the flask in his jacket wouldn't hurt, but not in front of Mary Beth.

Guest parking at the ranch had a dozen newish cars in it and two weathered pickups, including the one that pulled in beside Mary Beth. The driver of the red sports car, having parked quickly, was striding toward the man in the tan cowboy hat, jabbing a finger at him.

"Strings! Strings! You ugly son of a bitch!"

"Dirty man Boyle! Fogging up the air!"

Mary Beth and Daryl Onstott Sr. stood on either side of her Mercedes and watched them embrace and slap and hoot.

"Cocklicker!"

"You and that god-awful perfume!"

"Hey, I want you to meet somebody. Yvonne, honey! Come over here and say hello to Strings Stringfellow, the sorriest infielder I ever had the bad luck to throw down to in seventeen years of professional baseball. Damn, it's good to see you, Strings."

"You boys keep yelling like that, I'm going home to Mama."

"Ain't she cute? Go on, honey, give Strings a squeeze."

"Don't push on my sunblock too hard, Strings, and you'll get a kiss too."

"I might marry this beauty, Strings, so go easy. That's enough now, no tongue."

"*How* could a nice looking gal like you get hooked up with Dirty Burt Boyle, the stinkiest catcher *ever*?"

"Gee, I guess because he wouldn't leave me alone?"

"Does he ever slip out his premades and do his old guy?"

"Hey, I got me some better teeth since those old choppers. See?"

"Dirty man's the only guy I know can dip, chew, and drink beer all at the same time and not get any of it mixed up."

"Yuck," Yvonne said.

Boyle laughed. "I quit all that, Strings. Worst I do now's Viagra with a soft pop chaser."

"Hold on. Who we got over there?" Strings said, gesturing at Mary Beth and the old man.

They stepped forward.

"Mary Beth Urquhart," she offered her hand to Strings Stringfellow, then to Yvonne and Burt Boyle.

"Now, Strings, don't you go asking this lady who she played with—or what position she favored."

"Don't *you* start being dirty, Burt Boyle," Yvonne said.

"Oh, she knows I'm only kidding. Dontcha, darlin'?"

Mary Beth gave him a small smile. Then she turned to Daryl's father. "This is Mr. Daryl W. Onstott Sr."

The big grins on the faces of the two old ballplayers fell slowly away. Taking in this skinny little gent seemed to confuse them—*he's* the father of the man whose full-bodied heater once liquefied a batter's knees?—and he appeared to become smaller by the second, a clown of some odd make pretending to be spiffy and smart in goofy outdated clothes way too big for him. Wait—that hat—Burt was recalling—

But now a boil of raucous greeting rushed at them from the lodge: men their ages, hair thinning, waistlines rounding out, their shoulders and arms still muscular, however, still capable of heroic drives off the tee, the women with them tanned, attractive, moving expertly on high heels like leggy dancers running to center stage for their big number, the show-stopper, some dressed like Yvonne, some in bouncy skirts, one or two in T-shirts and jeans.

After the rumpus of hugs and greetings, Burt, who had been Stotty's battery mate during the great streak, took charge as a good catcher should and announced, "Listen up now, everybody, this here is Stotty's dad."

The old ballplayers shook his hand. It was an honor, they said. Stotty was a great guy, a gamer, one in a million. They were all so sorry about the present circumstances. The women nodded and murmured at these comments, but they held back from advancing and taking his hand out of a kind of deference to a man's turf. If Stotty's woman had been there, they would have gone directly to her. If his former wife showed up—Flo Barber said Shauna Lee was planning to be there—or better yet Phyllis the daughter—they would have complemented what the men did. Meantime, in the parking area of the Big Win Ranch, Daryl W. Onstott Sr. was sobbing and all the women could do was cry with him. A couple of the men looked away from the scene glassy-eyed; the rest began glancing nervously at Burt for direction. The old catcher was trying to shake clear a fuzzy memory: didn't Stotty once point out his dad in the seats behind third base—*the guy in the straw hat*—and then, in front of him, go out and lose his first game?

Watching from the porch of the lodge, Freddy and Seeley Boylen, Red and Flo Barber, and Clint Masters said nothing. Flo finally said she would put Stotty's dad in the Luke Appling cabin, where he usually stayed, and Seeley said, "Fine."

Jack Majewski woke up groggy: he'd arrived that morning around two o'clock and then drank a few beers with Red. Red told him how busted up Freddy was—not only was it his baby sister Heather's boyfriend who killed Stotty, but now Heather had a bunch of Chicago lawyers ready to defend the maniac, claim he was off his meds.

"Red, *why* would this boyfriend want to kill Stotty?"

"He's crazy."

"Of course, but—"

"Kept riding Clint in front of the guests and Stotty'd had enough—"

"Riding him?"

"Saying cowboy? cowboy? Where's your gun, pussy? Where's your authority? Like that. Stotty looked him in the eye and said Clint wasn't the pussy, pussy. Guy shot him three times."

They sat, holding their beers, until Red finally said, "What was it like playing with Stotty after they sent him down? He used to joke about that time a lot."

"Stotty was sad as a man could be most of the time, Red. And it was just a damn game."

Now, sitting on the edge of his bed, Jack could hear Flo Barber approach the cabin next door talking with another woman.

"They haven't seen each other, many of them, since they quit playing."

"I understand," the other woman said. "Please don't worry."

"I just didn't want you to think poorly of them, loud as they are. Burt Boyle, for instance, is very sweet. And the only one"—she lowered her voice—"from that White Sox team Stotty played with who's here. Bobby Trembly *wanted* to come, but the dear man's in a wheelchair. Did you hear about it?"

"No."

"Drunk driver. Bobby played center field that year. Stotty's year. Strings was with the Sox that year—he and Burt and Stotty all came up together—but he broke his ankle in the dugout before the first game even started. Can you believe such bad luck?"

"Oh, yes."

"Everybody else who's here played with Stotty in the minors before he made the big team. Except Jack Majewski. Stotty met Jack on his way down. Jack was on his way up, a real good pitcher, then boom, he quit. Just lost the taste, I guess. He's next door, by the way, in Billy Pierce."

"And I'm in—?"

"Nellie Fox. Hall of Famer. See the plaque?"

Jack lay back down and covered his ears with his pillow.

At the dinner Friday night, which was mainly for Stotty's former teammates and their families, Freddy Boylen stood up and banged his water glass with a spoon. He was a short round hard man who, until Stotty's death, had worked out in the gym three days a week and spent at least two more on one of his construction company's job sites in good clothes that got dirty. He loved being among men who knew how to put things together, and he loved baseball. In college he made the team by a fierce determination to fit in anywhere, sub at any position, but he didn't have a prayer of going pro, his heart's ambition. He followed the White Sox as a man follows a dream he can almost taste. When Daryl Onstott Jr. began his fabulous streak with the Sox, Freddy Boylen was there, in his box seat, and he never missed an Onstott-pitched game thereafter, home or away, until Daryl was sent down to the minors. Freddy took the mysterious disappearance of Daryl's gift personally and felt for him to the point of going to confession and making his Easter duty for the first time since college. When Daryl's wife, Shauna Lee, left him halfway through his last season and returned to Missouri, Freddy flew down and talked to her. He offered money, a mink coat, anything she wanted. Freddy said it pained him, too, that Daryl wasn't getting any better in the minors. She said that really didn't matter to her any more; she just wanted to live in Peculiar and be normal. Freddy said he knew how it must feel sitting in the stands with the other wives and hearing her husband get booed, called all sorts of ignorant names. She said she was over all that. Freddy said if she was fucking another man he would have her—and *him*—hurt bad. "Believe me," he said. Shauna Lee said there wasn't another man and cried so pathetically that Freddy left, ashamed of himself for his rudeness and for not getting Daryl his wife back. When they all learned she was pregnant, Freddy and Daryl went off elk hunting to clear their heads of that last dismal season way down in Class A and to think. That's when the idea of a dude ranch got formed. The daughter that Shauna Lee brought forth, Phyllis, came to prefer Wyoming and her dad to Peculiar and her born-again mom who wouldn't let the blossoming teen do anything hardly except praise Jesus. Then she went off to college, where she came to prefer books and older men—primarily her professors—to anything the Medicine Bow Mountains could ever offer.

"This will be short," Freddy Boylen said. "I guess it's the official welcome." He paused, appearing lost for a moment. Then: "I never got to play pro ball—my dream as a kid—but getting to know Daryl was just as good—no, better—because our friendship lasted longer than any career ever could."

Several guests smiled and nodded.

"The greatest thing Stotty gave me, though, was my wife Seeley. I first saw her at his first game, which he finished off by throwing nine straight strikes. She was over there in her box screaming and looking so great, so beautiful, because he looked so great. I knew I had to be close to her excitement, because it was my excitement, too, and when I went over to her, she fell into my arms as if she belonged there forever."

Freddy Boylen took a deep breath, rubbed his neck. "Okay, I'm glad you all could make it. I know getting here wasn't easy on short notice. Tomorrow at the memorial service you can say anything *you* want to say—or nothing. Just showing up to honor his memory is good. Okay, enjoy your elk steaks. Compliments of Daryl James Onstott Jr. who put that meat, most of it, anyway, in the freezer last fall."

Flo, in arranging the seating, put Daryl's family together at one table: his father with Mary Beth, his daughter Phyllis with her husband Handly, and the former wife Shauna Lee with her Chinese husband Tommy Lee. ("So her married name's now Shauna Lee Lee?" Flo said to Clint Masters earlier when he was helping her move tables around. "I don't know a thing about those people," Clint replied, "except their food goes through me quickern hay." "But you don't eat hay, do you, Clint?" He just looked at her.) Flo was also putting Jack and Strings at that table, she explained when they suddenly came in a bit early, to fill out the eight chairs and because they didn't have anyone with them.

"You mean Majewski's my *date*?" Strings said.

"You boys be good now," Flo said, and left.

"I *can* be fun, Strings," Jack said, pretending to be hurt, "if you'll let me."

Mary Beth, following behind them, overhearing, had to laugh. Jack turned to see where the laugh came from, and said, taking in her trim jacket and skirt, her classy shoes, "I'll bet *you're* not a girlfriend—*or* a new wife."

"What an odd thing to say. It's almost mean."

"Yes. Yes, ma'am, it is," he said on reflection.

"Perhaps," she said, glancing at the beer he carried, "you just came from the bar?"

"That is quite generous of you to give me an excuse, but also fresh—if you will pardon my candor."

"Oh, shake hands, you two, so we can sit down," Strings said.

"Jackson Andrew Majewski," Jack said. "And my apologies for that mean-sounding remark. *Actually,* I meant it as a compliment."

"Then I'll accept it as that. I'm Mary Beth Urquhart."

"Mary Beth Urquhart, I *am* a tad tipsy," Jack said.

"Would you like some coffee?"

"Heavens, no."

Jack noticed two bottles of wine on the table. He said to Mary Beth, "Would you care for an aperitif?"

"Thank you, the red, please."

After Jack poured her a glass, Strings said, "Here's to Stotty." They all drank. Then Strings said to her, "How's his old man holding up? I felt bad for him out in the parking lot this afternoon."

"I think he'll be all right," she said. "I *hope* so—he's very nervous."

"You have a connection to Stotty's father?" Jack asked her.

"Actually, I'm his chauffeur," she said.

"He wear a flat straw hat?"

"He does."

"A gaudy sport coat and pointy shoes?"

"We have the same gentleman in mind."

"I wonder," Jack said.

"Man," Strings opened his big hands over their table, "we're gonna have the whole family right here—even the ex-wife. Maybe shoulda stayed in the bar longer?"

"And miss having Mary Beth all to ourselves for a few precious moments? I think not, sir."

"Jack's an educated guy," Strings said to her, "but he don't mean anything personal by it."

"Do you boys always tease each other so?"

"Whoa, heads up," Strings whispered. "Here comes some family."

Shauna Lee stood a good foot taller than her husband Tommy, and looked pale and sad and uncomfortable as she sat down next to Strings. Her husband sat on the other side of her, next to Mary Beth, and appeared at ease. Except for Tommy's white shirt, the Lees were both covered in black. Jack suddenly recalled Stotty telling him last fall what his daughter had said about her mother and her Chinese husband: that they looked like a yard sale together.

"It's good to see you again, Shauna Lee," Jack said, then turned to her husband. "Your wife and I met, Mr. Lee, a long time ago—another life—in North Carolina. Stotty and I were with the Charlotte Knights." Jack, gracious and deferential, seemed suddenly sober.

"Yes," Shauna Lee nodded slowly, "that was a long time ago."

"Not a happy period for you, I'm afraid."

"No. No, it wasn't."

"It's good of you to come. Both of you. Did your trip go well?"

"Quite a lot of rain."

"Did you drive?" Mary Beth asked.

"Yes—from Missouri. From near Kansas City."

"Small world! That's where I drove from."

"Do you know Peculiar, then? South of Kansas City?"

"Oh my gosh. I was there just recently with Daryl's father. To visit Daryl's mother, who's in a care facility. With Alzheimer's."

"Yes, we know." Shauna Lee explained that she was born and grew up in Peculiar—which was true of Daryl as well—and that she returned home not long after that North Carolina period. Her husband, she touched his coat sleeve, practiced chiropractic therapy there.

"We visit Edith," she said, "as often as we can."

"Not as often as Shauna Lee's father," Tommy said softly. "A very good man, very dedicated. A widower. Edith believes he is her husband. For years now he doesn't try to explain. What difference does it make?"

Mary Beth said, "So when Daryl's father comes to visit . . . ?"

"Daryl's father," Shauna Lee said evenly, "has never visited her."

"Never?" Mary Beth said.

Jack leaned across the vacant chair between himself and Mary Beth—the chair reserved for Stotty's father—and said, "We should have a talk later."

"Okay," Mary Beth said, puzzled.

The other tables were filling up fast, the crowd in the bar moving *en masse* to the dining room. Flo Barber and the young waitresses scurried around helping people find their place names. When Burt Boyle and Yvonne came in, Yvonne called to Mary Beth, "Hi, sugar, don't *you* look super smart!" There was no head table. The ranch people sat together: Freddy and Seeley, Red and Flo, Clint and his girlfriend (whose tight Wranglers, Strings would observe to Jack before the night was over, *had* to be sucked onto her body by some powerfully wicked machine). The sheriff who helped bring in Stotty's killer—and his wife Jeffrey—also sat at this table. The chairs waiting for Stotty's father, daughter, and son-in-law remained empty until Freddy Boylen finished his welcoming speech and everyone was eating the former pitcher's elk steaks.

First, Phyllis and Handly Grant came in looking composed, elegant, and Eastern. Flo spotted the couple right away and rushed to greet and escort them to their table. "Mother!" Phyllis bent down and pressed her cheek to Shauna Lee's. Then she offered her hand to her mother's husband. "So nice to see you again, Tommy—it's been far too long, my fault entirely." Shauna Lee, her eyes wet, looked toward the big-horned heads mounted on a far wall as her daughter greeted the others. Flo said, "It has been years and years since we've seen this young lady. Welcome back, Phyllis, dear." It was Flo's turn to tear up.

Phyllis put an arm around the tall man in the dark blue suit beside her. "My husband, Doctor Handly Grant."

"Please, Phyllis," he protested, smiling, "Handly will do." Still smiling he shook hands with everyone, moving around the table with grace and skill.

He and his wife sat down between Jack and Strings and explained—Phyllis took over the explaining—that they had *just* got off a flight from Oregon and were *whisked* to the ranch by a sheriff's deputy waiting for them.

"I wonder if I look human," she said, a little breathless.

"Human enough," Jack, who sat beside her, smiled.

Handly said, "Strings Stringfellow—what a wonderful name, sir."

"Contrariwise to legend," Strings said, "my nickname goes all the way back to when I played a kind of banjo I invented in high school—*not* because my arms and legs were so skinny."

"Isn't he adorable?" Jack said. "So open, so all *there.*"

"You keep sweet-talkin' me like that," Strings said, "and I'll tell how I'm gonna vote for George W. Bush and make your face go all twitchy."

"Please don't spoil our evening, you big lug."

Handly said, "Maybe I shouldn't reveal that I'm a Yankees fan?"

"Boo," Jack and Strings sang together.

Mary Beth admitted to owning a Dick Howser Topps card. "Rookie of the Year in 1961," she said. "Also, I saw game seven when Saberhagen won the 1985 World Series for the Royals! Spilled beer all over my favorite mules."

Animated, using her long fingers to briefly touch those nearest her, Phyllis went quickly around the table gathering information. She learned that Strings effectively ended his baseball career just moments before his major league debut by tripping on the dugout steps and breaking his ankle. He now grew peaches in Colorado. She learned that Mary Beth was an attorney in Kansas City. She got Jack to tell that following his baseball days he taught junior high art in Iowa for twenty years, retiring to fly-fish in Idaho.

"Well," Phyllis said, smiling at each in turn, "we have a peacher, a teacher, a lawyer, and"—her tone sobering—"a preacher—my mom—and her chiropractor husband, dear Tommy. Not to mention"—she beamed at Handly—"a college president. I am proud to announce that my husband will most likely be leaving his present post to accept—"

"Now, Phyllis," Handly stopped her. "Let's not—"

Just then, Daryl Sr. walked in wearing his boater, sport coat, and spectators. He stood looking around as if enormously pleased—as if he'd just bought the joint—his freshly shaved cheeks red and shiny, chest stuck out, an unlit cigar between his fingers. He was rocking back and forth, waving the cigar, when Flo Barber took his elbow and brought him to his chair.

"Do you all know Stotty's father?" she said.

"They soon will!" He gave the table a swift, sly, proprietary once over.

"May I help you out here?" Mary Beth asked Flo.

"Do you mind?"

"Of course not."

Daryl Sr., the sly smile still on his face, had settled himself between Mary Beth and Jack and adjusted his shoulders. He laid the cigar among his silverware, lining it up just so. Abruptly he belched. "Well, excuse me!" he said to no one, and laughed. He seemed to have gotten rid of the last of that heavy weight on his stomach.

Mary Beth said, "Mr. Onstott, may I introduce you to our tablemates?"

He looked at her as if just now recognizing her. "Why, certainly." He straightened his back, gathered himself together. As an afterthought, he tipped his hat at her.

She started with Jack, to his immediate left.

"Oh, I know this guy—he played with my boy! Hiya, Jack!" Daryl W. put out his bony hand and Jack shook it. "Glad you're still aboard, Jackie!"

"Your granddaughter, of course," Mary Beth continued.

"My what?"

"Stotty's daughter, Phyllis."

"No kidding. All grown up now! How are ya, Phylly?"

"Fine, thank you," Phyllis managed.

"Her husband, Handly Grant."

"Handly? What kinda name's that?"

"How do you do, sir?" Handly said, affable, extending his hand. The old man reached across to shake it, almost knocking over Jack's beer bottle.

"Strings Stringfellow, who also played with your son, I believe."

"We met this afternoon," Strings reminded him. "In the parking lot."

"Sure did! You stay in shape now, kid, I got big ideas."

"Shauna Lee, Phyllis' mom," Mary Beth said.

"Wait a minute!" the old man almost shouted. "Said that's *who*?"

"I was married to your son," Shauna Lee said.

"Oh, no. Oh, no. You're *way* too old."

Mary Beth, her heart sinking, hurried on to: "Mr. Tommy Lee."

"You play ball?" Daryl Sr. demanded.

"Only as a small boy."

"Thought so." He dismissed the man as unworthy of his interest.

A waitress arrived with a plate of food and set it in front of the now scowling man mumbling to himself. "There you go," she said cheerfully. "Enjoy."

"Enjoy? You think I'm some old fart who can't remember? I told Daryl in Chicago, I told him when they sent him down. He was a *quitter*!"

Jack gripped the back of the old man's neck and gave it a squeeze. The squeeze seemed to release a fresh installment of alcoholic/cologne reek into the air, as if the man wore a ready supply of this mix in a sack under his collar. "Time out, pal. Coach says hold it right there." Then to Strings: "Stand by to give a help if it becomes necessary." Strings nodded.

After a short pause, Handly asked Mary Beth if she would ever consider selling that Dick Howser card. Blushing, trying to recover from feeling that a formerly friendly witness had turned disastrously against his best interests—and against her—she said, "Goodness, I don't think so." He felt the same about his Billy Martin. Phyllis, laughing, wanted to know *how* Strings managed to trip in the dugout. Somebody, he told her, had just released a stream of juice and he was trying not to get hit. Jack asked the Lees if they enjoyed fishing. He thought he'd try his luck in the morning, before the service, and would welcome their company. Shauna Lee, her voice just above a whisper, said she would like that. Tommy Lee said he would too. Mary Beth asked if she could join their party.

Daryl W. Onstott Sr. heard this talk. He saw Mrs. Lee's tear-shiny eyes. No one, he realized, wanted to look at him. The heavy weight was rushing back. He wanted to be with his boy.

In the dining room where a Wurlitzer juke box resided and people could dance, a small table held a vase of fresh lilies and beside the table, propped up in a chair, was a large framed photo of the young Daryl James Onstott Jr. in his White Sox uniform. A few feet away, a podium faced five rows of folding chairs. When the slain former pitcher's old teammates and relatives and friends came to sit in those chairs, they would see gracing the walls on either side of them enlarged photos of Stotty laughing with Hall of Famers Luke Appling and Nellie Fox and looking both shy and startled in the company of three bosomy starlets, plus a dozen other blown-up photos and half a dozen mounted heads of antlered game.

Flo Barber and Seeley Boylen had arranged the room and now as the guests began to arrive the two women approached the photo in the chair with a black ribbon. They had almost forgotten it and were nervous about where to attach the ribbon without obscuring Stotty's All-American smiling face.

Greeting arrivals at the dining room entrance, Freddy Boylen and Red Barber were also nervous. They hadn't seen the old man since he "slunk off last night" (as Freddy put it) from the welcoming dinner. Freddy could have strangled the old man for showing up drunk in those god-awful clothes. "Jesus," he hissed to Red, "I almost asked Bellfield to arrest him, that's how rattled the bastard makes me."

"Jack Majewski handled the situation," Red said.

"Maybe the old fuck's dead in his bed." Freddy smiled.

Red said, "Look, here comes Tim Noonan from the Laramie paper—with that cute photographer."

Sheriff Bellfield McLeod and his wife Jeffrey arrived just as Mary Beth did. The sheriff had taken Mary Beth's statement the day of the murder, but they said nothing about any of that now, only greeted each other as old acquaintances.

"All the way from Kansas City!" Jeffrey McLeod said. A white-haired lady with kind eyes, she held onto Mary Beth's hand a moment, whispering, "You look so sad, dear." Mary Beth thanked her, then moved quickly into the dining room to find a chair.

Jack Majewski and the Lees arrived and sat with Mary Beth. Handly and Phyllis Grant joined them. Then the former ballplayers and their women were at the door in a mob: many of them hungover, but the ones who had left the bar early last night and got up this morning to play golf were refreshed, ready to go out and play again after lunch.

They all sat, now, and listened to the Reverend Dick Nelly deliver the invocation. Mary Beth was hoping to see a sober and maybe repentant Daryl Sr. among the guests. What Jack had told her about the old man both surprised her and did not surprise her. And, yes, she probably did look sad, even though fishing with Jack and the Lees that morning was the best time she'd had since before the murder.

The Reverend Nelly's invocation was definitely sad, she thought, a standard dish of warmed-up piety.

Freddy Boylen took the podium. He pointed at the photo of Stotty in the chair. "We're here," he said, "to say goodbye to a good guy. Last night I got a little carried away. I was nervous then, and I'm nervous now. Stotty used to tell me he was nervous too, during his great run. But when he got to the mound, he took a deep breath and said to himself, 'Let's have some fun—'"

Just then the old man appeared, walking toward the front of the room. He wore what he always wore, holding himself erect, putting one foot in front of the other as if demonstrating he could follow a straight line. It was suddenly clear in a frightful way that he was aimed at the chair that held the photo. Mary Beth reached over and took Jack's hand. Freddy Boylen had stopped talking—stopped breathing, too, it seemed like. All eyes were on this skinny old man dressed like a kind of clown, who had now arrived at his son's youthful likeness. The old man retrieved the picture, hugged it to his chest, then sat in the chair with it, facing the guests, the black ribbon wound in the fingers of his right hand like a ragged glove. His manner and expression were that of a formerly powerful person—perhaps even a king—who had refound his strength—or enough, anyway—to come forward and repossess what was rightfully his; or his manner and expression were that of a somnambulant with staring eyes who by funny luck happened to be passing by and had no other purpose in life but to do what he just did.

Burt Boyle's girlfriend started laughing into her cupped hands. This broke the spell, and the gathered body could let out its collective breath.

But how to continue? The old man sat solidly *there,* embracing the picture—indeed was fixed to it as he was fixed to his straw hat, his coat of bright patches, and that scary stare containing God knew what—or so it seemed to the audience. And audience was the right word, it occurred to Annie Prosser, a waitress at the ranch since high school who was also studying theatre at the university, because here was *drama*, a real story, what great climax was going to *happen*? The old man didn't twitch, blink, blush—nothing. He was definitely into this thing—whatever it was—for the long haul. Everyone, including Freddy Boylen, saw it. Jeffrey McLeod sighed, "The poor man," sympathy attending those three words like motherhood itself hovering over a wound. Boylen was nailed. Where could he go from there but down if he did anything like collar the old fuck, which was what he wanted to do?

In the front row the photographer from the Laramie paper slowly raised her camera, the tip of her tongue playing around her lips. For years a record of that moment hung in her office. She loved it. Freddy Boylen wore the expression of a perfect lunatic, eyes bulging, mouth twisted. Of course the paper never ran the picture. By the time she took it off the wall, packing up to stay home with her two small boys, Freddy was long retired from his construction business and living quietly with Seeley in their home north of Evanston—attended to by Red and Flo and a full-time nurse. When Heather came to visit—not often—she stayed only long enough to smoke her cigarette, watching Freddy construct another human head out of clay, a therapy designed to help him regain his speech. Rodney Halkey, a.k.a. Shane Blaze, Heather's boyfriend, had been executed by the State of Wyoming. Adele also was dead; an hour after Daryl left on the bus for Laramie and the trial, she suffered a heart attack and lay undiscovered in her overheated house for almost two weeks, the TV in front of her continuing to bring forth its regular schedule of news and entertainment. When Daryl returned to Kansas City he found a room near Volker Park, where he spent many afternoons watching the joggers and walkers pass by his usual bench. Mary Beth retired from practicing law, married Jack Majewski, and caught trout with him in the Idaho panhandle. Burt Boyle married Yvonne. Handly Grant died in one of the planes that struck one of the Twin Towers. Clint Masters stayed on at the ranch after it was sold to a hunting club, performing a medley of duties: driving guests to the game sites, keeping the Jeeps washed. All the horses were sold. Phyllis Grant conducted self-help seminars in her home. Daryl Jr., who had won twenty-one straight baseball games in a stunning display of pitching that combined an exquisite physics with a kind of poetry, then suddenly lost forever the magic that had allowed him to do this, lay in the ground beside his mother in Peculiar, Missouri. His high school sweetheart and former wife kept fresh flowers on both graves throughout the spring and summer and when it turned cold she scattered seeds there for the cardinals and starlings and especially the sparrows, a bird that she and her husband, Tommy, were keenly attracted to because it seemed to ask for so little.

South of Wenatchee

A girl of high school age came directly across the park toward an old woman who was settled on a bench watching two white-haired men play horseshoes. She sat down beside the woman and with exuberance said, "It's Briana today, Aunt Gussie!"

"Who's winning?" said the other, frowning.

"Well," the girl said brightly, "let's see if we can tell."

"Please—school is over."

"School, Aunt Gussie?"

"Did you hear that helicopter this morning?"

"Not really," said Briana.

"Chasing after baby elk in the mountains! To put collars around their little necks. Four days old!" Aunt Gussie took hold of her hair with both hands—it was a wig of short red curls—and pulled it down tighter. Over her shoulders she wore a pink silk scarf.

"That isn't too hot today—your hair?" said Briana.

"What cute goats!" Aunt Gussie laughed suddenly and shook a finger in the players' direction. "I'm on the job!" she said. "You can't cheat!"

The two men were bending over a stake, counting their points. They were dressed in the kind of pastel-colored shirts and trousers that golfers often wear. After picking up their shoes, one of the men, preparing to throw, called to Aunt Gussie, "Quiet, you roughneck!"

"I plan to sing in a minute," she called back. "What is your heart's desire?"

Briana noticed that Aunt Gussie was clutching a string of pearls in her lap, and said, "Would you like to put your pretty necklace on?"

"These are my worry beads."

"Worry beads?"

"The clasp is broken."

"Maybe I can fix it?"

Aunt Gussie frowned at the sky. "I have come to no conclusion yet."

A tall, slim man in a baseball cap and Western shirt approached the bench. He was carrying a plastic grocery sack. White shaggy sideburns flew up the sides of his tanned face like wings.

"Got room for a stranger?" he said.

"Sure," Briana said. "Plenty."

Aunt Gussie said to him, "Are you in favor or against, as a rule?"

"Ma'am?"

"I'm conducting the usual survey."

He sat down on the end, next to her, and held the grocery sack on his knees. It seemed full of papers. His jeans, like his shirt, looked brand new, fresh from the store. His dusty black boots and faded blue cap, however, looked comfortably broken in.

"I might like this town," he said. "I see you got a movie palace and a Chinese eatery."

Aunt Gussie gave him a sharp look. "For or against!"

"Don't badger me," he said. "I'm resting." His eyes were straight ahead.

A horseshoe flew past them.

"I'm Briana?" the girl said. "I'm a volunteer at Fountains West? This is Aunt Gussie?"

The man faced them and nodded, touching his cap. Then, "Guess who I am."

"Oh!" said Aunt Gussie. "A new game!"

Another horseshoe flew past. It bounced off the stake, making a dull thunking sound. "Close," said a player, "but no damn cigar."

"You rugged beast," Aunt Gussie said, "you're on the nickel! What's in the bag?"

The man studied the sky as if something up there had called to him.

Briana said, "Oh, Aunt Gussie, don't tease him."

"My daughter talks the same way," the man said. "I can take it." He turned and gave them both a big smile.

"He's got his own teeth!" Aunt Gussie said. "Look!"

As if posing for a picture, he held the smile a minute. His eyes were sky blue, mischievous. Aunt Gussie, studying his face, said, "Well! This one will live. Next!"

"Let me show you something," he said. He searched in his sack and brought out a large black-and-white photo of a cowboy on a bucking horse. "That's me, on Cougar, in Madison Square Garden. But in seven seconds I'll be flying off like a frog."

Briana, leaning closer, said, "Oh, wow." Aunt Gussie raised her eyes from the photo and peered at the man suspiciously. She said nothing.

"Now here"—he pulled out another large photo—"look at this." A line of cowboys were down on one knee in a rodeo ring. "That's Hoot Gibson," he pointed. "That's Buff Brady. And this one here, he got his head blowed away one night by a jealous woman. Oh, and this one—he quit cold, went to work for Boeing and fell off a wing."

"Was he hurt?" Briana asked. "The one that fell?"

"Killed him," said the man.

"You killed him?" Aunt Gussie gasped, pressing a hand to her heart.

"And over here on the end is yours truly," the man said. "You can't see me too good on account of the shadows."

"You killed him?" Aunt Gussie gasped again, louder.

The man looked at her. "Killed who?"

Aunt Gussie gripped her pearls, bunched her lips and stared at him.

"I think she means the one who fell off the wing?" said Briana.

"Well, I reckon you could say he killed himself," said the man. "He'd've been better off riding bulls."

"A likely story," said Aunt Gussie. "Guilty as charged!"

"I hope he's ridin' again—up there," said the man, looking at the sky. "And hangin' on!"

"God hates backsliders. Just ask the ministers."

The players walked past them to the other stake. Aunt Gussie turned from the man to watch them. She sighed. "Yes, we must hang on. Who's winning?" she called to the players.

They bent down over the stake to see what was what. One suddenly slapped his leg. "It's on!" he said. "It's good!"

Aunt Gussie turned to the man beside her. "How would you like to wear a collar around your neck?" she demanded.

"Oh," he smiled, "I've been collared—more than once." Then he winked. "But not for long, sister." He went back to his sack, fished around, and produced another photo. This one showed a soldier and a young woman sitting side by side on the ground against a partially broken stone wall. "Anzio," he said. "That girl was a nice Italian we helped out. Oh, but it was loud there—loud and dirty. I spent my birthday in Anzio, and then I said to myself, 'No sir, I'm done.'"

"Is that you?" said Briana, indicating the soldier.

"Yes, it is."

"Handsome!"

"I was twenty-one."

Aunt Gussie began to sing "Happy Birthday." She sang until she got to the line that called for a name and stopped. "Happy birthday, dear who?" she said, looking at him.

"I told you—guess."

Briana said, "You're not John Wayne—he's not with us anymore. But you sure look like him in that picture."

"John Wayne is dead," said Aunt Gussie.

"Let me show you something," the man said. He took a wallet from his back pocket. Inside he found a card and held it up for them. "See that?"

"'P.R.C.A.,'" Briana read. "And 'Raymond J. Wheeler' is typed underneath. Would that be you?"

"It's my lifetime card."

"Gee," said Briana. "Lifetime. Wow."

"You won't see many," he said.

"Lifetime," Aunt Gussie snorted. "Preserve us."

"No sir, this is a rare card."

"Rare. My, my," said Aunt Gussie.

"What does P.R.C.A. stand for, Mr. Wheeler?" said Briana.

I told them to put "Ray" down, but they put the whole thing." He held the card out as far as his arm would reach and gazed upon it a moment. Then, abruptly, he searched in his sack and took out another photo—of a horse rearing up on its back legs while a man—a young Ray Wheeler—held its bridle. "See that one? I got a hundred and twenty dollars for putting a saddle on that wild critter."

The two players passed before them again. Ray Wheeler looked that way, as if seeing the white-haired men for the first time.

"Mr. Wheeler's a real cowboy, Aunt Gussie," Briana said.

"You can call me Ray," he said, still eyeing the two men.

"I thought he was a soldier," Aunt Gussie said.

"Well, he was a soldier, too."

"Not much of one," Ray Wheeler said, turning from the men. Then he laughed. "I slipped away, ladies. To Rome. They had a time finding me. But it was quiet there and I could breathe."

"Was that the Second World War?" Briana said.

"Yes, it was."

"Oh, wow."

"I had been planning to sing," said Aunt Gussie.

"You sang 'Happy Birthday' to Mr. Wheeler—I mean to Ray," Briana said. "Doesn't that count?"

"Don't be foolish."

"Hey, it was real nice," he said. "My birthday's a ways off, but that don't matter."

"Thank you, sir."

"I'll be seventy-five."

"A mere pup."

"You have a nice clear voice," Ray Wheeler said. "Do you know any good cowboy songs?"

Aunt Gussie looked down at her pearls.

"She used to sing professionally," Briana said to him. "Isn't that so, Aunt Gussie?"

"My husband would never forgive me," she said.

"For what, Aunt Gussie?"

"For being a party to such an outrageous fib!"

"But when we have Down Memory Lane Night and you stand up to—"

"I sang for the pleasure! At weddings and such. Don't make me out a liar."

"I'm sorry, Aunt Gussie."

The old woman then reached up and pulled off her red wig. She was nearly bald. She called out to the players, "Who's winning?" They ignored her.

Ray Wheeler, holding his card at arm's length, said, "P.R.C.A. means Professional Rodeo Cowboys Association."

Briana said to Aunt Gussie, "See, what did I tell you?"

Aunt Gussie dropped her pearls in the wig and rolled it up, clutching it in her lap like a purse. After a moment, gazing down, she said, "Woody lost both of his arms. But he could still play horseshoes. For hours! He'd slip his boot under a shoe. Have it resting there across the laces. Then he'd kick so quick and smooth you'd forget for a minute this wasn't the normal way. His full name was Woodrow."

She turned to face Ray Wheeler. They looked at each other as she continued: "It didn't stop him from farming, either. Didn't stop him from doing anything! I can still see him throwing his arms out after a kick…like a circus performer on a high wire…or a boy pretending to fly. Giddyup! I mean those arms he called his Fixit Tinker Toys."

Then she looked away, but Ray Wheeler did not.

"Everywhere else," she said, "he was lean, wiry. Like you, Ray. Twisting so hard sometimes you thought he might go all the way around and snap in half. 'Come on, honey…come on,' he'd say, praying for a ringer."

She looked back at Ray Wheeler, and he nodded. "That's right," he said.

"It is right."

"Yes, ma'am, it sure is."

"Ray?"

"Yes, ma'am?"

"I can't think of any cowboy songs."

"Oh, that's okay."

"Things have flown away. Most things . . . " She covered her mouth with part of her scarf.

Ray Wheeler looked down at his boots. Briana looked at her watch.

"Is my hair awful?" said Aunt Gussie.

"Let me see." Ray looked at her nearly bald head. "No, ma'am, it's fine. In fact," he winked, "it reminds me of that sleek look a duck has."

Briana said, "Should we start back, Aunt Gussie?"

"I'd like to be a duck," she said. "Let the water just roll off."

Ray Wheeler whispered to her, "Ever notice how one line in their V is always longer? Why is that, you reckon?"

She eyed him sidelong. "Because it's got more ducks in it?"

"Hot doggies!" said Ray Wheeler. "You're a good one!"

She touched her cheek. "Am I blushing?"

Briana said, "You should come visit us again, Mr. Wheeler. I mean Ray. You're fun." She stood up. "Well, Aunt Gussie, shall we go? John and Oliver have finished their game."

"I could sit here for hours."

"Well, why don't you? It's a free country," said Ray Wheeler.

"It would throw everybody into a pure snit."

"Throw 'em, Gussie!"

"Maybe I will!"

"Now, Aunt Gussie," Briana said, "don't be naughty."

"God in heaven," she said.

"Aunt Gussie has to take her medicine," Briana said to Ray Wheeler.

"I'm taking it."

"Not today you haven't," Briana said.

"It tastes like something you should throw out!"

"Throw it out, Gussie!"

"Mr. Wheeler!" Briana said.

"It tastes like a toilet cleaner smells."

"Oh, Aunt Gussie, please be nice."

"Nice?" said Aunt Gussie. "Nice?"

She closed her eyes. Then she opened them and, as if refreshed, began to sing "Happy Birthday" again. When she came to the line that called for a name, she put in Ray's, stretching the single syllable smoothly into two. All the while she looked at the sky, as he did.

When she finished, Ray Wheeler shook his head and smiled. "That was even better than the first time," he said. Then he looked at her.

"I did not expect this," she said.

"Me, neither," he said.

Well," said Briana, "life is full of surprises, isn't it?"

Aunt Gussie, sighing, clutching her wig, took the girl's arm and stood up. Ray Wheeler also stood. He touched his cap and winked.

"It's been a pleasure, ladies."

"A real pleasure, sir. I thank you," Aunt Gussie said.

"That goes for me, too," Briana said.

He watched them go off across the park, behind the white-haired men carrying their horseshoes. Then, gripping his sack, he headed off the opposite way, slowly at first, looking down, then looking up and stepping along as if he were late for something.

Gary Gildner has been publishing stories for more than fifty years in such magazines as *Antaeus*, *Grand Street*, *New Letters*, *Shenandoah*, and the *Antioch*, *Chicago*, *Georgia*, *North American,* and *Southern* reviews. *The Capital of Kansas City* is his fourth collection of them. He has received the National Magazine Award for Fiction, Pushcart prizes in fiction and nonfiction, and the Iowa Poetry Prize for *The Bunker in the Parsley Fields*. He has held fellowships from the NEA, Breadloaf, MacDowell, Yaddo, and Senior Fulbright Lectureships to Poland and Czechoslovakia. He lives with his wife Michele in Idaho's Clearwater Mountains.